The Jordan Tracks

by

Steven W. Wise

authorHOUSE

1663 LIBERTY DRIVE, SUITE 200
BLOOMINGTON, INDIANA 47403
(800) 839-8640
WWW.AUTHORHOUSE.COM

© 2005 Steven W. Wise. All Rights Reserved.

No part of this book may be reproduced, stored in a retrieval system, or transmitted by any means without the written permission of the author.

First published by AuthorHouse 01/21/05

ISBN: 1-4208-1360-9 (sc)

Library of Congress Control Number: 2004098962

Printed in the United States of America
Bloomington, Indiana

This book is printed on acid-free paper.

For my parents, Floyd and Norma Wise, whose love is like a river, requiring only a direction in which to flow.

The morning that follows the night of our lonely trial would, if we be faithful, find us new men, with a new name of help, and of promise, and of comfort, in the memory of which others would endure bravely, and fight as we had fought.

Henry Scott Holland

PROLOGUE

Rural Missouri, August, 1936

Clarence Bates plopped down heavily in his chair and looked past lazy eyelids across the supper table at the twelve-year-old son who would kill him within two minutes. The boy poked a chunk of bread into the white gravy puddled atop the mound of mashed potatoes on his plate, but the feel of his father's gaze caused him to hesitate before he lifted the morsel to his mouth. He glanced up at the man for only a moment before lowering his eyes, but it was enough to recognize the alcoholic haze, feel the scratch of dread in his belly, and he quickly ate the bite of food. Silently, his mother sat the plate in front of her husband and walked to the stove, returned with a pot of coffee.

"You want your coffee now, Clarence…or…later?"

He did not look at her as he spoke, the words thick on his tongue. "So you think I need my coffee now…huh? That what you think, woman?"

"I didn't…mean…that, Clarence, I just…"

He wrapped his fingers around the cup. "Yes you did. So shut up and pour it then."

She did not expect him to raise the cup, but he did, bumping the spout and sloshing the hot liquid over his thumb. The cup clattered to the table.

"Clumsy fool," he growled as he swiped blindly at her with his closed hand. The blow caught her squarely in the stomach, forcing her breath from her and knocking the coffeepot to the floor as she sank to her knees, stunned with pain. Now stirred by the initial blow and her pitiful nearness, the big man swung his clenched right hand in a vicious short arc that smashed into her nose and upper cheek with a sickening splat. Barely conscious and on her back, Nell Bates managed to raise her hands over her face in sacrifice to the blows that began to rain down. Her nose was broken, and blood trickled down the back of her throat, gagging her.

Ernie stood bolt upright in horror, his chair toppling to the floor. He had seen his father land glancing blows on his mother before, but the man had always instantly stormed from the house, hurling curses as he fled. This time it was horribly different. There was an animal intensity about the man as he set about the task of pulling his wife's hands from her face and attempting to strike her before she could again cover it.

"Stop!" Ernie screamed, "stop it, Pop!"

He threw himself from the side at his father's shoulder, only to be tossed aside by the frenzied creature he no longer recognized. Knocked off when Clarence had sprung from the table, the big wooden-handled bread knife lay on the floor a yard to the boy's right. There was no hesitation. He clutched the handle in his right hand and covered the distance separating him from his father in two long strides. From the corner of his eye, the man saw his son's approach, but he did not see the knife. Ernie swung it in a low arc just over the bloodied head of his mother, aiming at his father's arm. Clarence turned his head toward the distraction, lowering his shoulder in anticipation of another lunge. The long blade sliced into the hollow of his throat. As if outside his own body, Ernie watched the crimson explosion as the metal passed through the leathery neck skin and out the back at the collar of the cotton shirt. The doomed man's fingers grasped for the unseen torture instrument, located the handle, but the fingers had no energy and only twitched grotesquely.

For a moment undefined by a clear beginning, Nell's sobs and the wet, throaty death gurgles consumed the close air of the little kitchen. Life passed from Clarence Bates within seconds. Ernie cradled his mother's head in his lap and spoke in a calm, soothing voice that he did not recognize as his own.

"It's all right, Momma, it's all right now."

"Why...why'd he stop hittin' me?" she mumbled, struggling to regain her senses.

"He was gonna kill you, Momma...I swear...he was crazy."

Nell turned her head, spat a mouthful of blood on the floor, spied the still form sprawled on the floor. "Oh, sweet Lord Jesus," she cried softly, "sweet Lord Jeeeeesus!"

"Come on now, Momma, I'm takin' you to the doctor. You're bleedin' awful."

Arm in arm, they rocked slowly on the hard floor. As her brain began to clear, Nell stole another glance at her husband's body. Her hands, sticky with gore, framed Ernie's face and she spoke softly, pleadingly.

"It was me that did this...you hear me, son? Me! I grabbed the knife, and I was afraid he was gonna kill me...and I stabbed him, you understand?"

"I ain't afraid to tell the truth, Momma. He'd a killed you sure."

"Hush, child. I know you're not afraid, but that doesn't matter, don't you see. You're not gonna grow up with a killing hangin' over your head...even if it was needed. You're gonna tell them you were scared to move and that it was over before you could even figure out what to do. Promise me, son. Do it for me...please!"

Her tears mingled with blood and cut tiny pink rivulets down her cheeks, and she pleaded with her eyes. "They won't do a thing to me... everybody knows how he was. There won't be any trouble for me...I promise. Look at the mess he made of my face...they won't fault me. Promise me...it was by my hand!"

He nodded, said: "But I ain't afraid."

She embraced him, her hands stroking the back of his head. In the soft twilight, a great hunting owl hooted its low melody, and before the mournful notes faded into the dusk, the tattered remnants of Ernie Bates' youth passed away forever. The boy sensed it, knew that nothing within his power could halt its passing, and he did not cling to it, did not reach out and grasp with pleading, open hands. He did not even bid it farewell. Soon, it would be nothing more than the old song of an owl.

The man-child lifted his mother to her feet and steadied her trembling body. "We got to go to town, Momma. We'll be all right now."

They took two halting steps before Nell stopped, looked back at the body. "He was a decent man once, son…I swear…a good and decent man…I…don't…" The sobs shuddered through her small body, but as she slumped toward the floor Ernie gathered her up like a child and swept her from the room.

CHAPTER ONE

Christa Bates heard the violent intake of air pass over her husband's lips as the blackened stubs of legs flashed across the television screen for an eternal two seconds. The young Marine was being loaded into a helicopter with the cameraman so close to the stretcher that the image was momentarily jarred during the mad rush to secure the mangled soldier. The young face—drawn and hollow with shock—bore a striking resemblance to that of their son. Ernie Bates whirled from his chair in the small living room and dashed into the bedroom, sat down on the edge of the bed, his head cradled in his hands. Christa hurried to his side, curled an arm around his back.

"Ernie, it wasn't Aaron…you know that don't you?"

His eyes opened as he lowered his long fingers to the bridge of his nose. "You sure?"

"Yes, Ernie, I'm sure."

"I never saw one that looked so much…like…"

"It was not him."

Slowly, he lowered his upper body to the bed, pulling Christa with him. He rolled his head a quarter turn toward her, spoke the word softly, drawing out each syllable. "Vi…et…nam." He paused, turned his head straight up, stared at the ceiling. "Almost sounds like music when you say it slow."

From within his chest a sound grew—guttural and deep—and it caused the woman's brain to whirl with words that were little tools with which to quickly mend the beginnings of the crack in the man she loved. "Don't do this, Ernie. We've come too far now. There's not even four months to go, then we'll have him back for good."

"Right now that sounds like four hundred years, woman."

"It won't seem so long if you don't start to brood over it."

He nodded, glanced back at her before returning his gaze to the ceiling. "I'll try not to…but it's hard."

"I know…I know, but it won't help a thing. Not him, not you, not anybody or anything."

He huffed a mirthless little laugh. "You pray and I fret. That's the way it goes I guess, huh?"

"The same lines are open for you as for me."

"I'm not so sure about that."

Christa saw some of the tension melt from his features, reckoned that a little victory had been won, but she could not suppress the tiny whispers of dread within her. Four months in a war zone was a very long time.

They both thought of the boy's words now, knowing that they heard them in unison—almost whispers in the air. *"I want to be a Marine now…when it really matters. I'll go to the university up in Columbia and get a good job and all that. But now, I'm gonna be a Marine."*

Ernie pushed up from the bed, using his body to brush aside the phantom words like he would use his hand to swipe at smoke from a campfire that had drifted too close.

"I figure we'll have a pig-pickin' to beat all to celebrate him coming home."

Christa smiled, nodded her head. "Sounds good to me, even if it will be early winter."

"Yep…won't matter a lick. There may be a foot of snow on the ground, but it won't matter." Ernie smiled now. "It'd be a sight to see Fudd chomping his way through a stack of ribs in a snowstorm."

"I don't imagine it would slow him down much."

"No it wouldn't."

"Him and Harley doing alright?"

"Same as always. Those two can hang more turkeys than any three other men."

"Everything still on for next Saturday?"

"Yep, Harold's gonna butcher about a sixty-pounder for us. The usual bunch are all planning to come…last I heard when I left the plant this afternoon."

Christa snuggled close to him, stroked the close-cropped hair at the back of his neck, studied his profile. It was not a handsome face, at least not in the conventional meaning of the word, but there was an attractiveness in its simple masculinity. The heavy eyebrows were untamed, almost fierce in their disarray. The lines at the corners of his eyes were bloodless incisions, crookedly etched in the leathery skin. The nose was strong and prominent, the way a man's should be, Christa reckoned. The mouth perhaps a bit too narrow, but one that was able to form a sturdy smile. It was a face that a woman could easily love, a face that Christa did love.

She said: "It'll be a good warm up for the big feast in December."

Ernie nodded, glanced at his watch, closed his eyes. Christa knew what he was doing, where he was going, and she quietly pushed up from the bed and walked from the room. The time conversion was simple: ahead a half day and then add another hour. Ernie had called Aaron's high school geography teacher soon after the boy's departure for Vietnam. Ernie wrote Aaron of his intention to fall in step with him often, at any time of day or night. Aaron responded in his first letter back home, pledging to *"warp my time zone your way too."*

It was six-fifteen in Missouri, the summer sunlight still strong through the windowpanes. At seven-fifteen in the morning, Aaron would be up and moving with his unit, the day's operations already well underway.

Scenes from Aaron's final pig-picking before departing flashed through Ernie's mind in slow motion, like bittersweet memories from a beloved movie. Aaron and Harley, anchoring opposite sides of a whiffle ball game, both making an assortment of diving catches of the wildly swerving plastic ball. And then, just before the feast, Harley praying for Aaron's safekeeping, as the boy's big hand enveloped his mother's and squeezed gently, the thick veins bulging just beneath the bronzed skin, fixing at once the power and tenderness. Finally, as the gathering broke up at dusk, the last scene played out for Ernie. Fudd had lingered until the others had drifted toward their vehicles, then eased his way to

Aaron. As Fudd began to extend his right hand, the realization struck him like a blow that he desired to do something more. With their fingers inches apart, Fudd hesitated, and in that instant Ernie saw that his son understood the predicament. Ernie doubted that the earthy and strangely lovable man had ever embraced another man. Fudd was both bewildered and irritated with himself for creating the awkward moment. He had intended to clamp his most manly handshake on the boy and toss out a choice wisecrack. But the first look into the deep green eyes changed everything. Aaron took a short step forward and at the same time grasped Fudd's lost right hand. His left arm encircled the older man's upper back and firmly but gently drew their bodies together. It was easy for Fudd to allow his left arm to reciprocate, but the next few seconds brought another problem. Fudd's brain searched futilely for words to break the spell, but it was no use. A quiet panic set in and if Aaron had not again quickly rescued his friend, tears would have formed in the big man's eyes.

"Fudd, my main worry is that you'll get fat and make me feel bad when I come back and pin your arm down in our next match."

With a flood of relief and thankfulness, Fudd regained some of his composure, managing a brief goodbye.

The sound of Christa's singing drifted toward Ernie from the kitchen, and the curtains were drawn over the scene. He opened his eyes, allowed the sweetness of her voice to fill him, finally cleanse him of the horrific images on the television screen.

Eleven thousand miles distant, an eerie light flickers through the leafy green canopy as Aaron Bates looks down at the handsome Bulova watch that was his high school graduation gift. He closes his eyes for a moment, chases from his mind the oppressive might of the jungle, and listens to the harmonious offerings of a Missouri summer night.

Barely visible through the trees outlining the horizon, the sun cast a faint gleam on the railroad tracks as they stretched eastward—twenty-two miles to Jefferson City, and one hundred more to Saint Louis and the confluence of the Missouri and Mississippi Rivers. As was his custom, the man in the bright red cap and dark gray work clothes straddled the north track and peered toward the sun. The towering concrete walls of the slaughter house loomed two hundred yards to his left. To his right, claiming all the land between the tracks and Highway 50, lay the town cemetery. Like the tracks, the sea of stones rose with a gentle hill and dropped out of sight. Each workday morning, Harley Raines sorted out his thoughts from this vantage point. Within minutes, his body would be swallowed up within the hard walls to his left. Someday, his remains would lie with the stones to the right. Neither thought caused Harley the slightest dread.

"Till that day when I get to the stones, Lord," he prayed aloud, "till that day, let me live with good sense and not shame you."

He turned north and walked briskly toward the building and its birds and people. He shook his head, smiled, wondered what would be on Fudd's mind this morning.

This Monday morning in the late summer of 1968 would be no different than any other at the plant: it would mark the slaughter of fifteen thousand turkeys and it would consume the sweat and energies of the workers. Noisy, flapping, filthy creatures on the receiving dock, they would disappear within the walls of the plant and be transformed into neatly bagged food products, soon to be popped into the ovens and fall to the carving knives of eager diners. Few of these diners would ever think of the human toil that made this wonderful transformation possible. Fudd Ledbetter felt mild indignation at this consumer ignorance. He had about a minute before the first bird was to be hung on the line—just enough time for venting this nagging frustration.

Harley removed his St. Louis Cardinal baseball cap and replaced it with a dung-stained cloth cap stored atop the metal lockers in the corner of the lunchroom.

"Just think about it, Harley. In a minute or so these crap-scratchin' buzzards are gonna be pinchin' our hands and flappin' at your private parts just so some lily-livered guy with soft hands can stuff his face."

"He paid for it, he can eat it."

"That ain't the point, Harley. Point is that he's got no appreciation for what we go through out here. Probably thinks some robot snatched his bird off the truck."

"Nobody had a gun to your head to take this job, Fudd."

"That ain't the dang point. They ought to stop and think about the hard jobs in the world once in a while. You take a bite of turkey and you think about the workers that put it in your mouth. That ain't too much to ask, now is it?"

"I'm sure some people do think about it, but what does it matter to you? Like I said, they paid for it and they can eat it."

"Harley, I don't know why in heck I ever try to explain anything important to you. Just wastin' my breath."

Harley cracked a crooked little smile. "It wasn't exactly a problem for me, partner, but thanks anyway for your breath."

Dorsey Knowles, the dock foreman, swung open the heavy metal door leading to the evisceration room and popped his head into the opening. "Okay, let's hang some birds. They want two full and two empty 'til they see what they're looking like. They came from the same lot as that sorry bunch we worked Friday."

For Fudd, still charged with energy unexpended on Harley, the instructions were yet another minor irritation; he was ready to fill every shackle on the electrically powered line that conveyed the birds into the plant. His vise of a right hand darted into the metal coop and clamped two scaly yellow legs together. He drug the turkey to the edge of the coop floor, placed a leg into each hand, and then pinned the bird's left wing against his hip as he took one long stride to the line. With machine-like precision, Fudd secured the birds legs into the moving "Y" frame. Years gone were the days when he allowed the muscular legs to pinch his hands or failed to pin the wing; these were now only sources of amusement provided by a rookie hangar.

The grimmest combat was really a thing of the air, but it would take a while before the tiny demons—dust, feather particles, dried droppings—gathered full force and fouled the breath of life on the dock. Management offered paper face masks, but to a man, they were rejected as more bother than aid. "Paper pig snouts," Fudd called them. Born James Elmer Ledbetter, Fudd acquired his distinctive nickname from a Walt Disney cartoon character named Elmer Fudd. To his boisterous and often inebriated comrades of younger days, it was simply insulting to be called by one's given name. James had become Jimbo for a time, but it had little style. Seventeen years ago, this defective moniker was replaced one night by a buddy who had developed an affection for the blundering rabbit hunter in the cartoon who was always hilariously foiled by Bugs Bunny. Toward the end of a particularly rowdy gathering, the happy fellow announced to all assembled that anyone lucky enough to have "Elmer" for one of his names should dang well have "Fudd" to hang behind it. With roars of delight, the decree was approved, and Fudd was born.

Though barely six feet in height, Fudd carried well over two hundred pounds, with little of the weight clinging to his waist. His face was expansive, anchored by a bulbous nose and a fleshy gap of a mouth that always seemed to be open in laughter or speech, ivory-like teeth gleaming. "Horse's teeth," he liked to say, "hard as a drill bit. You can hear me eatin' my popcorn at the movies from the lobby!" The hands that hung from his long-sleeved work shirt were simply expendable tools. A half inch of the left thumb was missing in action, the result of a plow that had slipped off its repair block; half of the right little finger had succumbed to a feisty bull calf that had pinched his hand against the sharp corner of a new gate post.

Fudd had jumped at the job on the receiving dock as soon as he heard of the plant opening ten years ago. Weary from scratching out the meager income begrudgingly yielded from one hundred and sixty acres, the opportunity to earn $2.75 an hour on a steady basis was clearly a prize to be seized. He quickly refined the burdensome task of turkey hanging into a crude art form, though seen or appreciated by few.

Harley Raines, Fudd's proclaimed "hangin' mate," had come to the plant two months after its opening and fell in step on the hanging dock with his much larger partner. Harley lived contentedly on a small farm with his widowed mother, who possessed a sturdiness belying her years. Clara Raines managed the farm quite well, a fact that freed Harley to seek secure wages in town. His wiry arms and lean frame ground out the day's work with an ease that had always amazed Fudd, who operated in the manner of a bear swatting salmon from a river. Apart from piercing blue eyes, Harley's features were not distinctive, yet his smile was winsome, instantly overshadowing the plain features.

Fudd, a twenty-three-pound tom clamped in his hands, took a long stride to the line and slammed the dirty yellow legs into a shackle just as it lurched to a halt. "Aw, man...what now?"

"Don't know," said Harley, "these birds look a little better than Friday's. Maybe mechanical."

Fudd retreated to the truck coops and leaned back against the framework, waited for Harley to join him, then said, "Hope so, I hate to waste morning energy."

Dorsey's head poked from behind the evisceration room door. "Don't get your drawers in a knot, Fudd, it'll only be a couple of minutes."

Fudd aimed a little smirk at the foreman before he could close the door. "Reckon it's a miracle this line don't break down more than it does." He looked down the end of the line toward Ernie's solitary post as the tall man adjusted the chain-mesh guard covering his left thumb and forefinger. "Lord, Lord...every time I look down there I'm evermore sure that I could never be the killer."

"It's a tough job," Harley said. "I wouldn't want any part of it either."

Fudd shook his head. "That dadgum shocker table right beside you, hissin' and poppin' in your ears, and then havin' to make every throat cut just perfect so they bleed out proper. Whew! Hour after hour, them ugly heads passin' before his eyes, back muscles all corded up and tight from standin' in one spot. Me and the wife figured one day that he musta' killed twenty-five million birds since this place opened."

"You can't be serious...twenty-five million?"

"I'm serious as a six-inch hemorrhoid. You've seen that blood room floor when he gets done with the shift...looks like tomato paste a foot deep in there. Man, that's a lot of blood."

"He's a tough...I almost said "old," but he's not much older than me. He's a tough fellow, that Ernie. Lot on his mind now."

"I'll swear, but he has aged in the last year. I don't think Aaron ever leaves his mind. It's a mess over there. Me and Margie don't even watch the newsreels anymore...too depressin'."

With low-pitched groan, the line began to move. Both men cast a final glance at Ernie before turning to the coops.

CHAPTER TWO

Ernie Bates worked his arms and hands in precise mechanical fashion as he lifted the heads of the turkeys and cut their throats, but the precision was rote—simple muscle memory, with barely a glance at the white necks required. His mind was busy in other places, far from the noise and smells and feathery dust. It was not a mechanism that had come easily. Ernie reckoned that it had taken the best part of two years at the killer's position before he could will himself to other places and still perform flawless work. But that was long ago; now, if he desired, hundreds of birds filed by for his cut, leaving no impression in space or time with their phantom passing. Ernie was at home at the kitchen table, reading Aaron's latest letter home, the pages in his right hand, his left linked with Christa's. He could see the sturdy cursive lettering and read the words:

> *"Mom, you are going to have to make a chocolate pie every day for a month when I get back. Merange (I did not spell it right, I bet) 3 inches high. Pop, we are going to kill a sack full of quail this fall. I swear I can hear those babies tearing up the air when I close my eyes. Do not worry about me. We got a first class platoon. First class Marines from top to bottom. Sergeant Winfield watches us like a mother goose (he would knock me flat if he read that). Anyway, it is not that hot around here now. I clean this M-60 a whole lot more than I shoot it.*

Ernie's visions moved from the letter to the television screen and the jowly countenance of Walter Cronkite. The famous newsman's mouth moved but Ernie chose not to hear the words, and when the screen images moved with dark blurs of litter bearers and bloodied soldiers, he quickly erased them and led himself to the great woods behind his house. It was there that he could hide from the newsman and the sorrowful images. How long he stayed in the woods, Ernie did not know, but the feathered shrouds were beginning to come back into focus, and he allowed their coming until his reverie was broken.

He whispered the words. "Four more lousy months, then I can rest easy."

The commotion on the dock was diminishing. He looked down the line to his left and watched Fudd slam the last bird into its shackle and begin to walk toward him. It was Fudd's practice to stand beside Ernie as the last of the cuts were made, then wait as he hosed down his boots and pulled off his chain-mesh hand guard and stained plastic apron.

Fudd said, "Lord almighty, my belly's growlin', let's get them ham boxes down, Ernie."

Ernie stepped up out of the blood room, shook his head at Fudd. "How can anybody covered with turkey crap be that hungry?"

"Ain't nothin' ever slowed down my jaws in eatin' or talkin', you know that, Ernie." He paused, swiped at a feather clinging to his eyebrow. "If my Margie packed another egg salad sandwich I'll break down and bawl. Man's got to have a sandwich his teeth can feel, by dang. Good cookie needs to be soft, but not a sandwich!"

They reached the break room door just behind Harley and Dorsey. The three other hangers, one of whom was a bedraggled rookie, walked through the break room, toward the vending machines. After several gallons of hot water and two dozen paper towels were expended, the men pulled metal chairs up to the long Formica-topped table and popped open their lunch pails.

"That's more like it…spiced beef and onions," Fudd purred. "A man can make some energy with this kind of grub."

Dorsey shook his head and rolled his eyes toward the ceiling. "Why don't you just breathe on the birds while they pass by, and I'll turn off the shocker...they'll be stunned worse than electricity."

Fudd swallowed a gigantic bite and slowly licked his lips as he grinned at Dorsey. "Didn't know you were gettin' so dainty in your old age, boss man."

Dorsey had worked at the plant for eight years, the last two as dock foreman. He was well suited to the position, which mainly required maintaining a rapport with the hangers, specifically Fudd. Everything started on the dock; an even flow of birds was essential to a proper day's production. Neither too many nor too few—two full, two empty; three full, two empty; three full, one empty—whatever combination was demanded by infernal U.S.D.A. inspectors. There were seldom problems with disgruntled hangers; he was one of them—Moniteau County born and raised. The only condition that even resembled a problem was occasionally throttling Fudd, who deemed it absurd to allow too many empty shackles to pass.

Ernie wadded a foil sandwich wrapping into a tight ball and tossed it into the waste can. "Everybody good for Saturday?"

"Have I ever missed a pig-pickin'?" Fudd asked through a wide grin.

"Me and Mom will be there," Harley said.

"My crowd, too, Ernie," Dorsey added.

"Good," said Ernie, "Chick and his family will be there...and Evan Walker's brood. The gut line bunch too, I'm pretty sure. I got a pig that'll dress out around sixty pounds laid on at Harold's. I'll pick it up first thing Saturday morning and get him started around ten. You all come whenever you're ready for games and such."

At twenty-five minutes past three, the last turkey sounded its useless protest as Fudd dropped its long yellow legs into a shackle.

The remainder of the week passed uneventfully. Management was pleased with the weekly production of just over sixty-nine thousands birds. Weekend smiles and shouts filled the parking lot on Friday afternoon.

Fudd aimed his booming voice across the lot at Ernie. "I'm gonna eat light for supper tonight and tomorrow too, killer. That sixty-pounder might not be enough. Ha Ha! Haw Haw!"

Ernie laughed and waved at the big man, said, "I'm not too worried, Fudd, bring your best appetite."

CHAPTER THREE

Saturday morning dawned gray and windy with a steady drizzle peppering the windshield of Ernie's pickup. The rain presented no significant problem; the big metal cooker would work its magic from under the overhang of the machine shed. Pig-pickings at the Bates residence were not postponed due to inclement weather. Ernie preferred the usual location under the towering green ash tree that reigned over his back yard, and, if the rain stopped, the cooker had wheels.

Harold Cline was busy grinding sausage when Ernie banged the screen door open. "Morning, Ernie."

"Morning to you, Harold. My oinker ready for the fire?"

"You betcha. Go on back in the cooler and sack him up if you want."

Ernie was familiar with the routine. The white carcass was hung by one hind leg on the meat hook suspended from a steel beam. Ernie quickly made his visual inspection; Harold's work was always neat and professional. The body cavity was split open and well cleaned. A thorough scalding and scraping had rendered the smooth skin hairless. The head had been removed as ordered, this being a concession, initiated the previous autumn, to the teenage daughters of R. C. and Mavis. Fudd had protested long and loud; with a grin, Ernie remembered breaking the news to him.

"Well kiss my rear! Why don't we just put a dang blindfold on the prissy little ladies when they get close to the cooker? Didn't bother 'em when they were tykes. There's tender sweet meat in the head, and that mess of brains goin' to waste...Lord have mercy!"

Harold slipped through the open cooler door, said, "Well, is he a keeper?"

"Never saw one of yours that wasn't."

Harold smiled as he wiped his hands with a wad of paper towels. "My Susie made me promise to ask after Aaron...and, course, me and the wife..." Harold cleared his throat, surprised at the emotions dumped into the air by only a few words. "Well...we sure hope everything's goin' well over there with your boy."

Ernie felt something in his head, nearly physical, as if his brain had involuntarily shifted into a higher gear. "I...uh...thank you all for askin', Harold. Far as we know, he's doin' fine."

"How much longer?"

"Four months."

"Well...that ain't long, Ernie. Almost down to where a man can count the days."

Ernie looked at Harold, then through him toward the window beyond the open cooler door, saw the morning light, thought of the darkness now enveloping his son. "Harold, I been countin' the days since before he left the states."

"Well...I...uh...I'm sure you have, Ernie...I'm sorry I brought it..."

"No, No...I appreciate it, I really do, Harold. You tell Susie that Aaron's thinking of her too." Ernie turned around, walked toward the hog carcass.

Ernie wheeled into his driveway and saw Harley waiting under the overhang of the shed. What appeared to be Cardinal cap number three perched atop his head. The newest cap was reserved for fair weather only, with one of the older acquisitions worn in inclement conditions—number two for moderately bad, number three for the worst. The caps that he wore to work were not even worthy of a ranking.

Harley waited for Ernie to get out of the pickup. "Reckon this will break up?"

"Judging from that cap...what is it, number three?...you must not think it's gonna quit anytime soon."

Harley fingered the worn bill, said, "Can't be too careful with a Cardinal lid, might jinx the boys next spring by defiling a lid."

Ernie shook his head. "What in the world is it about baseball people and superstition?" Harley raised his hand, forefinger extended to the roof, but before he could begin a reply, Ernie said, "Don't bother. I wouldn't understand anyway."

The men set about the pleasant task in contented silence, the rain tapping a light staccato on the tin roof. Ernie spread ten pounds of hot charcoal over the floor of the cooker. The boxy contraption had been fabricated by an acquaintance named Raul Speckman, who pursued welding and metal work as a sidelight to a small construction business. Raul thoroughly enjoyed tinkering with such projects, and had convinced his wife that the labors were sufficiently lucrative to justify substantial expenditures of his time. In truth, it was widely known that he preferred the smoky metallic odors and the glow of his welding torch to the presence of a nagging wife. The fact that he had masterminded this little charade, even to the point of eliciting occasional sympathy from his spouse, magnified Raul's enjoyment of his work. This all worked to the benefit of many county residents who were able to conceive projects but lacked either the tools or the knowledge, or both, to bring them to fruition. Ernie lacked only the tools, and the cooker quickly took shape under his direction.

Ernie closed down the dampers to just past halfway. Old grease from previous cookings began to release a heavy, meaty aroma that teased the nostrils of the two men.

"Let's get this old boy to cookin' and go inside for some coffee," Ernie said.

They laid the carcass on the grill, skin side up, then Ernie eased down the heavy lid, transforming the blocky cooker into a giant oven.

Harley asked, "Don't suppose Christa would have a little cake around somewhere in the kitchen?"

"Ever been in there when she didn't?"

Christa was busy in front of her electric range, stirring the thick chocolate filling that would soon be ladled into the four waiting pie crusts arranged on the countertop. The rich, sugary aroma filled the small kitchen. As the men entered, Ernie followed by Harley, she glanced up and greeted Harley.

"I'll swan, Harley, judging from that cap, the weather's worse than I thought it was."

Harley removed the cap. "Reckon I could've gone with number two, Christa, but a man's got to be careful about such things."

"Don't get him started," Ernie said.

Christa laughed, nodded in agreement with her husband. *Harley*, the name whispered softly inside her head. There was only one Harley, and they were kindred spirits, bonded for years by a common Christian faith.

"Ernie claims there's cake somewhere around here," Harley said, peering at the spot on the counter normally reserved for Christa's latest creation.

"Well, it was a spice cake," she replied, "but now it's down to those two pieces wrapped in foil over in the corner. Clean it up, there's still coffee in the pot."

Ernie poured two steaming cups while Harley unwrapped the cake. Harley pointed to one of the pieces.

Ernie shook his head, said, "Eat 'em both, I'm just having this java."

"Pour me a cup too, Ernie," Christa said, "I'm through being Betty Crocker for a while."

She pulled out a chair from the kitchen table and sat down. As was her habit, even in her own kitchen on a Saturday morning, Christa was neatly attired in a light green print dress with a flat collar. On her feet were the soft moccasins Aaron had given her on her birthday. Her black curly hair was worn short, with several of the tight ringlets spilling down over the top of her forehead. The wide-set green eyes were expressive and changeable, conveying emotion as clearly as spoken words. This was a trait with which she had struggled in her teens, but was now accepted as a part of her being. She had long since grown at ease with herself, glass heart and all.

Her lips were too thin to suit her, but she reasoned that this just provided more space for her even, white teeth to brighten smiles and laughter. Though not fleshy, her face was round, cheekbones hidden. The many outdoor activities enjoyed over the years with Aaron and Ernie had allowed the sun to steal the smooth skin of her youth. When the mirror irritated her with its truthfulness, she would remember the laughing sun-drenched faces of her son and husband and acknowledge that the exchange of smooth skin for rough was a small price to pay for having been a part of the magic of it all.

"Aaron asked after you in his last letter, Harley," Christa said. "He asked if your horseshoe pitching had improved any."

"Tell that pup that I'll be waiting for him. How much longer is it?"

Ernie said, "Four months and counting. We're gonna have a pig-pickin' to beat all. He'll get back just after quail season gets goin' good, and I want him to have a long time to enjoy himself…don't care if he waits until next fall to start school up in Columbia."

"How's his outfit doing?"

Christa answered. "Real good bunch of boys, he says. He finally sent a picture. To see them, you'd think they were at some scout camp. Grins ear to ear, all hamming it up."

Christa retrieved the envelope from behind the toaster and removed the photograph, handed it to Harley. He smiled as he studied the snapshot. The three young men beamed from the shiny paper. Aaron stood in the middle with his long thick arms draped around two buddies. The close-cropped heads were uncovered and all three were shirtless, dog tags on long chains resting squarely on hairless chests. The boy on Aaron's right appeared a half foot shorter, and had an expansive European face with heavy dark eyebrows and thick lips. His pleasure at being the subject of a photograph was evident in his wide grin. His right arm and fist were cocked defiantly against his hip.

Harley poked a finger at the image of the short soldier. "That'd be Gino, I'll bet."

"Yep, best buddy," said Ernie, pointing at the photograph. "The other one is the Indian kid…they all call him Pima. Aaron says a combat photographer from *Leatherneck Magazine* took that and made sure that they got a copy."

Even the bleakness of the background landscape—essentially little more than a bomb crater—could not detract from the three subjects. Harley smiled, sensed the nearly palpable charm radiating from the tall youth in the middle. His face was a composite of the better features of his parents. He had his mother's coal black hair, wide-set eyes and even teeth, displayed to their fullest for the camera. The strong nose, prominent and manly, was his father's. At six feet four inches, the same height as Ernie, he towered over his companions.

Harley's thoughts drifted easily back to the last time the boy, then barely seventeen, had arm wrestled Fudd. The contests began several years before when Fudd jokingly offered to test his young friend's mettle, and had continued at the rate of three or four times a year. The exertion required by the older man in pinning the boy's arm had increased steadily to the point that the flushed strain once seen only on Aaron's face was obvious also on Fudd's. The last match took place after Aaron and two school buddies, along with Harley, helped Fudd put the first cutting of alfalfa hay in his barn. The challenge was delivered by Aaron, and the two friendly combatants braced for battle over three stacked bales, saved from the last load for this purpose. From the start, Fudd realized that he would encounter more than a little difficulty if he were to prevail. After three of the longest minutes of his life, Fudd finally pinned Aaron's forearm to the scratchy bale.

"Thought you had the old man, didn't you, you little pup?" Fudd wheezed, barely able to manage a weak grin.

"You'll be mine next time, Fudd," the boy warned as he flashed a toothy grin and slapped Fudd's heaving shoulder.

"That'll be the day! You'll have to get one of your buddies to help you pull against me."

Amid backslapping and mock insults, the three teenagers jogged toward the house for the fried chicken supper promised by Margie Ledbetter.

"Harley, what the heck does a hernia feel like?"

"Don't know, Fudd. Never sprung one."

"If it feels like you tore somethin' loose down low, I think I might have me one. I hope that kid don't get no stronger. I don't think I can hold out much longer. If the little dickens ever beats me, I'll never hear the end of Ernie's crowin'."

"He will," Harley solemnly intoned.

"Will what, dang it? Get stronger or beat me?"

"Both."

"Crapsakes! You're a big help to my mind. I'm gonna have to figure out some way to cheat."

"Won't matter, Fudd."

"Heck, you're prob'ly right. Hope he don't dare me again until I heal up some. Liked to turned my rear unit upside down...strainin' like that."

The episode had taken place over two years ago, with no subsequent challenges from Aaron. Harley wondered if this was due to the many distractions of youth, or to respect for Aaron's older friend. He strongly suspected the latter.

"It'll sure be good to see him," Harley said, passing the photo back across the table to Christa.

"Amen," she said, fingering the edges of the photo for a moment, then returning it to the envelope. "Clara coming this afternoon?"

"I imagine so. Says she's feeling some better. Mom's no more likely to miss a pig-pickin' than church, head cold or not."

"Good. Well, I've sat long enough," said Christa.

Harley pushed away from the table. "I've got some chores to tend myself. This rain isn't gonna last much longer. See you two this afternoon."

Ernie walked out with Harley. The breeze swirled through the yard as glints of sunlight fired golden darts earthward through the breaking cloud pattern.

"Gonna be a beauty," Harley said, as much to himself as to Ernie. "Lord a mighty, I love the sky."

Ernie smiled, clapped his hand softly on the hood of the pickup, and waved as the engine roared to life.

By two o'clock only clean, white clouds graced the blue sky and remnants of the wind that had pushed away the rain became warm zephyrs in the sunlight.

"Hey, you two!" Fudd boomed at the teenage girls, his voice carrying across the yard as if amplified. "Ernie saved the head and tail for you. Got 'em in the shed here. You can pick 'em up anytime. Ha! Ha! Haw! Haw!"

The men around the horseshoe pit joined in the laughter. The girls flashed their tongues grotesquely in Fudd's direction. This caused his bellowing laughter to reach near convulsive levels as he dropped the horseshoe he was holding and squatted to the ground to catch his breath.

Margie Ledbetter, a porcelain bowl of cole slaw cradled in her forearms, popped open the kitchen door, and with no more than a glance at her husband and the rapidly departing girls, filled in the previous ten seconds. "Fudd, I will declare…won't you just leave the poor little things alone about the head."

"No, little woman, I don't intend to do no sucha thing," said Fudd, "until they tell Ernie to have Harold leave it on."

"Shaaawww," she exhaled loudly as she thumped the bowl down on the table.

Ernie wrapped a thick rag around the cooker handle and called out over his shoulder, "Ready for the grand opening."

Fudd led the pack at a trot toward the cooker. When Ernie opened the top, the meaty smoke billowed out as Fudd's head and shoulders disappeared like a ship entering a fog bank. From the smoke came the voice: "Have mercy! I may just snort this oinker smoke up till I croak and die evermore a happy man."

Ernie waited until the smoke cleared and Fudd took a step backward. With a butcher knife he opened long crisscross slashes in the roasted carcass, then laid the knife aside. He picked up a half-gallon glass jar full of his special hot pepper vinegar concoction and shook the contents vigorously before sloshing the sauce over the steaming meat.

"Let's gather round and do it," he said. "This pig wants eatin'."

After the group formed into a loose semi-circle, Christa nodded toward Harley. "Return thanks, would you please, Harley?"

Harley removed Cardinal cap number one and prayed in a steady, even tone. "Father, in your sunshine and love we stand among family and friends, thanking you for all of life's blessings. And we pray those blessings for those not among us today as we await their return to our midst. Hold us now...both those here and those far away...in your arms, now and forever. Amen."

Ernie moved away from the cooker as the children were ushered to the front of the line. Harley's words were a whispery echo inside his head. Years before, when he first heard Harley pray, he registered great unease; it did not seem proper to be so intimate with the great God Himself. But with each subsequent prayer uttered by the wiry little man with no hard edges, the feeling faded, and was now gone. *"I wonder if I could do that too...but I wonder if You are there for sure."*

As was his custom, Fudd was last in the food line. In his hands he held a serving dish, about fifteen inches long and nine inches wide. This was his "pig-pickin" plate. After having whined long and loud to Margie after the first feast about the inadequacy of paper plates at such a sumptuous affair, she opened a lower cabinet door in the Ledbetter kitchen and fished out the old meat dish and pressed it against Fudd's wide chest with the words: "That should do it."

The dish was soon burdened with enough food to satisfy a normal family of four. The left half was laden with carefully layered side dishes—cole slaw, baked beans, potato salad, and green beans—and the right half supported huge chunks of tenderloin and ham, with four ribs carefully placed around the perimeter. Fifteen minutes and three cupfuls of iced tea later, and with a ten-minute break to settle the first load and chit chat with the others, he re-armed himself with the dish and proceeded to replicate his original creation. He returned to the same spot against the tool shed, and in fifteen more minutes, bared the dish. He arose, stretched like a cat in the sun, and returned to the table. Three pieces of Christa's chocolate pie remained, and he took two. He nestled a huge chunk of Margie's red velvet cake next to the pie, then reached for a handful of Mavis's chocolate chip cookies, with a handful equaling eight. A fresh cup of tea in hand, he was now ready for the grand finale. After clearing his palate with half of the drink, he lovingly consumed every crumb of the sugary delights.

It would be over an hour before he attempted to gain the standing position. Dorsey eased down next to him and meticulously filled the bowl of an ancient looking pipe with Sir Walter Raleigh tobacco, lighting it with a silver Zippo.

He smiled, cat-like, as he savored the first puff. "Didn't hurt yourself did you, Fudd?"

Fudd belched wetly, offering no other verbal reply. Dorothy Lou, the plant nurse, approached with a folding lawn chair and a cup of coffee. She placed the chair upwind from the smoke of Dorsey's small fire. "Good Lord, Dorsey, that stuff smells like somebody dropped a stink bomb in a cherry soda."

"Never knew a woman who could appreciate the aroma of a fine tobacco," Dorsey replied, tamping his pipe carefully.

Fudd chuckled weakly at Dorothy Lou's playful insult and raised a hand a few inches off the ground in a pleading gesture. It would morning at the earliest before he could safely laugh at full throttle.

This terrible occurrence had taken place at the previous pig-picking, with the result being a violent bout with what Dorothy Lou had dubbed the "hic-a-belches," a strange and noisy blending of hiccups and often simultaneous oral expulsions of stomach gas. The malady had rendered the big man to such a sorry state that Margie and Dorothy Lou had seriously considered taking him to the doctor. Several of the men half dragged the tortured figure to the bed of his pickup while Margie arranged several old towels offered by others as a makeshift mattress. Fudd was laid out in funeral fashion. After ten minutes or so, the intervals between eruptions grew longer and the noise less intense. This was to the relief of all assembled except for the younger children and a particular set of twin teenage girls, who viewed the episode as wondrous entertainment.

Soon the clutter of bowls and serving dishes disappeared into the kitchen, and busy, expert hands restored order to the yard. More lawn chairs popped into place around the perimeter of the shed, and the brown bouquet of coffee wafted on the light air. The whiffle ball game erupted again, this time without Harley, who sat cross-legged between his mother and Christa. A blue mug of coffee rested on the wide plastic arm of his chair. The three were engaged in jovial conversation, with Harley content with mainly listening, inserting only an occasional comment.

Dorothy Lou and Dorsey were joined by Dorsey's wife, Sue, who enjoyed the sharp wit of the sprightly plant nurse and the verbal sparring with Dorsey that seemingly never ceased. All three were drawn to a laborious movement near their feet. Fudd looked up and managed a faint smile, the great body listing to starboard against the shed, the right hand jammed into the grass in partial support.

"Fudd, I'm tempted mightily to make you laugh and start the show," Dorothy Lou said.

Fudd clamped his eyes shut and slowly rolled the back of his head from side to side over the rough wood siding.

Dorsey said, "Great day, woman, you trying to shut the plant down Monday? He's got to be back on the hanging line in thirty-six hours, and looks to me like he'll need most of 'em to recover."

"Oh shoot, he'll probably be munching on a half dozen eggs and a pound of bacon at breakfast." She glanced down at Fudd, whose features were contorted from the image conjured up.

"For pity's sake, Dorothy Lou, you're supposed to be an angel of mercy, not torment," said Ernie.

"Whatever...I guess I'll refrain, but my what a temptation."

Ernie walked to the edge of the gathering, his hands slowly moving underneath a damp cloth. He surveyed the soft, summery chaos of the scene and registered the usual discomfort from Aaron's absence. Dusk had descended like a delicate blanket, and by twos and threes and fours, the guests filed by Ernie and Christa and smiled, spoke their thank yous, and departed. Ernie returned their smiles and words, but he was already in another place, half a world away. He walked slowly to the edge of the yard, and then into the knee-high fescue as dusk yielded to darkness. As if suddenly painted in bright white above the treetops, the half moon beckoned from a quarter million miles, and the man assented to the tug of childlike innocence, reached out toward it with the fingers of his right hand, said: "No more feasts without you, son. That was the last one without you."

In the eerie light flickering through the jungle canopy, Aaron glanced at the Bulova. He closed his eyes for a moment and listened to the Missouri night sounds, sorted through the tree frogs and crickets and coyote howls until he heard the lonely hoot of a great owl.

"Gone again on me ain't you, Missouri boy?"

Aaron blinked away the scene, turned his head toward Gino Polites, said: "Yeah, guess I was at that."

"Winfield don't like that, you know…driftin' away out here in the badlands."

Aaron nodded, said, "That's why he's a good sergeant, watchin' over us, fretting' about everything."

"I thought that was your God's job."

Aaron shook his head, blew a puff of air through his lips. "Come on, man…I'm not up for a round of…"

"No, no…I'm not pickin' at you, it's a serious question."

Aaron stared at him, saw the earnestness. "I didn't hear a question."

"Well, is it God's job or Winfield's job to look after you so you make it back to Missouri?"

"Gino, for crying' out loud…Winfield…he's a man, with a job. God…is just…God. It doesn't seem right to look at it the same way."

"Well, if I was you, good buddy, I'd be hopin' that God was acting' like he had a job with you."

"Why just me, you don't think he cares about you?"

"You're a believer…me, I'm just a wonderer. I ain't sure of nothin' anymore." Gino chuckled, said: "It's like my Aunt Rosa, good old Rosa, more momma to me than my own momma…got a moustache like Zorro, whip any man in the family…you in Aunt Rosa's family—even somebody as sorry as me—and she'll thump anybody looks at you sideways. But if you're not in the family…well…you're on your own, you know what I mean?"

"It doesn't work like that, Gino. God's not like your Aunt Rosa."

"Seems like it oughta be that way, you ask me."

"I didn't ask you."

"Oh, so you're tellin' me then, huh? You got it all figured out, like the Pope or somethin', that it?"

"This thing is goin' nowhere, man."

"So now you're irritated…just like always. I'm just trying to sort out all this mysterious stuff and you're a genuine Jesus freak, and every time I ask a simple question, you get steamed."

Aaron pinched the bridge of his nose with a thumb and forefinger. "I got it all figured out for you, buddy…you ready?"

"More'n ready."

"NOTHING is simple."

"Oh, that helps…that just fixes everything. What a religious genius."

The soldier in front of Aaron looked back, motioned with a wave of his hand, said: "We're movin' out and I'd appreciate it if you two'd shut up and pay attention."

CHAPTER FOUR

On Sunday morning Christa allowed the weekly hope to kindle in her chest as she finished the breakfast dishes. Ernie, thumbs hooked in the straps of his bib overalls, stood in front of the window watching a pair of squirrels flit along a thick branch of the ash tree.

"The choir is doing a real pretty number this morning," she said, reaching for a towel. "I've got a little solo part."

He shifted his weight, said, "I know it'll be nice...but I need to work on the cooker some. The dampers don't work to suit me."

"Well...I'll go on and get ready."

The Sunday morning service at First Baptist moved at its usual brisk pace. Jack Bowden, the music director, led the congregation through vigorous renditions of *All Hail the Power of Jesus' Name*, and then *Rock of Ages*, before Pastor Fred Riggins welcomed guests and made announcements detailing the coming week's activities. Another hymn served as the offertory song, after which the plates were passed by the ushers.

Jack turned to the choir, smiled his encouragement at the beaming faces, and winked quickly at Christa, discreetly flashing the thumbs-up sign with his right hand. He knew that Christa required no fortification; it was a little ritual developed over the years between director and soloist, and both relished in the silent bond.

The hymn to be sung was *He Hideth My Soul*, a beautiful old piece written by Fanny J. Crosby before the turn of the century. Christa was to sing the verses, with the choir joining her on the refrain. Christa had first sung it as a child at her mother's side, watching the long forefinger march in time across the page, fingernail taping beneath each word or syllable. The words of the hymn came to her with the first notes of the piano; she would not once look down at the page of the brown hymnal cradled in her hands.

A won-der-ful Sav-ior is Je-sus my Lord,
A won-der-ful Sav-ior to me;
He hi-deth my soul in the cleft of the rock,
Where ri-vers of plea-sure I see.

The soprano voice was strong and vibrant, as pure as the call of the whippoorwill the woman often heard from her kitchen window. Her head gently drifted from one side of the congregation to the other, her eyes meeting those of her listeners as she offered her soul's energy. She sang with eyes glistening with the few tears that always came when she sang a hymn. Never so many that her eyes overflowed, only enough to cause a soft shimmer. It had been so from her first solo as a teenager, when she feared that they would cascade down and render her to a blubbering failure. But they ceased with the first few words, and on that day she offered a wordless thanks to the maker of her tears. Although untrained beyond the level of Wednesday night choir practices, Christa knew that her voice was far beyond ordinary. Her mother had told her that it was a gift from God, to be shared and cherished—a powerful force that could make the difference in the direction a soul might take, a powerful tool that could preach a sermon as surely as the finest evangelist.

The four verses passed too quickly for her audience, and even as Pastor Riggins rose to deliver the sermon, the final notes hung in the air.

He turned to face the choir. "Thank you, choir, and Christa for that special music. I'll declare, Christa, it's surely a blessing to listen to you, but something of a curse to have to follow you."

The congregation joined him in laughter and then settled back down as he opened the big leather-bound Bible that lay before him on the lectern. The text was from Luke, a book that had remained among the most cherished from his early ministry. A great many of Fred Riggins's sermons were developed from the words of Christ, and Riggins was a master at conveying the depth and beauty of the teachings. Many of his contemporaries had long since settled into large city churches and some of his fellows had gently chided him about what appeared to them to be a mismatch of talent and ambition. Indeed, he had turned down the entreaty of more than one pulpit committee sent on pastor searches by a larger church.

Fred Riggins preached what he fervently believed in—an omnipotent Creator, salvation and eternal life in heaven through acceptance of Christ, and the equal surety of eternal condemnation through rejection of Christ. He was forty-seven years old, sturdy and square of frame and countenance, and a pastor for twenty-six years—years filled with peaks and valleys of his own life as well as those of his flock. He had been a widower for the last twelve years. He and his beloved Ruth had not been blessed with children, and soon came to the conclusion that God had denied them this pleasure so that they could minister to church members without regard to familial duties and restrictions. The church would be their family; they would be parents to many, not just a few. The bond between the couple and the church began as a thread and grew to a cable.

And then came the bright autumn afternoon when the couple was halved by the grinding of metal and glass. Ruth had just departed the house to visit a sister in Eldon, twenty-two miles south down Highway 87. She left in a rush, without her purse, and Fred noticed it on the kitchen counter as she backed out of the driveway; he was unable to attract her attention before she drove onto the pavement and disappeared from sight. He wondered at the time how soon she would reach down with her right hand and notice its absence. She drove less than two miles before turning back to meet her death. Two teenage boys, one sixteen and the other seventeen, were locked side by side in a drag race as they roared southbound over a blind hill. The heavy Ford sedan in the wrong lane was traveling at over twice the speed of Ruth's car. Her death was instantaneous. The boy in the wrong lane was mangled horribly; his racing partner bore only mental scars.

Pastor Riggins knew well things of the heart. Every sermon he had preached since the fateful day was dedicated to the woman who now knew the Lord by sight, and with whom he would share the coming reunion across the Jordan.

The sermon flowed powerfully from within him; his voice inflection and style were distinctive—from crescendos down to whispers—as he implored his flock. When he surveyed the faces before him, he expended all of his energy toward the souls they represented. The inner man was what mattered—"the forever part"—he liked to say. As long as God granted him breath, he would toil in love to claim the precious forever parts for the next life, the life without end.

The hymn of invitation was given, Jack Bowden stepping slowly to the edge of the podium to lead the song with subdued arm and hand motions. Christa sang softly with the other choir members. Her silent prayer was always the same; she prayed by name for a single soul whom she knew had never made the walk down the aisle to confess his or her allegiance to her Christ. Although a disproportionate number of prayers had been offered in her husband's name during the years he accompanied Aaron, Christa always had two or three other people on her heart.

On this morning, the son so far away was the focus of her prayer, though one of thankfulness rather than longing. She looked down at the red carpet, closed her eyes, saw the boy trundling forward toward the waiting arms of Fred Riggins. It had come as no surprise. For the previous two weeks, Aaron's questions of his mother had taken on a serious tone that indicated that the time of accountability was at hand. Questions about Christ's life, His crucifixion, the resurrection, the promise of eternal paradise—they all came tumbling out. Christa was joyously deluged with the queries, and had simply opened her heart's door for her son.

Throughout Aaron's early childhood, she had previewed the conversation many times and assumed that it would be relatively simple to lead her son to take the final step. After all, it had been a continuing process for the last couple of years, this merely the culmination. But the vulnerability and responsibility of it all was surprisingly discomforting. The inquisitive green eyes bored into hers, probing for truth, and at the same time searching for any doubts she might harbor. Then it was finished. Satisfied with her explanations and the conviction in his heart, he took her hand in both of his, looked a final time into her eyes, and with a solemnity that belied his years, slowly nodded his head. Within the span of a few moments, his childhood returned full force. Now unburdened from the weight of the conversation just past, he was out the back door and calling for Hound, the energetic beagle. A romp around the yard ensued, the excited yaps of his little dog filling the air.

The final notes of the hymn faded into the high ceiling of the sanctuary. Christa's eyes glistened as if she had just offered up a solo, and in fact she knew that she had after a fashion. It was a solo to the Keeper of her son.

Monday morning dawned hazy, the humidity an unwelcome blanket that bode ill for the day. Fudd spotted Harley as he ambled from the railroad tracks toward the plant, the undulations of the bright red cap marking his approach.

"Let's get after these buzzards, I feel strong as a bull," Fudd implored as he stalked toward the dock.

"Easy, Fudd, they're not going anywhere."

Fudd's desire to charge full throttle into the action was soon thwarted. The hangars had barely broken a good sweat before Dorsey poked his helmeted head through the doorway to the evisceration line. The hangars had already noticed that the line speed was down considerably.

"Back off, you guys. They want two out of five hit. We got chiggers."

"Lord have mercy!" Fudd roared. "I'm gonna have a peek in there."

He ducked under the line and stomped across the dock, banged the door open with a forearm. Even from a distance of thirty feet, the angry red dots stood out in dark contrast to the white skin of the wet carcasses, speckling the legs and lower breasts. Fudd peered farther down the line, saw the Department of Agriculture inspectors and Dorsey engaged in urgent conversation. Then Dorsey half trotted away as Fudd watched with the line workers at the beginning of what would be a very long day for the six women to be reshuffled from work stations to the chigger patrol. Fudd had heard the tale many times from the gut line crew; the variations were minor. Pinch the slick skin up with a thumb and forefinger and snip as closely as possible below the bite location with the razor-sharp scissors. Pinch and snip, pinch and snip, and then, after a half hour or so of the tedium, one of the luckless snippers would grow arm weary, disrupting the delicate coordination required, and a small but agonizing excision would be performed on either thumb or forefinger. Then off to Dorothy Lou's office for a tetanus shot, salve, gauze bandage, and some pain pills to combat the demons that lived in fingertips that would throb into the night until fitful sleep finally came.

And on came the birds—white, wet, naked—with the red dots shining in mockery at the efficient machinery of the plant, now slowed to a crawl. Fudd shook his head, turned away from the doorway.

Two days drug by until the infested birds were processed through the plant. At his farm, Fudd redirected surplus energy unexpended at work toward an assortment of afternoon chores at his farm. His fifteen-year-old son, Tad, whose frame was beginning to resemble that of his father's, stood silently awaiting further instructions as Fudd tugged at the bottom strand of loose barbed wire. He drew it tightly against the fence post and waited patiently for three seconds, finally glancing up at Tad, whose gaze was directed over the adjoining pasture.

"For cryin' out loud, son, how long you gonna let me squirm like a rolled up bug down here?"

"Oh…uh, sorry Pops." He quickly knelt, placed the steel brad over the strand and hammered in into place.

"Thank you very much," Fudd huffed. "Pay some attention to my labors, okay?"

The boy nodded absently, again fixed his eyes on the pasture. He was in the throes of his first serious courtship, with the object of his attentions being a sprightly pony-tailed blond named Peggy Conroy. "Pops, I can't make her pay any attention to me, and it's about to bug me to death."

"Tommy, I've never claimed to be the world's greatest Romeo, but I do know enough to tell you that you can't trail her around like a young bull. Somehow, a female wants to be noticed, but not…too much."

"That doesn't make any sense."

"Well sure it makes perfect sense…she's a female. Their minds are strange things. What you need to do is pay attention to some other little girl and make sure she's watchin'."

"But none of the others look as good as she does."

"Crimminy sakes, boy, you just gotta PRETEND that you're not interested in her."

"But what if she gets really ticked off by that?"

"Great day, Tad…I thought you were sure she was sweet on you."

"Well, I am sure…at least I think I'm sure."

"So then, if she does get a little ticked off, that's great. Then you'll know for sure that you're the one she's sweet on."

"Sounds risky to me."

"Well then, son, you'll just have to think of somethin' yourself, cause that's the only advice I know to give you."

"If I just had my driver's license, I wouldn't have to be messin' around on foot at some dang ball game or such. I could make some real headway then."

Fudd turned, arms akimbo, and contorted his features as if a great pain had exploded inside his head. "Oh, heck yes! I can't wait! Layin' wide awake in bed at midnight while you two are foggin' up the windows on some back road. Me and your Momma wonderin' if we just been made grand folks. Yeah, you and your driver's license…I just can't wait!"

"Pops, come on…I didn't mean that. Haven't you ever heard of movies and cheeseburgers at Jimmy's?"

Fudd drew a long breath loaded with his next salvo, but he raised his right hand like a fingered flag, released the empty breath. "I don't want you to ask me any more questions about females for a while, okay?"

"I don't remember askin' you a question to start with, I just…"

"Hush, hush, for cryin' out loud. It must be ninety out here and we got a lot left to do without yellin' at each other any more."

The boy shrugged, offered his palms to the sky. "I never yelled once, Pops."

"I know, I know…it was me, gettin' a little loud, didn't really mean to yell though."

"You didn't."

"Good then."

They fell back into the rhythm of the fence work, did not speak for several minutes. Fudd stood, slapped his hands on his lower back and arched his body toward the sky before looking down at Tad. The big man was not weary, but irritated with himself, and in a vaguely hurtful sense the irritation was linked to his affection for the Bates family. The fact that he had raised his voice to his son had grown from a little scratch inside his chest to a claw; he could reach out and touch his son, while Ernie and Christa Bates could only worry about their son who was half a world away in a violent land.

"Why you starin' at me like that?" Tad asked.

"I'm not…starin'…exactly, son, I was just lookin'."

"You don't usually look at me like that without a reason."

Fudd crossed his arms, looked up at the hazy sky, said: "I was thinkin' on Aaron…over there. If you were a couple years older…"

"Yeah, could be me, huh?"

Fudd nodded. "I reckon…if you had a mind to be a soldier."

"Hadn't thought about it much."

"Well, this thing'll be over surely, time you're outta school."

"What if it's not?"

Fudd looked back at him, held his eyes for moment before looking back at the sky. "Me and your momma'd just as soon you wait till it was…if you're still thinkin' on the service, that is."

Tad stood, wiped the sweat from his forehead with the back of his forearm. "Can't we knock off for a while? I'm dyin' for a cold Pepsi."

Fudd clamped a hand on the boy's shoulder. "Yeah…sure, me too. Let's go to the house."

During the third week of September the heat relented, the promise of autumn alive in the sassy pre-dawn breeze. The bedroom window was open a few inches, allowing the air to nudge through the screen and tease the sheet against the hair of the man's lower legs. For as long as Ernie could remember, this had been his time of day. Even in childhood, there was never a need for an alarm clock. It would be another hour before first light. The next few minutes would be devoted to the harmonic sounds filtering into the room. From the comforting, scratchy babble of the tree frogs and crickets to the melodic notes of the night birds, these offerings of nature were bits of treasure to the man who accepted them as a balm to his spirit.

His thoughts turned to the day at hand; thankfully, it was Friday. The birds had been good all week and he had toiled steadily in his concrete space of blood and feathers. Yes, Friday, sweet Friday, and cool air for further refreshment. It would be a good afternoon to visit his forest cathedral.

The day passed uneventfully, save for a new bird hanger requiring a visit to Dorothy Lou's office and an early trip home. Fudd explained the incident at lunch, between and during mouthfuls of a gigantic meatloaf sandwich and dill pickle spears.

"Heck, I knew it was comin'. Been here dang near a week and he still wants to grab 'em by one leg. I says, 'boy, you keep grabbin' them buzzards by one leg and sooner or later that loose leg's gonna churn up some loose crap specks and zip 'em right into your kisser.' He'd go back to two leggin' 'em for a while, then he'd get lazy again. Knew it was comin'. Reckon when Dorothy Lou gets done Q-tippin' his crap-clogged eyeballs, he'll be takin' my advice Monday."

Ernie and the others chuckled at the animated explanation, more at the narrator than the hapless hanger.

The short drive down winding Highway 87 was peaceful, with Ernie's thoughts floating ahead to his destination. Christa was in the process of removing a load of laundry from the clothesline in the yard when she turned to meet the familiar rumble of the approaching truck. Ernie ambled toward her, his fingers kneading the small of his back in a futile attempt at unknotting the nagging musculature.

"Bad day?" she asked.

"Good day for the plant. Nice birds all day long. Yeah…kind of a long day, for everybody except Fudd. We must have averaged five out of six shackles all day long."

Ernie shook his head and smiled along with Christa as they both thought of their indefatigable friend.

"I'm headed for the place."

"Be a nice day for it. See you later."

A considerable portion of the worth of his refuge derived from its proximity to the house; Ernie could reach it easily within five or six minutes. When he sought to purchase land prior to Aaron's birth, one of his requirements had been that the bulk of the acreage be in woodland. He had no intention of ever raising livestock or crops for his livelihood. What the serious farmer considered wasteland had long been treasure to Ernie. The woods near the home place of his youth were suitable for a time, but soon proved to be full of dark memories. Christa had been perfectly satisfied with the land, and had intentions of fixing up the house, but she acquiesced to her new husband's inexplicable desire to sell and seek another home.

He was almost there. His senses began their glad transformation from unwilling receptors of mechanical din and bestial stench to covetous organisms that held fast each offering of creature voice and delicate fragrance carried by the breeze.

The shrill alarm of a blue jay announced the man's approach. Ernie looked up and caught a glimpse of the regal plumage and crested head of the vociferous guardian of the forest. As the clamor of the bird subsided, the soothing trickle of Paddy Creek filtered through the trees. A few more steps brought him to the edge of the bank, with the level of the shallow water six feet below. Thirty inches below the edge, swift waters driven by countless rainstorms had exposed his place of rest. The curving, snake-like root of a cottonwood tree protruded from the bank in a tight arc, offering eighteen inches of chair bottom. The grassy bank above the root inclined gently away from the creek, providing comfortable back support. When Ernie desired a change of position, the curve of the bank allowed him to pivot on his buttocks, draw up his right leg to the level of the root, and lean it against the bank. This slightly reclining position was his favorite, and he slipped into it with practiced ease.

Once secure, he tilted back his head and inhaled forcefully through flaring nostrils. The expulsion of air over his loose lips would be the only human sound intruding into the serenity of the hideaway for over an hour. The dank, heavy odor of the sandy earth encircling his back was welcome. The great lady Earth, he mused. Her presence should overrule this place; it was only proper. Still, she permitted a commingling of subordinate aromas for his pleasure—green smells of grasses and leaves from above, and below too, on the rocks crowned with moss and dock. And when the breeze swirled from behind him, the memory of springtime perfume wafted from a patch where ox-eye daises had begged for a bit of the glory.

In the spring, the man was given a panorama of blossoms bathed in white beyond the opposite bank, framed on the right by dogwood and hawthorn, and on the left by black cherry and wild plum. His gaze drifted slowly across the sweep of trees about him. From stately to lowly, they lined the banks of the creek. The giant cottonwood that provided his wooden chair rose skyward with the impudence of the mighty.

"Careful, old tree," he whispered, "she'll see you be too proud and send a lighting bolt that'll bring you back to her."

A double-trunk hickory reigned over the far bank, thirty feet distant, providing ideal sites for the untidy knots of squirrel nests far in its upper reaches. The trees, the beautiful trees; they were both wall and ceiling to his open-air cathedral, permitting just enough dappled sunlight to paint the water and rock of the creek bed. And when the breeze possessed energy to expend in the branches, songs were sung—leafy and melodious in the fullness of spring and summer, and in the nakedness of winter, high-pitched and plaintive.

There were days at the plant when he needed the promise of the tree songs. Days when he had bloodied fifteen thousand throats and, with shoulder and back muscles turned into daggers, still faced the coming of a thousand more. Days when the disharmonic roar in his ears would torment his brain and reduce life to an existence measured by the cadence of knife swipes. But through it all, part of him always clung to his place on Paddy Creek, the surety of it equal to the turmoil surrounding him. The thousand birds would become five hundred, and the five hundred would melt to one hundred, and then he could steal a glance to his left and see the hangers shuffling away from the line, the last turkey secure in the rigid grip of the shackle. Then he would know that solace was nearly at hand, with the trees and the creek waiting patiently six miles away.

Only Christa and Aaron knew of his place. They had both acknowledged its beauty, but Ernie knew that they took their greatest peace from other things. For them, the preacher's words, a hymn, prayers to God, a favorite scripture—these were the treasures of their hearts. He was not resentful of this fact; they were the two people whom he loved above all others, and their joys were his joys. But the sources of their joy were different from his. No, they would never know the true worth of his place. No one could but him. It was one man's place, his place.

CHAPTER FIVE

To the delight of Moniteau County Fair officials, the mild weather pattern extended into the last Saturday of September, the annual opening day of activities. This event was the crown jewel of the community, and, according to the flyers posted about the county, the longest running county fair west of the Mississippi River.

The fairgrounds were located at the northeast edge of town, adjacent to an outcropping of newer brick homes along one boundary, with an older residential neighborhood along the other. For fifty-one weeks of the year, activity was infrequent on the grounds that consisted mainly of a grandstand above a soil arena for livestock and horse shows, adjacent stables, two well maintained exhibition buildings, and ample flat grassed area for the midway carnival and vehicle parking.

The total area encompassed less than five acres. Devoid of the crowds, it appeared much smaller during the dormant months. The land and structures were owned by the town and were well cared for. Over the years, the fair had elevated the status of the small town beyond that enjoyed by larger-sized sister communities in the mid-Missouri area. The vast majority of townsfolk became involved in one manner or another during that one shining week of glory, with supporting roles ranging from mere attendance to more important organizational duties.

More than anything else, the fair was a celebration of the small-town way of life. A soft chaos enveloped the grounds and offered sensory pleasures to the rank and file of the town—farmers, housewives, factory workers, schoolteachers, shop owners, young and old, healthy or infirm—as they all melted into one great pot of humanity. There were beaming, scrubbed faces of schoolboys and schoolgirls who attended manicured heifers and bulls, the stately animals secure in the reins of the diminutive masters. There were the leathery visages of sixty-year-old farmers, gnarled fingers caressing a grandchild's stuffed bear, as the child squeals in glee on a slowly circling pony. And there were rows of artistic cakes and pies, their creators resplendent in print-dress finery.

Ears were flooded from all directions with sounds somehow discordant and yet enchanting. The low-pitched chugging of the diesel engines powering the carnival rides mingled with the scratchy music and delirious laughter of riders whirled helter-skelter through the thick night air. Farther east, organ notes cascaded from loudspeakers above the grandstand, only to be overwhelmed by spirited applause and cheers given to horse and rider, strutting in showy cadence. Everywhere, the great voice of the fair ebbed and flowed. To the inattentive listener, the voice was garbled and meaningless—something to be contended with. But it was much more, a living thing that could be broken down into individual, distinct voices, some halting and raspy in old age, others smooth and vigorous in the prime of life. Some were marked by the exuberance of youth, with the words tumbling forth, tripping over one another. The voices were nearly unanimous in their merriment, anger or sadness quickly swept away by the stronger current.

Mingled about the place were dozens of scents. The sugary aroma of cotton candy teased the nostrils, only to be nudged aside by the promise of fresh popcorn or the meaty, tantalizing exhaust pouring from the hamburger stand. The ubiquitous cloud of tobacco smoke hovered over all, a thin gray layer like the ghost of a long-forgotten battlefield. And in the milling throng and packed bleachers of the grandstand wafted perfumes and hairspray and after shave lotions and perspiration, all colliding in the air. From the livestock shelters came earthy odors of hay and manure and the heavy scents of large animals—odors of the farm brought to town.

It was into this great slice of life that parts of three families—Bates, Ledbetter, and Raines—joined in an annual rite. Tad Ledbetter led the group into the carnival midway, carefully maintaining a distance sufficient to disguise any parental attachment. His sister, Elizabeth, was perfectly content to walk beside her mother.

"Be back at the car by ten-thirty, young man," Margie Ledbetter instructed.

Without looking behind him, the boy raised his right hand in halfhearted acknowledgement.

Ernie said, "I think Fudd and Harley and me are going to take in some of the rodeo show. You three want to come?"

"I think we're headed for the exhibition building, Ernie," Margie replied. "We're going to check on all those cakes and pies with blue ribbons on them that aren't as good as Christa's."

Christa huffed lightly and shook her head as she smiled at the compliment.

"Let's meet back at the Ferris wheel in an hour, okay?" Ernie said.

"See you then," Margie answered.

Fudd lurched to a sudden halt at the top of the grandstand. "You all be pickin' out some seats, I gotta have a bag of popcorn. That dang smell's been workin' on me since I opened the car door."

Armed with a tall paper bag of popcorn in one hand and a cup of Pepsi in the other, Fudd motioned for his friends to proceed. Once seated, Fudd offered the bag to Ernie and Harley, each shaking his head.

"I don't know how in heck you two can watch a show and not munch a little corn. If a man's butt is on the bleachers, he's supposed to eat popcorn. I think it's a law, ain't it?"

"Fudd, we just finished supper not twenty minutes ago," Harley said.

"Harley, that was supper, this here's a show. Man can't half watch a show without munchin' on something."

The attention of the men was soon drawn to the soil battleground below them where the calf roping contest was underway. For the most part, the contestants were local youths who fancied themselves as misplaced cowboys. Lack of rodeo skills was compensated for in large measure by the sheer desire of the riders. It all made for great fun, with the boisterous crowd roaring with each effort of man and beast. After several rounds of the dusty combat, the men were caught up in the action, cheering and groaning for the would-be cowboys.

Ernie leaned his head near Harley and said, "I need this. It's hard to worry at a fair."

"Yeah, I've been thinking about him too. Every time I see some tall, stout kid with black hair, I think about him."

Both men shared the moment with easy, knowing smiles and then allowed themselves to be lost again in the young men they could see and cheer for. The hour passed swiftly for the men; Ernie glanced at his watch and motioned to his companions that it was time to rejoin the women.

Christa and Margie were waiting near the ticket booth for the Ferris wheel.

"See any cowboys?" Christa asked as they approached.

Harley answered. "No, but we had a barrel of fun watching them try to be."

"The calves won hands down," Fudd added, "always do. Where's Elizabeth?"

"She found a girlfriend from school. They're going to run together for a while," Margie answered.

"Come on, woman," Fudd urged, "let's get on this wheel and mess around at the top, you good-lookin' thing."

"You two sure you took him to the rodeo?" Margie asked. "Sounds like he sneaked off to a peep show."

"Haw! Haw!" the big man bawled as they began to walk toward the ticket booth. "Now you know that they don't have such a thing around here."

Harley persuaded Christa to ride the Octopus with him. The sprawling contraption bore a striking resemblance to its namesake. Long steel arms protruded from the central engine, with the rider buckets affixed to the ends in a manner that allowed them to spin wildly with the centrifugal force generated. The great arms whirled about the center while simultaneously changing elevation—thirty feet in the air one instant, nearly scraping the grass the next.

"There's room for three in the bucket, Ernie," Harley said.

"You two go ahead. I don't want to see my supper again."

After the machines slowly ground to a halt and the riders walked from the exit gates, the little group reassembled. They meandered through the midway, pausing now and then to enjoy the sights and sounds enveloping them.

Ernie said, "Me and Christa got room for some popcorn now. Anybody else?"

"I'll pass," said Harley.

"I'll be ready again in a little while," Fudd said. "We'll meet you two down by the Bullet. Me and Harley's gonna talk Margie into a really wild ride."

"I doubt that," Margie replied.

"Come on, let's just go watch it for a spin or two. You'll get worked up to it," Fudd assured her.

The three proceeded, giggling like teenagers, toward the infamous ride. Their merriment would be short-lived. Throughout the fairgrounds, an Old West theme was being played out, with several townsfolk portraying roles that included cowboys, saloon girls, lawmen, and gunfighters. They had been operating in earnest for the past hour, and had now worked their way to the far end of the midway, near the Bullet.

The sheriff of a small but rowdy posse soon became the focus of attention. The man in the sheriff's role was self-appointed. Long known within the town for his loud and abusive manner, Bud Alexander delighted in any situation that offered his brand of fun, no matter how uncomfortable for others. He worked in an auto repair shop, carefully removed by the proprietor from customer contact. He had been married years before in Sedalia to a woman who had ended a tempestuous relationship by firing a .38 caliber bullet in the general direction of his head. For this, and no doubt other reasons, he was single now, and had lived for the last five years in a rooming house two blocks from the shop.

Though barely five and a half feet tall, his tattooed forearms were thick and corded from a life of manual labor. His hands were gigantic squares, the fingers punctuated with permanent black dirt and grease stains half-mooned under the nails. His floppy cowboy hat sat atop an unruly mop of reddish-brown hair, spilling over cruel little eyes.

The organizer of the western theme groups had attempted to place him in a less conspicuous role, but in the end was intimidated, and finally acquiesced after a promise from Alexander ensuring him that nothing troublesome would take place. His fragile trust was misplaced. Bud had fished a dirty, coarse length of thick rope from behind the seat of his truck. With this he fashioned a hangman's noose that served as his main weapon. He soon embarked upon an entertaining evening, highlighted by capturing unsuspecting victims whom he paraded about for a few minutes before release. He had chosen men for the most part, with the only women victimized being younger and in all-female groups. The men went along with the game rather than make an issue of it, and the younger women were too taken aback to offer resistance. With each success, he paid less and less attention to the gender, age, or companionship of his next target. It was with this growing bravado that Bud Alexander and his posse spied the trio nearing the Bullet ride. Dirty noose in hand, Bud approached Margie from behind and with a little flip of his wrist pitched it over her head, the heavy rope scraping her right ear on the way down. Her hands reached up instinctively in an effort to protect the tender skin of her exposed neck. Incredulous, she quickly turned and looked at her antagonist.

Fudd's face instantly turned into a crimson mask of rage. He reached for the rope and carefully lifted it over his wife's slightly bowed head. Her neck was splotched with red from the chafing of the rope. Fudd then took the noose with both hands and formed it into a loose ball, his eyes never leaving Bud's face. Before the man could raise his hands, the rope shot from Fudd's hands and impacted squarely on his chin, causing him to take a step backward.

"Get outta here, man," Fudd growled, "that's the best and only offer I'm gonna make."

Now having gathered himself and feeling the stares of his companions, Alexander spat out: "Ain't nobody throws somethin' in my face!"

"Well, I tried," Fudd said, more to Margie than to Alexander.

"Fudd, I'm all right…there's no use doing this," Margie pleaded as she placed her hand on his clenched right fist.

"Leave me be, woman. I'm gonna jerk this idiot's lungs out through his nose holes 'cause he needs a lesson."

Harley had remained motionless since the beginning of the ugly incident. Two steps separated the protagonists, and as Fudd began to close the gap, he felt Harley's firm grip on his left forearm. Harley spoke directly to Alexander, who by now had raised both fists to waist level.

"For shame, man…for shame. Think about what you've just done. A man doesn't throw a rope around a lady's head."

Alexander formed a curse on his lips and raised a forefinger toward the smaller man, who quickly raised his hand in a demand of silence. Their eyes were locked now—Alexander's more quizzical than angry, Harley's steady and penetrating.

"I'm not through yet. If you want to say something when I'm finished, you can. Whatever made you think you could treat a lady like a horse…and right in front of her husband?"

Alexander glanced furtively at Margie, her chin quivering with emotion. A small gathering had formed a loose circle around the disturbance. Harley continued to speak evenly, without menace, like an older brother speaking to a younger brother who had just disgraced himself. "I can't figure out how somebody can live as long as you have and not have decent manners. Look around you at all these people who came here to have a good time and not worry about any ugliness. What right do you have to change all that?"

Harley finally received the signal he was looking for in Alexander's eyes, which had softened noticeably, and in his hands, no longer clenched. He also felt a relaxation of the bands of muscle in Fudd's forearm.

Alexander's brain struggled mightily with tandem problems, one of which he knew demanded immediate response. All of the negative attention directed at him had become an intolerable burden—palpable, given life by the scrutiny of the onlookers. The second problem, totally befuddling, was his inability to interrupt this meddlesome little man and get on with the business at hand. Three different times during the preceding minute, suitable curses had formed on his lips, but none could be uttered. Against an obviously unworthy physical foe, he had been rendered mute. It made no sense to Alexander. He had dispatched the likes of this fellow more times than he could remember with nothing more than a simple sneer. And yet the man stood before him, clearly unafraid, asking questions that stung, and for which he had no answers.

Harley spoke his final words. "I imagine everybody here wishes none of this would've happened. Me and my friends are going back to what we came for, and that's having a good time." He paused, sighed. "Just walk away."

With a final snort of exasperation, Alexander reached down and snatched up the rope, wheeled around, shouldering his way past the bystanders as he melted into the larger throng of the carnival.

"Come on, you two," Harley said to Margie and Fudd, "I'm going to buy us all a nice big Pepsi."

With Fudd in the middle and Harley's hand softly patting the small of his back, the three began to make their way to the refreshment stand. Ernie and Christa, approaching from the opposite direction, exchanged curious glances as they neared their subdued friends.

"That crazy ride take the starch out of you all?" Christa asked.

"Wasn't the ride," Margie replied with a weak smile.

"We had a little run in with Bud Alexander," Harley added.

"What's that character up to?" Ernie asked.

Margie briefly recounted the confrontation for Ernie and Christa. Once finished, she summed up her feelings simply and thankfully. "I'm just glad Harley didn't go get a Pepsi with you two."

Fudd, silent while his wife spoke, finally cleansed his mind after a colossal exhalation emptied his lungs. "Kinda scary, getting' mad like that. I reckon I'm glad he didn't either. I was ready to go to the grass, and Harley ends up lashin' him with his tongue worse than I could've with my fists."

"I've heard a lot about him," Ernie said, "I'm surprised he didn't jump you, Harley."

Fudd said, "He dang sure wanted to, I'll tell you that much, but he just couldn't pull the trigger." He paused, slowly shaking his head. "Course, neither could I." He looked at Harley who was busy fidgeting with his cap.

"I still want that Pepsi, don't you two?" Harley asked, already in motion.

"Let's go find some grandstand seats," Christa said. "I think a little dose of the rodeo would suit everybody fine."

"Sounds good to me," Ernie said.

"Let's do it," Fudd agreed. "I'm tuckered out. That was worse than hangin' a day's worth of birds by a long shot. I'm too old to be gettin' that mad."

After three bull rides—all of which were won by the bulls—the memory of the incident began to fade into the raucous cheers of the crowd. Christa watched the cowboys, but her thoughts were united with the friend seated on her left. She doubted that Harley's full attention was being given to the action below.

She glanced at him and smiled, then leaned close to his ear. "Blessed are the peacemakers."

He returned her smile, nodded his head slightly, said, "Thank you."

Christa read his lips for the words, lost to everyone except her as the sudden roar of the crowd consumed them.

Fudd sat down on the edge of the bed, pulled off a sock and tossed it in the general direction of the closet. "I been thinkin' about it all the way home, and it still doesn't make sense, Margie. I wanted a piece of his hind end so bad I could taste it. I was decidin' where I ought to hit him first, and then I feel Harley's hand on my arm—not hard, mind you—I just felt it. And he starts talkin' and all of a sudden I can't move. It was plumb unnervin' at first. And then, before it's over, I'm dang near feelin' calm about the whole thing. I mean, I'm not ready to shake Alexander's hand or nothin' like that, but I didn't want to hit him no more either. No way to be that mad and then have it simmer down so quick, I tell you."

"That's just Harley for you," Margie said, "he's got the knack for doing the right thing somehow. There's just some people like that, I guess…who've got living religion."

"Yeah, I know it's got somethin' to do with his religion, but heck, I've known a bunch of religious people that weren't a thing like Harley.

He's changed me some through the years without me even thinkin' much about it."

Fudd flopped backward on the bed and spoke again even before the bouncing of the mattress ceased. "Remember the time way back when we started hangin' birds and I used God in a cussin' way…I told you about that time, didn't I?" Margie nodded but Fudd proceeded anyway. "Anyways, he looks at me and says, 'I'd appreciate it if you wouldn't ask God to damn anything.' And I says that I wasn't really askin' God to do any such a thing…I was just usin' a good strong cuss word. But he told me it meant a lot more than that. But I still don't get mad at him, and I'm thinkin' something ain't normal here—I should at least be a little agitated—but before I could cogitate on it, he's steered us away toward something else…and, boom, it was all over. I'll swear…he ought to have been a preacher or a priest."

Fudd nodded his head in wonderment, a half-smile on his face.

Margie looked down at him, said, "Maybe he is a preacher."

"Oh, Margie, he's a turkey hangar, just like me…a real good man, better than most, me included for sure…but…"

"Where does it say that a man has to have a whole church full of people to be a preacher? He preached a little sermon tonight, and it was harder than standing in front of a bunch of folks all dressed up nice and smiling at him. There's something behind all that. Bible doesn't say a thing about what you've got to look like or talk like to be a preacher."

"Since when did you come to be an expert on the good book?"

"I've had my share of church learning, mister."

Margie had, within the past few years, taken the children to services, but only sporadically, and only for their betterment. In truth, she was only slightly more inclined than Fudd to consider the weightier matters of life. Fudd was aware of this, and the knowledge made him wary of her assertions.

"And I'll tell you another thing, too. It wouldn't hurt any of us to go to church once in a while. Maybe he's listened to Fred Riggins for so long that he's come to be a little preacher in his own right. Something made him like he is, and that's got to be at least a part of it."

"I thought you said a man didn't need any formal trainin' to be a preacher, and now your sayin' that the same man's a preacher because he's listened to another preacher who'd been formal trained. Have mercy, woman, you're gettin' me plumb turned around on this thing!"

"Oh, Fudd…I don't know exactly what I'm trying to say. I just wish everybody could be more like him. And Christa, she's just like him, and she goes to church regular too. And I think about the kids…it just got me to thinking—you so close to wrestling in the grass with that bully—and don't get me wrong, I appreciate you taking up for me, but it turned out so good when it could've turned out so bad…and I think about what makes Harley and Christa like they are. I'm gonna get up in the morning and me and the kids are heading for services. I just feel the need to."

"Great day, I start talkin' about Harley and you wind up talkin' about church."

"It's the same thing…same thing." Margie sighed, the weariness leaking from her with a puff of air across her lips. "I'm going to bed, I'm worn out."

"Suits me too. My mind can't take any more churnin' tonight."

Harley walked into the house and greeted his mother. "Hi, Mom. You gals have a good time at the fair?"

"You bet we did. I'm likely to be back down there another time or two before the week's over. How about you, son?"

"Pretty good night, all told. Any tea left?"

"There's plenty, bring me a glass too."

They sat in the tiny living room and talked for another twenty minutes before Clara arose, exchanged a cheek kiss with her son, who had not mentioned the confrontation with Bud Alexander. Harley entered his bedroom and sat down in the rocker next to the night stand. He reached for the black, leather-bound Bible and turned on the lamp. The words he sought were in the book of Matthew, the fifth chapter. He knew the passage, but there was a deep contentment in seeing the red lettering that formed the words of Christ.

> *Blessed are the peacemakers, for they shall be called the children of God…let your light so shine before men, that they may see your good works, and glorify your Father*

which is in heaven.

He closed the book gently and placed it back on the night stand. He removed his clothes and pulled on the worn pajama bottoms, flicked off the lamp. Then, with the silver moonlight cleansing the room of all things earthly, the man knelt at his bedside as he had since childhood, folded his coarse hands beneath his chin, and prayed.

It was during the second stanza of the opening hymn that the woman and her two children scurried up the concrete staircase of First Baptist. Margie was dressed smartly, the two youngsters freshly scrubbed and in their best clothing. They slipped into the last row of the center section of pews. Margie took a hymnal from the rack and glanced at the page number. As she looked up, her eyes met Christa's, dancing in song from the choir loft. Christa smiled a warm greeting, and Margie returned the gesture.

Christa flipped back the Sunday calendar pages in her mind; this was the first service in nearly four months that Margie and the kids had attended. She was pleased but not surprised by their attendance. The near disastrous incident of the previous night had obviously served as a catalyst, although she could not know precisely how this had come about. She was certain that the greatest portion of the motivation had come from witnessing Harley Raines, who lived out his beliefs. The joy she felt for the Ledbetters grew to include Ernie, who spent every workday with her beloved friend. Harley could do more toward leading her husband to the faith than ten thousand words from a preacher, even one as splendid as Fred Riggins. Just as she believed that it was no accident that Harley had chosen not to go to the refreshment stand the night before, neither was it mere chance that his life had come into contact with Ernie's.

Yes, she assured herself, Harley would find a way to lead her man, and it would not be astray.

CHAPTER SIX

After two days of good birds at the plant, Wednesday brought an unwelcome surprise. Before leaving the parking lot for his morning session at the tracks, Harley made a brief inspection of the first load of turkeys waiting in the dock driveway. He took several steps in the direction of the trailer before looking up. Had he looked up before starting his walk, he would have saved the steps. One look at the black feathers crammed against the coop doors was all that was required.

"Dadgum," he mumbled under his breath, "bronze birds."

The turkeys came from Arkansas, as did nearly all of the bronze variety. The birds closely resembled their wild cousins in both appearance and behavior; the latter characteristic presenting significant problems for the hangars, who were in no need of more. The white-feathered domestic birds, which made up ninety-eight percent of the total production, were a pleasure to handle compared to the bronze. The hangar could throw open the coop door one time and never again worry about the white birds, which, for the most part, faced away from the hangar ignorantly awaiting the hand of man. Not so for the bronze. The generally accepted procedure was for the hangar to open the door for his bird, and then quickly slam it before the next malcontent flapped toward freedom. This soon became a nightmarish chore for the hangars, and by mid-afternoon the pace of work on the dock slowed to levels that usually brought a visit from the evisceration line foreman, who would inquire indelicately regarding the slowdown.

Although from no lack of energy, even Fudd succumbed to the doldrums caused by hours of battle with the disobliging creatures. Harley hoped that only one day's worth of the birds was scheduled. When he returned from the tracks he found Fudd waiting at the edge of the parking lot, arms folded across his chest, staring at the trailer.

"I'll be switched with barbed wire if I can figure out why they buy these black devils," he muttered. "Outta the jillion, nice white birds roamin' the earth, they round up a bunch of these critters. Crapsakes! It just beats the heck outta me, Harley. I think they do it once in a while just to show us they can."

"I doubt that, but it doesn't seem worthwhile to me either."

"If one of the wild devils jumps on my back today, I'm gonna wring his neck and carry him to the plant manager's office and go home, I swear."

After two terrible days with the bronze birds, smallish hens were scheduled for the next day, making for what should have been a trouble-free day, both on the dock and inside the plant. But it was not to be. Torment, sometimes great, sometimes small, was always on the prowl in the building. There was too much power, coupled with hundreds of razor edges, for man to control unerringly; it was simply the nature of the place.

An hour after lunch break, Harley finished hanging a turkey and was turning back to the coop he was working when he saw the speeding vehicle zip away from the parking lot. It was Dorothy Lou's blue Mustang. The passenger side of the car faced the dock opening and Harley caught a glimpse of the hunched form of a man, and what appeared to be an arm coming over the back seat that was wrapped protectively about the shoulder of the man. Harley felt a chill pass through the pit of his stomach. She was headed for Doc Kenyon's office, and she was in a great hurry. A man's life had just taken a turn for the worse. Harley only hoped that the damage was repairable. He turned to Fudd and passed on the bad news.

"Somebody got hurt inside," he shouted over the din.

Fudd slammed a bird into a shackle and moved toward Harley. "How fast was she goin'?"

"Fast. It doesn't look good."

"Must've been clear over on the done side," Fudd said, "this line ain't slowed down since dinner."

The "done side" was the section of the plant where the turkeys spilled from the chilling tanks onto a conveyor belt line. Once the birds were re-hung on this separate line, there remained only one dangerous task for the workers to contend with—the neck cutting station. Two men were equipped with an air powered pistol-gripped cutting machine that was suspended from overhead. The cutting blades were two three-inch curved scissor arms, honed to razor sharpness. With the pull of the trigger, the arms converged in a quarter of a second, neatly snipping even the thickest neck of a big tom turkey. What made the operation doubly dangerous was the large flap of loose skin that dangled annoyingly in front of nearly half of the cutter's target. The flap of skin was deemed a necessary hazard by management; it provided a covering for the neck end of the cavity, and besides, it sold for the same price as the choice parts.

Word filtered over from the evisceration line at afternoon break. Terry Basinger, Mavis's nephew, was the victim. Lost a finger, somebody said. Carl Schmidt, the veteran cutter under whom Terry was training, was inconsolable, somebody else heard.

Harley, Fudd, and Ernie stood in the parking lot, waiting for the done-side workers to emerge from the plant. Mavis and Carl were friends, dating all the way back to the early days of the plant, and Terry was a kid about whom Mavis had hounded the personnel office until he had been given a job. It was more than curiosity that brought Ernie and the hangars to stand vigil near Carl's car. When the plant wounded a worker, everyone bled in spirit.

Carl, flanked by two friends, shuffled toward his car. His eyes were red and he clutched a checkered handkerchief in his right hand. He appeared thankful when he looked up and saw the men waiting for him, but both Fudd and Harley knew that it was Ernie's presence that moved him. The two men were the only continuous employees remaining from the opening day of the plant, and they had become minor legends due to their work ethic and skills. Ernie stepped forward and firmly gripped Carl's right forearm as he wrapped his other arm around his shoulder.

"Man, I'm so sorry, Carl."

Carl nodded his head and drew in a jagged breath, swiping at his nose with the handkerchief. "I should've been watching him closer." He shook his head.

"There's no use in blaming yourself," Ernie said softly. "Mavis said he'd been doing fine for a couple of weeks now."

"It was the neck flap…he got tangled up in it and didn't back off…didn't just start over and find the neck…" the words tumbled out now, needed to come out. "He was always worried about getting behind, and I told him a hundred times that I'd catch him up for a year if need be…just go steady, I told him." He blew out a breath. "But he's a young'un, proud and all…didn't want me doing more than my share."

"A man can't help that, Carl…can't do a thing to prevent that," Ernie said.

"I saw it, his thumb…fell out from behind the flap and bounced on the toe of his boot…ended up on the drain grate, but before I could grab it, it fell through. Man oh man…you think they could've sewed it back on?"

"Not likely, Carl," Ernie said with a shake of his head. "It's a long way over to Columbia…even if they would've had a chance."

Carl spoke in a raspy whisper: "Worried his thumb off for two dollars and fifty-five cents an hour, that's what the boy did."

Ernie clapped him gently on the shoulder before releasing him. "You listen now…there's not a finer worker…or man…in that plant than you, and I'm tellin' you that there wasn't a thing in the world you could've done. He's young…and proud."

Carl nodded and dragged the handkerchief across his face. "Thanks for saying it, Ernie." He turned in unison with his two companions and walked away.

Ernie spoke a subdued farewell to Fudd and Harley and walked toward his pickup. Fudd looked down and inspected his left thumb, marveling as if for the first time at the wonderful function of the digit as it worked in harmony with the fingers. "I've nipped off a couple of tips, but it'd be terrible to part with that thing."

"Tough row to hoe for a young fellow, there's no doubt about that," Harley said.

"You gonna think about the kid up on the tracks Monday mornin'?"

"I expect I will before then."

"Figured that. See you Monday."

Christa was in the kitchen peeling apples for a pie when Ernie opened the back door and walked straight to a chair at the table.

"Tough day?" she asked.

"Not for me. Was for that nephew of Mavis who was neck cutting."

"Oh, no…what happened?"

"Cut off his left thumb. Carl said he was tryin' too hard to keep up."

Christa placed a half peeled apple and her paring knife on the counter. "Bless his heart, dear Lord, bless his poor heart. I expect they'll take him to Jeff City…or Columbia?"

"Doubt it. The thumb got knocked in the waste line. Probably couldn't have got it back on anyway. It's just a question of whether or not Doc Kenyon thinks he can do a proper job on the stub."

"You want a cup of this?" Christa asked, pouring herself a mug of coffee.

"No, I'm headed for my place."

He paused in the doorway and without turning back to her, said, "He's Aaron's age, you know. Just tryin' too hard to keep up. Aaron would've been the same way."

"Yes, he probably would've been."

Ernie continued to stand poised in the doorway, and Christa sensed that he was probing for unattainable answers. "It's just a hard piece of life, Ernie. It grieves me deeply."

He remained motionless, silent. Christa said, "How can you tell a young man not to try to pull his own load?"

Ernie raised his hand as if he was going to speak, but he quickly lowered it and softly closed the door behind him.

The tree line in the distance was awash in shades of red and gold. Within ten days, the hues of autumn would reach their exquisite apex. Rainfall had been above average during the late summer, interspersed with days bathed in sunlight, assuring high sugar content in the trees and vigorous leaves that would cling tenaciously to their season, succumbing to nature only after long days of pleading artistry.

Ernie's pace was swift as he consumed the distance separating him from his goal. He eased his bulk onto the cottonwood root and comfortably braced his back against the stream bank. The afternoon breeze was spirited, nearly chilly. The last several days had been unseasonably cool, portending the winter that would sweep down on the jet stream from Canada in late November.

He rested his head against the bank, allowing his gaze to rise along the great trunk until it reached the soft blanket of leaves, swirling like a misplaced field of yellow wild flowers. He lowered his head, took in the offerings of black oak and hickory—muted shades of red and buttery ambers. And on to the proud sumac, blood-red and radiant as it captured the sunlight. For long minutes, he forced his thoughts to drift in accord with the beauty surrounding him. But thoughts returned, as he knew they would, to young men and their sorrows.

He spoke to the trees as if to revered counselors: "A hard piece of life, the woman says. Sure is that. A boy trying to make some money to help his family, and harm takes him. I got one trying to be a soldier in a place that takes more than thumbs. Place boilin' over with bullets and hate…and yet there isn't any hate in him. A man can't make all that straight…can he?"

The leaves answered in scratchy whispers.

"Hard piece of life, oh yeah. A boy craves his daddy's love…ends up killin' him at suppertime. Same boy gets a son of his own, loves him for all the world, and has to worry about him day and night for fear some other daddy's son will harm him. Daddys and sons…there just ain't any straightenin' it out."

The leaves above him blurred as he looked up again, all light and color and softness as the scene unfolded yet again in his mind, and he could not shut it out—the first sickening blow to his mother's stomach…the sound she made as she doubled over…the flurry of his father's fists…the long knife on the floor, beckoning…and then the blood, and finally the howling silence, like a great wind in his head. He blinked his eyes, attempted to hurry the thing away, but he knew it would be a futile effort. The scene had a life and will of its own, and it would not be hurried.

He knew that it had passed when he felt the cool breeze on his face, and he shifted his weight on the cottonwood root. Warm tears crowded for space under his eyelids, seeped onto his cheeks. "If caring and hoping matters at all…or if tradin' my own life would do it, surely harm will leave my boy alone. He doesn't have but a few weeks to go. Just let him hang on…just a while longer…please."

He pulled up the sleeve of his jacket and stared at the hands of his watch. It was four-thirty in the morning in Vietnam. Above the man, the Missouri leaves sighed, but would not answer him.

Gino Polities held up the dirty sliver of paper that bore the penciled block numerals "17." He turned the paper over and over in his fingertips, studying it in the manner of an art collector contemplating a rare find. Behind him, sitting on a steel helmet next to Aaron, was the soldier with reddish-brown skin and hawk-like features known as Pima. He was twenty-one years old, from Enid, Oklahoma, and a devout Baptist whose father taught Sunday school. In his rucksack he carried an illustrated New Testament and his grandfather's feather-trimmed hunting hatchet. He carried the hatchet as a reminder of his grandfather's distrust of the white man—though it was a splotch deep within Pima that he acknowledged only on occasion.

Pima took a sip of Kool-Aid from his canteen liner, then said softly, "Chu Lai not far away, huh?"

"Tomorrow maybe," said Gino, "the day after for sure, Sarge says."

"Maybe we won't run into a tunnel this time."

Gino looked back, smiled wryly as he rolled the paper into a tight ball and tossed it at Pima. "If it's our main mission to find 'em, I imagine we'll find us one or two…and the big number seventeen belongs to my little Chicago butt."

Pima drained the last of the Kool-Aid, ran the tip of his tongue over his lips. "So it is. It has been a long time since you went down though."

"Not long enough." Gino looked at Aaron, said, "You big guys whine about all the stuff you have to hump, but gettin' out of tunnel duty makes up for all of it."

Aaron tapped a finger against the ammunition belt draped on his shoulder. "This M-60 and the ammo strung over my shoulders weighs thirty-eight pounds, man, and unless I'm asleep I wear it like clothes."

Gino shook his head, said, "Still ain't fair. They ought to grease you up and poke you down there like us little boys, right, Pima?"

"Naw…it all works out in the end…what's fair and what's not."

Gino turned toward Pima and Aaron, then traced his gaze up the crooked trunk of a tree at the edge of the little clearing. "I've known you two long enough now to admit that I'm scared stiff down there." He paused, continued to stare at the tree trunk. "Didn't know that, huh? Didn't think I was scared of anything, did you?"

Aaron and Pima exchanged glances, then Pima said, "It is not a bad thing to be afraid. It sharpens a man's senses."

Gino made a sound in his chest that was at once a hum and a sigh. "Not mine, brother Indian, not mine." He paused, gathered his thoughts. "I pissed my pants last time I went down." He swallowed hard. "You tell anybody else and I'll hurt you somehow, I swear. You hear me, you two Jesus boys?"

"You know we wouldn't say anything," Aaron said.

"It was the rat that caused it…big as a cat, I swear. He came from a little side tunnel, just popped in my face…didn't pay no attention to the flashlight at all. Just, boom…right there a foot from my nose, on his haunches, teeth bared, hissin' like a snake. Froze me like an ice cube…couldn't move a muscle. Then, he just disappeared, like some nasty black ghost, and for a second I thought I'd just imagined it…the long teeth and the beady little eyes…all of it. But then I felt the pee on my legs. He was real."

"It was involuntary," said Aaron, "would've happened to anybody."

"I think it was an omen…like I ain't supposed to go back down there."

Pima said, "Let Keller go down for you. It's a standing thing, everybody knows. He comes all unglued about goin' down…loves it…weird guy. Nobody would think a thing about it."

Gino looked back at him, said, "Then how come nobody's ever took him up on the offer?" Pima scraped at the ground with the bottom of canteen liner. Gino nodded, "that's right, it's an offer that nobody can take, and still hold his head up."

"So, me and Aaron will pray for you if you go down."

"Yeah," Gino said, "you boys pray your butts off…can't hurt I suppose."

"Can only help," Pima said.

Gino stood, brushed off the bottom of his fatigue pants. He walked to Pima, reached down and tapped his rucksack. "How come when you go down you take that old hatchet instead of the lieutenant's pistol?"

"It was my grandfather's."

"But it ain't a pistol. There's not room down there to use that thing much beyond poking a V. C. in the face." He paused, tapped the rucksack again. "It's an Indian thing, ain't it, Pima? You got a little Bible in there, and that hatchet, and I'll bet the hatchet means more to you."

"They are both things of honor, in different ways."

"But which one do you trust most?"

Aaron stood, said, "Come on, Gino…for cryin' out loud, don't…"

Pima held up his hand, shook his head for silence. "It is a fair question." He stood up, faced Gino. "One is of God and one is of man, but man is of God. How can I rank such things?"

"You're talking in circles, bro," Gino said, "I'm still waitin' for the answer."

"That is the best I can do, my friend."

"Sheeeze!" Gino spun on his heel and stalked away.

Aaron bumped his fist softly against Pima's shoulder. "He doesn't mean anything bad by that…you know."

"I know. He is a searcher in the spirit world, and searchers leak anger sometimes. I am not offended."

"I think it's a good sign he's all churned up. The Holy Spirit must be working on him."

"I think this is so." Pima turned to walk away, then stopped after two steps and turned back around. His features were stone-like, his eyes riveted on Aaron's face. "What do you believe is the color of the Holy Spirit's face, white man…like yours, or like mine?"

Aaron felt a hollow punch in his stomach. "I…uh…why do you…"

It was then that the corners of Pima's mouth began to twitch, quickly followed by a burst of laughter.

"You…you sneaky little jerk." Aaron jumped toward Pima, but he vanished into the green edge of the clearing. "I owe you one, buddy… that one's gonna come back at you."

It was Thursday of the following week before the plant workers regained their sense of balance. The memory of a bad accident always hung like an ugly cloud for several days, especially for those who labored near sharp edges or the might of machinery. A bloody accident was an unwanted reminder of the flimsy veneer of flesh and muscle, strands made trivial by the metal edges.

It had been over three days since anyone on the dock had laughed from the belly, and for Fudd, this was an intolerable situation. He arrived at work Thursday morning bent on rescuing his fellow workers from this sorry state, but it was not until noon that he found proper fodder for his cannon of mirth. To his dismay, Margie had failed to pack something sweet in his lunch pail, and he had trudged to the main lunchroom for a package of cookies from a vending machine. He returned to the dock break room with only six minutes remaining before the resumption of bird hanging. It was ample time.

"I never been to that crazy place but what I don't see somethin' amazin'," he began, laying out the bait.

"What could be amazing in a room full of mostly screechin' women and cigarette smoke?" Dorsey drawled.

"You hit it square on the head, boss man. The things some of those gut line women can do with their mouths is truly amazin'. They're all the time in a big hurry, and that's the cause of it, no doubt. Always dillyin' around in the bathroom, and havin' no time left to eat, you know."

Fudd had everyone's attention now, even though no one had the slightest notion where this latest tangent would lead.

"Anyway, I'm standin' there unwrappin' my cookies and I start watchin' two of 'em sittin' right across from each other, just jabberin' a blue streak. The big blond—I think she's a gizzard cutter—she's chompin' on a wad of gum like an alligator, and smokin' a cig. She unwraps a chocolate cupcake, and I'm figurin' the gum will have to go…but heck no…she commences to stuffin' the cake down the hatch. So, I says to myself…dang, gum on one side, cake on the other, and still talkin'. Surely she'll forget the cig, right?" As I live and breathe, she didn't miss a single drag on that thing either, and still yakkin' along like a blue jay!"

His audience was chuckling and the animation rose with the positive response.

"I'll kiss your behind on the courthouse steps if that ain't four things at once! I figure if she can do four, surely I can to three. I'm not gonna smoke, so I'll chew gum, eat my cookies, and talk, right? So I eased over to the table, couple spots down from her, and bummed a stick of Juicy Fruit and got it goin' good on one side. I popped a cookie in the other side, and commenced to munchin' that. I'm havin' to concentrate pretty hard on keepin' them apart, but what the heck, I says to myself, I'm just tryin' for three outta four…so I turn my head and start to butt in and say something, and I got the devils mixed up in my mouth. I'll tell you something…Juicy Fruit and Hydrox cookies don't mix all that well, and I got to chokin' like a man dyin' from consumption. The dang gum felt like it was goin' down my windpipe, and the blond heifer…she's poundin' on my back so hard she's knocked my cap off in the floor. And even while I'm concentratin' on not dyin' I'm thinkin' I'm a son-of-a-gun if she ain't doin' five things now…cause she's askin' me if I'm all right and blowin' smoke jet in my face, and she hasn't swallowed the gum or the cake, and she's poundin' the shirt off my back!"

Laughter rocked the little room as Fudd pushed away from the table. "I was plumb embarrassed by then, and I hightailed it outta there, but I'll tell you, it was worth it. There's circus people can't do things like that…and it didn't cost me a cent."

He was one step from the door, adjusting his filthy cap for battle. "I feel stronger than an old man's pee at dawn…let's hang some of these buzzards."

Fudd sensed the breaking of the solemn spell, knew that the tale would spread throughout the plant. The following Monday, Terry Basinger's replacement arrived at the neck cutting station, and the steady drone of the plant filled the air.

The letter from Aaron arrived on the third Wednesday in October. Harley pulled down the mailbox door and found the envelope atop the small stack. He registered mild surprise; this was the first direct correspondence from Aaron. Previous letters to his parents had contained several requests to pass on greetings or light-hearted comments. Harley settled into the rocker in the corner of his bedroom and cut the top of the envelope with his pocketknife.

> Dear Harley,
> You are probably wondering why I am writing to you, and maybe I am a little too. But we neither one should be. Outside of my folks, I feel closer to you than any other person. I need somebody to talk to about some things on my mind. I don't want to worry them. I know Mom could handle it all right, but I can't very well write to just her. And you are really the one to say this to. I can tell right now this will be a long letter, so I will say up front that I am sorry for unloading on you. Things have been hot lately. Enemy movement has picked up and our platoon has had its share of contact. We have lost five guys in the last two weeks, three killed and two wounded. It is not that I am afraid so much as that I

just know how quick it can happen over here. We never see them first. The shooting just starts and it is where they want it to. Anyhow, I have thought lately about in the Bible where it says that life is but a vapor. I think I know what that means now. I am sounding heavy now, huh? Pop has been on my mind lately. Him and Gino Polites. He is a Greek kid from Chicago—a little fire plug of a guy. The folks have shown you the picture and told you about him I am sure. He told me he is in the Corps because a judge gave him the choice of doing some time or joining up. He grew up rough, but we came together close somehow. He has got no use for God, or so he says. But he is just like Pop. They know God is there, but they do not trust Him for the big picture. My Indian friend, Pima—you have probably heard about him too in the letters—is a Baptist like us and we have talked to him some. But he asks some hard questions that neither one of us can answer very well. He enjoys the stories I tell him about you helping me with stuff when I was a kid. Remember that time when I was in sixth grade and the teacher made me wash crud off of Virgil Slawson's neck? Poor kid kept coming to school dirty as a pig and finally Mrs. Kuhlman put me in charge of cleaning him up. You remember. I was mad as a hornet and then you read me the story about Jesus washing his men's feet. Anyway, that moved Gino for some reason. He said that he did not figure the Christ for a foot washer. I get words on the tip of my tongue that I need to say but I can never get them out right. I know I will get the chance to say the right thing sometime. If he could hear Mom sing, huh? Ha! I would love that. I guess I have beat around the bush long enough. What I am asking is that you help Mom with Pop if something happens to me. There—I have said it and will not mention it again. On to better stuff. Fudd had better put another mattress in the bed of his pickup at my first pig picking back there. I plan on matching him bite for bite. I have told Gino about them but he can't quite get the picture. I want him to come and visit when we have one. We will break him of that Greek food for good. Hope Pop gets a nice fat deer next month. I have been thinking about smoked venison too. Most of these guys do not have a clue about real country food like we do. Wish I could have watched some of the World Series with you, even if the Cards did not win. We got all the details here but I did not get to hear any on radio. What the dickens made Lou Brock try to score without sliding in the fifth game? We got to talk about that play. Can you believe this letter? Ought to have a binder. I got to stop. It feels good just writing to you and I look forward to seeing you soon. Sorry about the heavy stuff, but I had to get it out. You must feel like a priest on the other side of that little screen. Ha! A Baptist priest. Remember me on the tracks.

Love from your friend,
Aaron

Harley placed the letter in his lap and drew in a deep breath. The letter had been an emotional roller coaster. He wondered if the boy had experienced a premonition of some sort. Harley had long known that Ernie's lack of faith troubled Aaron, as well as Christa. Aaron would surely come back, Harley assured himself; he had unfinished business with his father. Harley reasoned further that Aaron's witness to his buddy, Gino, would be more effective back in the states, back in rural Missouri. Back where a voice like Christa's could soften the edges of a tough city kid's heart.

He felt better now. The old rocker creaked soothingly as he looked out the window. Yes, there would be a pig-picking to beat all in November.

CHAPTER SEVEN

October passed in the autumn serenity of sun-drenched days and cool, crisp breezes. The cold fronts that pushed through hurried off contritely to the east. The invigorating tingle of the fall air infused the vast, white processing plant and its workers, who picked up the pace markedly. Management noticed the phenomenon each autumn, and attributed it to the higher energy level of the laborers, now freed from the sweltering bondage of summer. The hangers were especially favored on the open-air loading dock. The cool breeze swept in and at once refreshed the hangers while pushing the heavy odors away.

Fudd greatly enjoyed this bonus of nature as he offered up a thunderous rendition of a Johnny Cash tune.

"I fell in….to a burnin' ring of fiiiire
I went down, down, down, as the flames went higher
And it burns, burns, buuuuuurns…the ring of fire
The ring of fiiiire."

Harley shook his head in resignation and smiled wryly at the inexpert crooner.

"Now Harley, you got to admit that wasn't half bad."

"You're exactly right, Fudd, it wasn't half bad, it was totally bad."

"Haw! Haw! He! He! You're just jealous, I can tell. Me and old John, now that'd be a pair for sure. Him strummin' that big ole guitar and me backin' him up. Go on now!"

Dorsey sounded retreat through the doorway and the men, except for Fudd, scurried to the break room for lunch. Fudd stepped down to ground level at the rear of the trailer and faced the wind sweeping in from the west. He removed his cap and tilted his head slightly upward, drawing the air into his nostrils with all his might. After three vigorous inhalations, he was ready for lunch and conversation.

"Indian summer, by dang, you can't beat it with a stick!" he proclaimed as he entered the lunch room.

"I'll go along with that," Ernie said. "This has been a beauty so far."

Fudd unscrewed the lid of his thermos as he licked his lips in anticipation.

"What you got in there?" Dorsey asked.

"Some of the meanest chili this side of west Hades, boss man. Plenty of onions and red pepper, and beef and beans…man oh man… just take a whiff and blister your nose hairs." He extended the open container to the men around the table.

Dorsey shook his head and frowned. "There's no doubt in my mind but what there's a law somewhere says a man can't eat chili like that." He shook his head. "Margie and your kids eat that?"

"She makes a special batch for me, and one for them." He spooned down the first steaming bite and smacked his lips. "You know, I been thinkin' all morning about this weather around here. Danged if I can figure why anybody would want to live somewhere without four seasons." He paused for another spoonful and a cracker square. "About the time you get a belly full of summer, fall comes kickin' in like this, kind of breakin' you in for winter. A few good snows and some cold weather to kill off the bugs, and here'll come April and May, all sassy and green. Then you're ready for some heat again. All works out just about right."

"I don't know, Fudd," Dorsey said. "I can remember a couple of Januarys that like to froze my tail off and had me thinking about some beach out in California."

"Oh, for pity sake, boss man. Three or four days of sand in your drawers and havin' to look at them dang hippies with flowers stuck in their ears and you'd bust your butt hurryin' to get back to Missouri. I ain't interested in nothing west of Kansas City or east of Saint Louis. I'm what you'd call providential about my territory, I reckon."

"That's not right, Fudd," Harley said.

"What's not right?"

"Providential…it's provi-something…provincial…I think, but I'm not sure that's altogether what you mean."

"Harley, if you know so dad blamed well what I really mean, why bother to straighten out my wrong word?" He waved his hand dismissively. "Anyway…this here's the only sensible place a thinkin' man would live. I reckon north Arkansas or maybe parts of Illinois or Kansas would be all right, but I figure I'd have found Missouri even if I hadn't been hatched here. Wait till Aaron gets back. He'll a been all over the world, and I'll bet he'll tell us the same thing."

"I imagine it will look mighty good to him," Ernie said. "Says he's going to bring back some city kid from Chicago to visit. Fudd, you can try your hand at converting him to the country life."

"Chicago! Have mercy! Poor kid. He'll think he's died and gone to heaven when Christa lays one of them chocolate pies in front of him. And you and Aaron get him in the middle of four or five coveys of quail. He'll be wantin' you to adopt him."

Ernie laughed softly at the scenes conjured up and nodded in agreement with Fudd.

"I can't believe it's the first of November already," Dorsey said, "what's he got left, Ernie?"

"Little over two weeks. I'm about to breathe easy at last. All he writes about in his letters is eatin' his Mom's cooking and such…doesn't seem too worried about the war."

Harley fidgeted with a small bag of potato chips, shifting his weight in the metal chair. Fudd said, "Let's lay the pig-pickin' on for just before Thanksgiving, Ernie. Whatcha' think?"

"Sounds about right to me. I plan to have fresh venison tenderloin in the cooker too."

"Go on! I like the sound of that," Fudd said. "Dorsey, how about tradin' me the other half of that good-lookin' ham and cheese for the last cup of this chili? Give you something to fight back with."

"Why not…anything to keep you from eating all that fire soup yourself."

The chatter continued around the table, but Harley had little to offer. His thoughts were lost in the neatly penned words of the letter tucked in his top dresser drawer.

Christa set about her regular Friday afternoon chore. She considered herself a bit irrational when she first cleaned her son's empty room only a week after he departed, but she reasoned that there was no harm in it. She cleaned the other rooms of the house; why not keep his fresh too. It was a good way to stay in touch. The place was a kaleidoscope of pleasant memories—food for her soul. The bedroom, once so large for the baby boy nineteen years ago, had seemed to grow ever smaller with the passing of each year. After she stripped the bed and made it with clean sheets, she raised the window a few inches. The clean air quickly permeated the room as she dusted the dresser top and small nightstand. The two rugs were taken outdoors and shaken with unnecessary vigor. She stopped in the doorway and surveyed the room.

The bed...dear Lord, the bed of a thousand memories. The place where comfort was sought and given during earaches and leg pains and scary dreams and little-boy tears. The place of questions, and answers—some good, she assured herself—others admittedly poor. A place where the mother hoped some wisdom had been imparted, and where she knew wisdom had been gained.

The bed was a place of shadows. She could envision at will the long shadow of her husband cast over the sleeping child, the man kneeling on his right leg and resting his big hands on the small body so that he could feel the rhythm of heart and lungs. And when the moon had light to share, the flickering images of leaves and branches crowded through the window and caressed her son. Yes, beautiful images all, but memories now. Only memories. This thought created no despair in the mother looking at the empty bed. More than anything else, this life was but a long string of memories. The next life would be lived without the constraints imposed by time and place. Her eyes shifted to the oval-framed picture of Christ's face, hanging on the wall beside the window. He too was shackled on earth by time and place, and Christa took great comfort in the fact. His bondage, like hers, was temporary. Memories would suffice for now; they were good things.

The picture had hung in its place for twelve years. It was a gift from Pastor Riggins's wife, who was Aaron's Sunday school teacher at the time. Aaron was seven when the tragedy on Highway 87 jolted the town. Christa broke the news to him just before lunch on that Saturday. They both cried their tears and she offered all of the consolation that she could, but little was said until she sat on the edge of his bed that night. She remembered the words as if they had just been spoken, could see her young son's face as it stared up at the picture.

"Momma, how does anybody know what Jesus looks like?"

"They don't, son. People who paint pictures of Him just paint what they think He might look like."

"Mrs. Riggins knows for sure now, doesn't she, Momma?"

"Yes...she knows for sure now."

Then he looked at her face, his eyes penetrating even in the faint light. "You'll see Jesus before I will, won't you?"

She smiled through her tears at the innocence. "Yes, son, I expect that I will. That would be the natural order of things."

She sat on the bed until sleep claimed him, and she prayed the same words then as she now did, standing in the doorway of the empty room. "Dear Lord, please let the natural order of things be for this family."

The platoon stopped for the night and set up a perimeter near the edge of a narrow river. In the morning, they would cross the muddy river and begin a slow ascent toward a nameless village reputed to be Viet Cong infested. At nightfall a steady, penetrating rain began to fall, and the men pulled out their rubber ponchos and huddled under them like little tents, knowing that in all likelihood the rain would pelt them through the long night. The men first up for guard duty on the perimeter included Gino, who sloshed off with three of his fellows to points designated by Sergeant Winfield. An hour later, Aaron and Pima lay on their sides, bodies angled toward the ground, poncho hoods pulled low over their eyes.

Although Aaron could barely discern Pima's outline, he knew with an eerie clarity that his friend's eyes were fixed on him. "Why you staring at me?"

"I cannot see your eyes, how can you see mine?"

"I can't, but you're staring at me, aren't you."

Ten seconds dripped by in the cadence of the rain drops. "Yes."

"You gonna go ahead and tell me why, or do I have to ask a bunch of stupid questions?"

Pima made a sound in his throat, part sigh and part groan. "I have looked into tomorrow…I have seen things."

"You mean like…a premonition?"

"Yes, that is the word." He paused, shifted under his poncho. "It is not good."

Like a big spider crawling up his spine, Aaron felt the chill creep upward and lodge in his throat. "Well…I reckon you're gonna tell me, right?"

"The spirit world of my people and the spirit world of the Christians are not so different. We do not even argue about that anymore."

"I didn't really think that we ever…argued about it. Besides, you are a Christian, you believe in the Holy Spirit. What's that got to do with all this?"

"I do not want you to think what I must tell you is…only an 'Indian thing,' as Gino says."

"Pima…spill this on out…now."

"Tomorrow, in that lousy little ville up the hill…I think that one of us will die."

The chill rippled through Aaron's throat, and he swallowed against it. "Why…me or you?"

"Gino…I think. It has something to do with him. We are the only true believers he has as friends."

"Then it seems like we should…stay alive, and lead him."

"His heart is hard."

"Man, you're really spookin' me, you know."

"I am sorry, but…how could I not tell you?"

Wet seconds oozed by as the breeze swished through the leaden boughs above them. "My father's heart is hard, too," Aaron said.

"I know…and that is why I think it will be me. My parents are in the faith. You need to go home to your father and help your mother with him."

Aaron opened his eyes as wide as he could, wished he could see the long grass, and the trees, and above them, the sky. But the rain leaked down from his brow and he could only blink at the wet darkness. "I'm not so sure." He felt his lips form a little smile, though he did not know where it came from. "I wrote a letter home."

"To your parents?'

"No. To my best friend back there."

"So, you felt something before I did?"

"It didn't really…feel…that heavy, when I wrote it. But now…"

Within the span of a few seconds, it was finished—complete and sturdy, like a great chain pulled taut by a heavy load—and neither of them desired to speak of it again.

Pima whispered through the rain. "I will pray for us tonight until sleep comes to me."

"So will I."

The hot grease in the black iron skillet hissed a mild protest as Christa carefully arranged three pork chops. Dipped in a batter of milk and egg, then thoroughly floured, the meat would fry slowly under the lid. She retrieved a quart jar of canned green beans from the pantry and dumped them into a large sauce pan to simmer on the adjacent burner. Two baking potatoes had been in the oven for a half hour, the pleasing aroma now mingling with that of the frying meat and brewing coffee. Ernie clumped in from the shed where he had been tinkering with one of the dampers on the pig cooker.

"Smells like chops to me," he said, sniffing the air.

"You bet, and cut thick, just like you like them."

He washed his hands in the kitchen sink and dried them on the dish towel hanging on the oven door handle.

"You get it fixed?"

"Yeah, just needed a little filing on one side. Smooth as silk now."

He poured himself and Christa cups of coffee, handing one to her as she stirred the beans.

"You clean his room today?"

"Yes."

He smiled as he curled his arm around her waist. "Won't be empty much longer."

"It's getting close."

They ate the meal slowly, savoring the simple but hearty fare, the conversation light and chatty.

"There's cake still on the counter," Christa offered.

Ernie held up a hand and shook his head. "I'm to the full line." He patted his stomach. "I saw two does and a spike buck down by the edge of the woods a while ago."

"It's getting to be about that time, isn't it?"

"Saturday is opening day. Aaron will just miss the season this year."

"Reckon you'll see that big buck this year?"

"Can never tell. Maybe, if he gets love struck at the right time. Aaron would have a fit if I get him, wouldn't he?"

They both chuckled at the prospect. "I imagine he would."

"I'll probably end up bagging a yearling buck. Be better eating anyway."

Christa began clearing the dishes from the table. "How have the birds been this week?"

"Real good. It's been a good week. Fudd's training a new hanger."

Christa laughed as Ernie looked at her and shook his head slowly and grinned. Ernie's tales of Fudd in his tutorial mode had been the centerpiece of many supper conversations through the years. Ernie's work station position allowed for a periodic glimpse of mentor and student, laboring mightily in their strange endeavor, and then, at lunch breaks, Fudd's colorful narratives would complete the picture.

"This guy won't last two weeks, but Fudd's working him for all he's worth. Heck, he might not come back tomorrow for that matter."

On Friday, the day before the opening morning of deer season, the lunchtime conversation was soon directed toward Ernie's prospects for success in his annual quest, and also toward the latest recruit in the hanging wars, a fellow named Tully Bledsoe. Periodically, the personnel office became disenchanted with the turnover rate on the hanging dock, with the previous rookie's brief tenure causing a closer scrutiny of job applications. Three days passed before the latest position was filled. Tully had taken to Fudd's tutelage remarkably well, a fact explained by Dorsey through a mouthful of potato chips.

"Joe up in the personnel office told me he'd been a catcher down in Mississippi a couple of years ago. No wonder he's not scared of the birds."

"Heck fire," Fudd moaned, "and all mornin' I been thinkin' it was my teachin'. He didn't say a thing to me about any bird catchin' down south. Closed mouth sort of fellow, ain't he?"

"Who'd know if he was or wasn't, Fudd?" Harley asked. "Between you blasting at him with dos and don'ts and those big toms tryin' to fly away with him, how could he have much to say?"

"Harley, you wouldn't recognize a good hangin' teacher if he was close enough to bite you in the butt. You got to keep talkin' at 'em or else they'll make bad habits from the start. Got to keep those wings away from their private parts. That's how I messed up with the last rookie. I let him get his jewels whacked on the first day, and he never got over it. Man can't stand an early jewel-whackin' out here."

"Sounds like the solemn truth to me," Dorsey said. "Say, where did this new guy go anyway?"

"Said he was goin' to eat a sack lunch in his car and rest for a while," Fudd said. "Lay you three to one that he's laid out in the seat like a cadaver."

"He'll be all right, I think," Dorsey said. "If he can just hold on until he gets in shape. I never did any bird catching on a growing farm, but it's got to be some help in learnin' to handle them." He glanced at Fudd, quickly adding, "But no doubt you're breaking him in right, Fudd. Stay on him for me. I don't want to hear any more crap out of the front office for a while."

Dorsey cranked his neck, looked at Ernie. "Going after those monster bucks in the morning, I reckon?"

"Going after something, but a man never knows what he'll get into. Big wall-hanger would be nice, but they're hard to come by."

"Now don't dilly around too long and not shoot somethin' nice and fat for the cooker," Fudd said. "I can just see those two big strips of tenderloin laid over the coals next to the pig at the Thanksgivin' pickin'. Have mercy! Pig and deer tenderloin side by side on the grill. I can't stand the thought."

"I'll get us a nice fat young one, Fudd. I'm a bit partial to that tenderloin myself."

"I wish Margie would ease up on me a little. I'd shoot one myself like I used to. Heck, it's been four years now, and she still pitches a fit when I bring it up."

"Can't hardly blame her, Fudd," Dorsey said. "A man takes a tumble from a tree stand like you did without breaking himself up good…well, you can expect a woman to hold on to that for a long time."

"Whatever," Fudd huffed, "but I tell you that I'm goin' next season as sure as the Pope's in Romania."

"The Pope's in Rome," Harley said.

"Now don't start nit-pickin' me, Harley. There's probably a Pope in Romania too."

"Not but one and he's in Rome."

"Crapsakes, I can't stand no more Pope lessons. I'm gonna talk to the birds for a while. They got better manners."

Fudd stood, belched wetly, and banged out the door on his way to the dock. The afternoon passed uneventfully. Tully had indeed retired to the back seat of his car and fallen asleep. Dorsey had retrieved him with a mild reprimand about the pitfalls of lying down during such a brief lunch break. The penitent man redoubled his efforts on the line, and was beginning to look, according to no less an authority than Fudd Ledbetter, like a "real bird hanger."

When the dock crew scattered in the parking lot, Fudd left Ernie with a final reminder. "Nail one early, hunter man. Don't dog-butt around and pass one up. You might not have much luck later in the week."

Ernie smiled at the friendly admonishment and tossed a wave of his hand in parting.

Wearing only long flannel underwear, Ernie peered out the glass top of the back door. It was five o'clock in the morning and the November night winds had delivered a chilling rain that pecked on the storm door. In his younger days—or if Aaron had been there—he would have donned a plastic poncho and never given a thought to the elements. But it was no longer so. A hot cup or two of strong coffee before Christa awakened, and then fried eggs and spicy sausage with the dawn—yes, the deer could wait until the afternoon.

Just after dawn and before sunset were the preferred hunting times for the whitetail deer. From a properly placed tree stand near the edge of a feeding area or along a trail, many of the hunter's opportunities were presented as the animals returned to the woods after night feeding, or, in the late afternoon shadows, as they returned to the fields. Ernie had intended to spend two or three hours in his stand both morning and afternoon. But with the season nine days in length, it made little sense to give up the warmth of the kitchen. He smiled at his lack of resolve, and reckoned that his age was beginning to show.

By mid-afternoon, the rain lost its passion and slowed to a sputtering drizzle. Patches of blue flashed through tears in the swirling mass of gray clouds.

"The weather man got one right, it looks like," Ernie said as he peered intently past the windowpane over the kitchen sink.

"Looks like you'll be in the woods this evening," Christa said.

"Yep, that'd be my plan."

By three o'clock he was ready to leave the house. He had bathed and donned clean clothing. The brown coveralls he wore had been stored in a cedar-lined chest. He wore rubber boots that were reserved for treks in the woods, and which were never soiled with man odors such as petroleum products or cleaning fluids. And all this to foil the greatest enemy of a successful hunt—the nose of the white tail deer, possessed of a sense of smell a hundred times greater than man's. The firearm of choice was a .30-.30 Winchester lever-action carbine. It was a short, easily maneuverable weapon, and had sufficient range for the hunter not given to wild shots. Ernie was such a hunter; if the heart-lung area was not clearly presented, within seventy-five yards, he passed up the shot. No wounded animal to run away and die a lingering death. He believed that the creatures were his to take for food, but not with reckless abandon. For field dressing chores, he carried a quality hunting knife in a leather sheath, which hung from his trouser belt under the protection of the coveralls.

"See you after a while," he said, wedging his way out the back door.

Christa followed him into the back yard. "Good luck, hon, it ought to be a good afternoon for you."

Within minutes, the man was swallowed up by his beloved forest.

In another forest, halfway around the world, where no soft, autumnal colors graced the tree tops, darkness still reigned as the boy waited patiently. In time, the strange light of dawn gave shape to the verdant life surrounding him. The angel of death was not fearsome to behold. Had he sat where the first streaks of sunlight could have touched him, his hair, like that of his ancestors for centuries, would have shone with a blackness like that of a raven. The hair was crudely shorn about the sides and back of his head. The upper line of his smooth forehead was broken by two jagged tufts that drooped down to be nudged by the slightest puff of wind.

His features were delicate, with the beginnings of masculinity encroaching. The oval curves of his face were giving way to lines that would define cheekbone and jaw. Though drawn to slits as they strained in the weak light, his eyes could not hide the softness of youth. Duc Thon was six days beyond his twelfth birthday. He wore no shirt, with his brown skin stretched tightly over frail collarbones and pointed shoulders. The movement of his rib cage was nearly indiscernible with each shallow, rhythmic breath. His arms were long for his torso, with elbows resting easily on upper thighs as he sat against the trunk of a large tree. The foliage encircling him was thick enough to render him invisible to anyone more than twenty yards distant, yet he could see for sixty yards through two small, well spaced breaks in the vegetation.

His thin fingers were wrapped around a battered Soviet-made AK-47 automatic rifle that had been shoved into his hands an hour before by the Viet Cong soldier. The magazine held only three rounds of ammunition; the black-clad soldier had not bothered to check it. The boy was positioned on the least likely avenue of approach into the village. The Viet Cong leader and his small band had set up an ambush two hundred yards away at an approach point they considered the most probable. The Viet Cong who positioned the boy reasoned that he was merely an expendable bit of insurance. Whether or not he actually struck the Americans with a bullet was of secondary importance to the alarm he would set off in the event of contact at his location. He had been given no instructions on how to react after he fired at oncoming troops—primarily because the Viet Cong who placed him was certain that he would be cut down by the withering return fire he would surely draw if indeed a firefight broke out.

Duc Thon knew that he was in harm's way, but he was not troubled. He should have known fear; he was alone. He had listened as the footsteps of the departing soldier grew ever fainter in the darkness, and he knew that the man would not return. The weapon that he had never before handled provided little consolation. When the fear first crept toward him, Duc Thon concentrated on remembering the day of the photographs.

Two weeks had passed, but the images were crystal clear. Every family in the village was herded into a central point for photographing by the Americans. One by one, with a family member holding a small chalkboard nameplate, the photographs were made. One American soldier explained through an interpreter that they were attempting to identify and eliminate the Viet Cong infrastructure suspected in the village, and that everyone's photo was necessary in this effort. Duc Thon did not understand this. He did understand the humiliation he felt as he stole a glance at his revered mother, sheepishly holding the nameplate against her breast. He saw his brothers and sisters with bowed heads looking at their feet, heard the snarled command from a nearby soldier as he shoved them closer together. He watched intently as the muzzle of the short, black rifle prodded his mother's chin higher, the wielder of the rifle cackling with satisfied laughter at his involvement in the process. Yes, these things Duc Thon understood and remembered well.

Before that day, he harbored mixed emotions about the big strangers. Indeed, he had seen relatively few of them close hand. But on that fateful day, his perception forever changed. It had been easy to respond to the Viet Cong who came to his hut in the night. It would have made no difference in the outcome had he not been willing to go, and both he and his family realized this fact. But he arose and followed the man willingly. For on the day of shame to his family, he chose sides in this strange affair, and his Oriental heart was committed unto death for the honor of his family.

And so it was that the child who should have known fear and been a stranger to hatred, became one who feared not, and who followed the bony, crooked finger of hatred.

Enshrouded by the shadow world of early morning, the tiny angel of death waited patiently.

CHAPTER EIGHT

Eleven thousand miles distant, the sunlight given to Vietnam was being taken from Missouri. Ernie had been in the tree stand for over an hour now, with perhaps another half hour of adequate light remaining. The silence was broken only by the intermittent staccato chatter of two squirrels. Ernie watched two does feed in the edge of a field at a distance he judged to be two hundred yards. The does were of little interest to him, but he watched intently the half circle of woods behind them.

The ancient burr oak that supported Ernie had proven to be the best of the three stand sites he and Aaron had built over the course of the past several years. He had not occupied this stand since the season before last. The previous year he killed a nice yearling buck from another stand on the second day of the season. He was content to make the early kill and allow Aaron the remainder of the season to concentrate on the buck that they had named The Ghost. Two other hunters had also reported glimpses of the animal over the past two years, within a general range of four miles. Both Ernie and Aaron had been fortunate enough to espy the creature last season, Ernie from closer range than Aaron. The most recent accounts of the body and rack size varied from two hundred twenty-five pounds to as much as two hundred seventy-five pounds, and from twelve to fourteen points on the rack. Ernie judged him to be closer to the upper end of the reported range in both categories. At either parameter, he was an extraordinary animal, and had lived, by Ernie's reckoning, into his fifth of sixth year.

Hypersensitive to noise and motion, and with the incredibly acute sense of smell, he had managed to evade the hunter's bullets and grow to full maturity. The does and younger bucks always led the way into the open areas, while he peered warily from a safe distance, usually waiting until the comforting veil of darkness nearly enveloped his body before venturing forth. But during the rut, when the does were in estrus, his usual caution diminished as the powerful urge to mate overwhelmed him.

Ernie watched as the larger of the two does raised her tail to a half-erect position. They had fed casually and steadily in his direction, and were now less than one hundred yards from the burr oak. Ernie could see that the doe's action was that of urination, and this pleased him. The breeze would carry the scent of fresh urine into the woods. He could only hope that an eager buck would be in a good downwind position.

Deep within the forest, and downwind from the field, the ghost buck lifted his moist, black nostrils skyward and drank in the offerings of the air with deep inhalations. His loins quivered slightly in anticipation—the scent of fresh urine was unmistakable on the cool air. With a low, pig-like grunt and the flicker of his tail, he began to glide across the forest floor, toward the field, the does, and the armed man sitting high in a tree.

And the hunter waited patiently in the thick evening shadows.

Marine First Lieutenant Ross McHenry had been in country for only three weeks, his predecessor's tour having ended in death by the hot, jagged metal of a mortal shell. The de facto leader of the platoon was Sergeant Winfield; it was a rock-solid certainty that comforted McHenry and the platoon members. They were nearing the village when Winfield suddenly trotted forward to Gino Polites, who was walking the point, then raised his right fist in a signal for the platoon to halt. As Winfield walked back to McHenry's position, Aaron turned around and locked his gaze on Pima's eyes until the Indian boy raised his fist to his shirt and tapped twice over his heart. Aaron nodded, lifted his right hand from the weapon and tapped his chest twice.

Winfield spoke in a slow, measured tone to the young lieutenant. "Only other time we came up on this ville, it was from the south…but it doesn't feel right this time. We don't know who Charlie's eyes and ears are in there. I got spooky vibes in there last time. We're gonna go in from the east, with the sun behind us. Let's swing the boys over that way. The little Greek's on point, and there ain't nobody better at it than him. We're in good shape."

As if tethered to one another with an invisible rope, the platoon members nudged forward through the undergrowth, carefully avoiding the beaten path that led into the village. Aaron, grim-faced, and with the black M-60 hanging by a strap from his shoulder, followed directly behind Gino. Two positions behind Aaron, Pima trudged, his features drawn taut, black eyes darting from side to side.

The column of soldiers walked west now, the new sunlight forming tiny dancing images on their backs as it darted through openings in the tangled, green mass hovering over them. In less than sixty seconds, Duc Thon would spy the small form of Gino Polities.

Ernie's attention was drawn to the quick motion from the does. The foot-long tails flickered nervously, the white undercoating as conspicuous as large handkerchiefs. Simultaneously, the delicate heads jerked toward the woods. Ernie made a hasty calculation of their line of sight, squinting into the owl-light near a large thicket guarded by several mature hickory trees. The pace of the man's heartbeat quickened as the form of a huge deer took shape in the gathering gloom. The magnificent rack adorning his head identified the buck instantly—it was surely the ghost buck, and his guard was down. Ernie glanced to his left in order to locate the does that had already begun the long, graceful bounds that would place them in the woods fifty yards to his left. It could not have been a better situation had he diagrammed a plan on a chalkboard. He was between the coquettish does and their suitor, whose attention was riveted to the females. The buck would pass within thirty yards of Ernie, and his gait, though quickening, would allow for an easy shot with the carbine. Ernie drew a steadying breath as the great animal picked his way through the brush. The long tines of the rack reached skyward like white daggers, undulating in perfect cadence with the muscular body.

Just seconds now, and the prize would be claimed. Nothing could go awry; the ghost buck's passion had sealed his doom.

With a slight motion of his buttocks and bare feet, Duc Thon purchased a bit of relief from the callous touch of tree bark. His moment of relief was short-lived. There was movement, barely perceptible, to his front. And then again. It was the head of a soldier, the camouflaged helmet clearly visible now, and then the American soldier's body materialized. He carried a short black rifle that Duc Thon recognized as the instrument of his mother's humiliation. The soldier was advancing almost directly at him.

The child's body tensed. Another body, much larger and carrying a menacing heavy weapon, had taken shape behind the small man. There were more, many more perhaps. The boy's brain wrestled mightily with the situation. The questions hammered against the inside of his skull. *How long should I wait? Should I stand up before taking aim? Should I kneel? Where should I run after I fire?* The fear, absent until now, reared its ugly head, and the boy struggled to conjure up another image of his family, but it was not to be. Four Americans now, and a fifth emerging from the jungle. The small soldier in front was forty paces from the boy, then thirty. The words formed at once as a plea and a scream—"*Stop! Stop! Turn around!*"—and though the boy was certain that his voice pierced the jungle, the only sound heard by the soldiers was the soft swish of the long grass.

The boy's sweaty forefinger groped for the trigger as he strained to hoist the heavy weapon to firing position. He did not know that the selector switch was in the full automatic mode. Gino Polities discerned the tiny movement near the tree, but before he could shout a warning the three-round burst of fire pierced the air. Within the span of the next second, many things took place. The first bullet churned up the earth and thick grass a yard in front of Gino's feet. The second passed knee-high, six inches from his right leg. The last round, rising ever higher as the recoil drove the muzzle upward, creased the tip of his pointing right forefinger. The bullet struck the bottom edge of his helmet, leveling its upward trajectory as it hurtled toward the flesh of Aaron Bates.

To Aaron, the noise of all three rounds was a single horror, simultaneous with the unnatural force of the dull punch against the right side of his chest, and then he was on the ground. Tall blades of grass waved eerily in his peripheral vision and he could hear shouts of excitement mingled with the automatic return fire of his comrades. He heard a wet, rasping sound, but did not yet realize that the source was the air being drawn through the hole in his chest. There was no pain, only a grotesque numbness—a void—in the center of his body.

Twenty-five yards away, the tree that had given its begrudging shelter to Duc Thon became a gigantic execution stake as the spray of bullets pinned him against the rough bark. Lifeless now, the small body slumped like a doll slipping through the fingers of a child.

Unaware of his minor finger wound, Gino hovered, frozen and panic-stricken over his fallen friend, alongside Pima, who had raced forward. The ringing in Gino's right ear was deafening, magnifying the detached horror of the scene.

Suddenly, Winfield was at their side, jerking the pressure bandage from Aaron's rucksack strap. "Do something, son! Press this over the hole and keep it there while Little Doc works on him." Winfield turned and searched through the confusion of men behind him. "LT, get on the horn and get us a chopper in here. I'm gonna disperse the men. The kid was a decoy...we gotta set up a perimeter right now!"

McHenry trotted forward and motioned toward Aaron, asking a silent question. Winfield shook his head, pursed his thin lips. He stood and moved quickly toward the men, shouting orders as he ran.

The struggle to breathe and the heavy loss of blood quickly weakened Aaron. It had all become a simple matter: It was time to die. He blinked Gino's face into focus, then Pima's. Gino's voice was high-pitched, plaintive. "I swear, Aaron, I seen worse! You can make it if you try! Just gut it out till the chopper gets here!"

The big hand reached up slowly and clung to Gino's shirtsleeve, pulling him closer, but the jagged whisper was directed to Pima. "We know now...don't we...brother?" Pima placed his hand on Aaron's, then bowed his head, could not speak.

Winfield appeared and grabbed a handful of Pima's fatigue shirt, jerked him away, shouting orders after him.

"Gino...me and Pop...always liked the dawn. It was dawn when... the angel said...'why do you seek the living among the dead?'"

Gino felt the grip on his sleeve relax, saw his friend's eyelids half close, then set, saw the gory fingers of the medic reach down and gently close the eyelids. Then Winfield's voice hammered in his ear, the words lost to the chaotic whirl inside his head. Winfield's open-handed slap rocked his head sideways, but it only made the whirling worse, and Gino dug his face into the grass, his fingers raking over the ammunition bandoliers covering Aaron's body.

Winfield turned toward Pima, jerking him upward by one arm. "Snap out of it! Nobody else is gonna die here today. Move!"

The sergeant shoved Pima toward the perimeter, shadowing his first few steps before veering off in another direction. Neither man looked back at Gino.

The chill began as a prickly tingle in the bottom of Ernie's stomach, but as his arms lifted the cocked carbine into shooting position the tingle quickly magnified—cold and electrical—and spread throughout his upper body. The buck's pace slowed; it should have been the simplest shot the man had ever taken. Ernie was dumfounded by the shuddering mass of muscle and bone his body had become. He had not been out of control in a hunting situation since boyhood. There was simply no logical reason for this; it was time to shoot. He attempted to aim, but only for a split second; his trembling right thumb and forefinger worked in unison to pull the trigger and ease down the hammer. He lowered the butt of the carbine stock to the top of his boot, grazing it before it bumped roughly on the wooden floor of the tree stand. With the sound, the animal skidded to a halt, sending a shower of leaves and loose soil over its front hooves. The great head, at once haughty and inquisitive, swung directly upward, the black nose pointed at the man. Ernie was spellbound by the piercing gaze of the plum-sized black eyes. The deer instantly recognized the unnatural silhouette in the tree, and in the lingering second that followed, Ernie Bates sensed the presence of his son as keenly as anything he had ever experienced. And then it was gone. The deer shattered the silence with a loud "whoosh" of alarm, bounding away with long, zigzagging strides.

Ernie was completely unnerved, knew that he needed time to calm himself before beginning his descent from the tree. He shoved his back forcefully against the tree. The hum of energy in his body was gone now, leaving in trade a wondrous, airy mystery that lingered in the tree limbs for a span of time lost to the man—seconds, minutes, hours, days, years, or was it a lifetime?—then it vanished like the hum, and his soul chased after it for only a futile moment. He held his wristwatch close to his face and read the hands: six forty-five A.M. in Vietnam. They would be on the move now, he surmised, and the fact that he registered no danger to his son brought tears to Ernie's eyes. But what had happened? Something out of the ordinary must have taken place. Something would be in the next letter, if in fact the boy sent another so close to the end of his tour of duty. No, not a letter, he thought, he would discuss it face to face with his son in the glad days to come. He would just have to wait. Ernie's thoughts turned to the buck, and with the thought came a weary smile; it was perfectly fitting that the creature was alive.

He was eager to return to the house, although unsure of his desire to share the experience with Christa. He wondered if she had sensed something similar, would soon know with the first look into her eyes—eyes incapable of hiding her innermost thoughts.

Christa looked up from the stove and smiled as Ernie shouldered his way into the warm kitchen. "See anything?"

"I saw a couple of does and…one nice buck. Couldn't get a shot to work out though."

"Well, it's just the first day of the season." She clanked the edge of a spoon on the side of the saucepan.

Ernie drew a glassful of cold water from the tap and quaffed it, then looked out the window into the darkness. *So it is between me and the boy. So be it.* He sucked in a deep breath, exhaled luxuriously. There were many ties that bound them; this was yet another, and it was the most unique of all. It was of the spirit, beyond flesh and bone and blood. It was of a father and a son.

First Sergeant Olin Gerhardt sat behind his desk with his hands clasped behind his head, reflecting on his Monday morning. The Jefferson City noontime traffic had returned to normal on High Street, the vehicle sounds now less intense outside the window of his small office. The office door stood open and Gerhardt read obliquely the neat lettering on the glass top: UNITED STATES MARINE CORPS RECUITING OFFICE.

"Recruit, my butt," he mused aloud, "business is a tad slow on the old home front."

Gerhardt had been at this assignment for three months, with relatively little to show for his efforts—at least according to his superiors. Central Missouri was not exactly the population center of the country, he diplomatically reminded them from time to time. And besides, Vietnam play-by-play on the nightly newscasts was more than a little unglamorous these days. Not surprisingly, their response was always less than sympathetic.

"Well whatever..." he whispered under his breath at the empty chair in front of his desk, "don't want to be a lousy desk jockey for long anyhow."

The jangle of the telephone broke his train of thought. Gerhardt casually placed the receiver in the cradle of his neck and shoulder. "United States Marine Corps Recruiting Office, Sergeant Gerhardt speaking."

Slowly, as if coiling his body in preparation for an athletic maneuver, Gerhardt sat forward in his chair, his left hand darting to the notepad. For the next sixty seconds the only sound in the room was that of his pen inking the grooves he traced into the paper pad. "Yes sir...yes, I understand perfectly."

He looked down at his notes: Aaron Wayne Bates KIA—Sunday morning— telegram coming THIS afternoon—personal contact with next of kin BEFORE it comes—Ernie Bates, wife Christa Baptist Rural Route # 7 Box 114 California MO.

Gerhardt's fingers fumbled for the pack of Camels and he shook it twice, brought it to his mouth and pinched a cigarette between his lips. He flipped open the silver Zippo, thumbed the wheel, carefully inserted the tip of the cigarette into the yellow flame. He took the smoke to the bottom of his lungs, shot out a tight stream. *Well, there you go, good Sergeant Desk Jockey…try that little piece of duty on for size.* He pushed against his eyebrows with a thumb and forefinger. What would he say to them? How would he say it? What if he couldn't find them before the telegram arrived? He took another deep drag on the cigarette as the dark scenarios flashed through his mind.

Halfway through the cigarette his composure returned, and he contemplated the proper steps. Thankfully, the little town of California was only a half hour drive down Highway 50. He would go to the post office—surely it was large enough to have a post office—and get some solid directions to the house. But wait…Baptist they said…yes! He would find the Baptist preacher to accompany him to the house. The preacher would know them, would know what to say if he faltered.

It was not total relief that Olin Gerhardt registered as he settled behind the wheel of the car, but it was a beginning; the situation was not so bleak after all.

"If I can just find that preacher man," he muttered as the engine roared to life.

CHAPTER NINE

Twenty-four miles of hard driving west down Highway 50 placed Gerhardt near the intersection with Highway 87, the location of the only traffic light in town, and a flashing red at that. Three of the four quadrants were service stations sites; Gerhardt chose the Sinclair on the right and wheeled the sedan to a stop near the door.

"Can't hardly miss the post office, soldier," the attendant drawled. "Just get on 87 here and follow it for a half mile or so, then make a right at the stop sign and go another block. Big ole 'merican flag out front."

Gerhardt parallel parked in front of the brick building and mounted the steps two at a time. The man behind the counter was sixtyish, with thin graying hair poking through the open top of his visor. He crinkled the corner of his left eye at the Marine in full dress uniform.

"I'm in need of some directions, please, sir."

"I imagine I'll know where it's at."

"I'm looking for the Bates home. I've got a rural address." Gerhardt pushed the paper across the counter.

"Don't need the paper, I know where they live." The man paused, adjusted the bill of his visor. "I know they got a boy in the service, too. Reckon that's why you're here, huh?"

"Yes, sir…it is. Please direct me."

"Take 87 north outta town, go about five miles to a gravel crossroads. No name posted, but there's a boarded-up old store on the right. You go left, about another mile…second house on the left. Name's on the mailbox."

"I appreciate that. One more question, sir. Is that big Baptist church I passed the only one in town?"

The man's shoulders slumped visibly. "Looking for the preacher, huh?"

Gerhardt could not hold the man's gaze, looked down at the counter, searching for words, but the man spoke first. "Only thing I was gonna ask you was if he was dead or wounded. Now I don't have to." He muttered unintelligibly under his breath. "Preacher's name is Riggins, Fred Riggins. Office door's on the south side of the building. Wish you'd stopped there first."

Gerhardt swallowed hard, said, "I…uh, should have. Wasn't thinking straight."

"He was some kid…that Aaron. Everybody knows him…or did…now."

"I'd really appreciate it if you kept this to yourself until I've had a chance to talk to his parents. I ought to be able to find them within the hour, with any luck."

The man nodded his head in compliance. Gerhardt thanked him again and turned to leave. As he reached the door, the solemn voice stopped him. "Can't blame you for getting the preacher, soldier. I'd rather sandpaper a lion's ass than go out there by myself."

Gerhardt offered no reply, quickly shouldered his way past the door and trotted to the car. Within a minute, he stood in front of the door to the church office. "I don't believe this!" he said aloud, softly bumping his fist against the neatly printed note taped to the door.

> *I WILL RETURN BETWEEN 3:30 AND 4:00. PLEASE CALL LATER, OR LEAVE A MESSAGE ON THIS NOTE. THANK YOU. PASTOR RIGGINS*

Gerhardt shuffled to his car and sat motionless behind the wheel. The initial panic returned full force. He could not wait for the preacher and risk arriving behind the telegram. Fate had dealt him a lousy hand; he would simply have to deal with it as best he could. At least it would be over with quickly. He had no responsibility beyond informing them. When the body was shipped back in two or three weeks, some other unlucky Marine would accompany it, and stay until the burial. If the parents chose to have a military funeral, Gerhardt know that he would be involved, but it would be with a detail of men, and the initial shock would have worn off of the family by then. But for now, he was alone, and the parents he was about to face were going about their daily routine, far removed—or so they thought—from death's black shadow. The words he spoke would change their lives forever; Gerhardt felt the weight of it all press down on his shoulders as surely as if invisible hands draped a heavy blanket over them. He steeled himself, thought for a fleeting moment about a cigarette, then shrugged against the weight, switched on the ignition. As he pulled away from the curb, the final words of the gray-haired man echoed inside his head.

Ernie emerged from the tool shed mildly curious about the sound of a vehicle coming to a stop in the driveway and the ensuing whump of its closing door. The house blocked his view of the car until he sauntered around the rear corner. The blocky image registered, ever sharper, with each step: dark green sedan—right foot—late model—left foot—Plymouth—right foot—white lettering on the door—left foot—UNITED STATES—right foot—MARINE CORPS. His boots softly crunched to a halt in the edge of the driveway. He felt the hammering inside his ribcage, like a determined, frantic bird seeking freedom, the swishing thuds full in his ears. His eyes moistened and the image on the car door blurred, yet within his peripheral vision he could see two human forms standing on the front porch. The precise, white letters appeared to undulate, and were replaced with the image of the ghost buck—the great, black eyes piercing his soul. And then the eyes of his father, wide with shock and fear, as they turned toward him, seeking the wielder of the knife just thrust into his throat. He closed his eyelids tightly and strained with every fiber of his being to wipe away the images and think clearly. Why had he not at least felt apprehension when the boy's spirit touched him? Or why not some horrific dread? Within seconds he would learn if his only son was severely wounded or dead. A sense of overwhelming betrayal descended on the man, its source a crushing power—unknowable, immutable—a discordant hum in the air.

He turned his head slowly toward the life-size figurines on the porch, frozen in time, saw a Marine in full dress uniform, his overseas cap wrung like a wet washcloth in his hands, saw Christa, her left arm wrapped around the porch post, face ashen, blank of expression. Ernie's eyes sought Gerhardt's, but the Marine could not will himself to hold the dreadful gaze.

The voice rasped into the bizarre silence. "Just one question…is he…dead…or wounded?"

Gerhardt had intended to gather them both and go inside to sit down, but the situation was already out of control, like a firestorm sweeping up a steep windblown slope. The tortured man in the patched coveralls was waiting for an answer, and he would not wait long. Gerhardt managed to draw only a shallow breath before speaking.

"Mr. Bates…I'm very sorry to have to bring you this news…but your son…died in combat on Sunday morning."

The tall man emitted a guttural sound and vanished around the corner of the house. Christa ran to the edge of the porch as fast as her trembling legs would carry allow, called after him in futility. She watched as he ran clumsily toward the woods, his destination soon apparent. He was moving in the direction of the giant cottonwood tree at the creek. With her right arm suspended as if to reach out and bring him back, she watched as his staggering gait covered a hundred yards before he lurched to a halt, then hunched over as he retched. Christa lowered her arm when he disappeared into the trees.

She turned back to the stricken soldier who was looking at the floor of the porch, his mouth hanging half open, as if he continued to search for words that no longer mattered. Christa willed a bit of strength into her legs, tiny spurts of prayer echoing in her head—*Jesus…help me…oh, sweet Jesus…now…I seek thee…now*—until she realized that the help she sought would come only through the help to be given; there was a task before her, wounds to bind. She gently locked her left arm around Gerhardt's and escorted him through the open doorway and into the living room. She released his arm, looked at the nameplate over the breast pocket of his uniform, then at the white cloth stripes on his shoulder.

"Please…Sergeant, isn't it…Sergeant Gerhardt?"

"Yes, ma'am."

"Sit down with me, won't you? I don't imagine your legs are too strong either just now."

"No, ma'am, they're not." He sat down beside her. "Ma'am, I know that I'm probably not the right person, but I'd be willing to go with you to try and help with your husband."

"That's mighty kind…and brave of you to offer, Sergeant, but it wouldn't do any good for either of us to try now."

"Mrs. Bates, I know I've done a sorry job of this, but they just gave me the word a couple hours ago…and I've never had to do it before, and…"

Christa held up her hand to silence him, smiled through her tears. "You did just fine, son…just fine. I can't think of a harder thing to be asked to do. My husband didn't give you a chance to be proper about it. I'm beholding to you for caring so much about our feelings." She paused, looked down at the knots of flesh and bone clenched in her lap. "I never altogether understood why my son was so bent on being a Marine, but if there are more like you…then…I understand better now."

Gerhardt nodded a thank you. Christa stood and he quickly followed her lead.

"I know you must be uncomfortable here, and you need to go on about your business, but I didn't want us to part without my thanking you for what you did. You hold your head high, son. You did a fine job."

"I appreciate that more than you'll ever know, ma'am."

"Is there anything else I need to know right now?"

"No, ma'am, not really. There will be an official telegram soon."

"How long before they send…him…home?"

"It'll be two weeks or more, most likely, Mrs. Bates."

Her strength waning, she offered her hand to Gerhardt and drew him close, placed the side of her head against his chest, squeezed his hand firmly with the finality of parting. She led him to the front door, said, "Goodbye, son."

"Goodbye, Mrs. Bates."

Gerhardt slid into the car seat, carefully closed the door, then loosened his tie. His albatross had been lifted, but the sweet relief coursing through his veins was tempered with sadness. He shook his head in wonderment. *The father was a nightmare...the mother was...an angel...a comforting angel.* He was not certain that he could ever sort that out, only knew that he would remember it that way—a nightmare and an angel—for as long as he lived.

Christa sat on the edge of the bed in Aaron's room. The tears flowed freely now over trembling lips, and she made no effort to staunch them. She hoped that Pastor Riggins was right when he once said that tears of the brokenhearted were the blood of the mourner's soul, never shed in vain. This would be the hardest goodbye, and she would say it only once. She reached up to the top of the bedpost, clutched the baseball glove to her bosom, then fell to her side, allowed the sorrow to carry her away.

She arose a half hour later, replaced the glove, composed herself with smoothing motions of her hands over her dress and hair. She walked to the telephone and dialed the familiar number. Clara Raines answered.

"Clara...this is Christa. There's no easy way to say this...we've lost Aaron. A soldier just came with the word."

"Lord Jeeeesus." The words came softly, like a prayer. "Oh...I..."

"It's all right, Clara, I know there's nothing you can say. Listen, though, please...I'm worried about Ernie. He ran off to the woods. Is Harley there?"

"Yes...yes, he's out back. I'll go get him."

"No, you'll have to break it to him. I want him to come quick and help me with Ernie. I'll be on the front porch. Call the preacher and tell him we'll talk later."

"I'll go get Harley now." She hesitated. "Christa...I..."

"I'll need you later, Clara. Thanks."

Clara hung up the receiver and jerked the back door open. Harley was walking toward the barn when he heard his mother call out his name. The strain in her voice signaled something terribly amiss, and he came at a trot.

"Harley, it was Christa on the phone. It's Aaron…they've lost him in Vietnam."

"No…no…" he whispered as his eyes clouded over. He knelt on one knee, could only shake his head.

"Christa says Ernie's bad off and she wants you to go over and help her with him."

He ran toward the pickup, tossed the words over his shoulder. "I don't know when I'll be back."

Christa pushed herself up from the metal porch chair as Harley turned into the driveway. He walked quickly toward her, saw red, swollen eyes, the brave effort at a smile that would not form. They embraced on the porch, rocking gently to and fro.

"Oh, Harley…I always believed he'd come back to us."

"Me too. I thought he had more to do here." He held her at arm's length. "Are you holdin' up?"

"I suppose…I'm cried out for now, and I feel about a hundred years old, and I'm not up to dealing with Ernie..without you."

"You got me as long as you need me, you know that."

She nodded her gratitude. "We've got to go now. I want to bring him back before dark."

They walked a straight line to the cottonwood root at Paddy Creek, approached the edge of the creek bank, peeked down at the long face etched in stone. He did not acknowledge their arrival, but he spoke first, his voice devoid of emotion, save for the tinge of bitterness.

"I know the minute he died. Wasn't God that told me, it was a big buck deer tried to tell me, but I was too dumb to figure it out."

Christa and Harley exchanged worried glances, the silence betraying their thoughts. "No, I ain't gone crazy. Thought I was gonna be when I got here, but now there's nothing but empty inside of me…empty.

You two wasted a trip down here because I'm not goin' anywhere for a long time."

"Ernie, we didn't come to make you do anything you don't want to," Christa said softly. "Me and Harley just came to sit with you... don't want you to be alone."

Ernie raised his right hand in a gesture of apathy. Harley said, "You love him, Christa loves him, I love him...a lot of people love Aaron, Ernie. There's hurt in us too. Don't shut us out."

"Oh, I did love the boy...I did love him," the voice trailed off into the dusky woods, the bitterness unrestrained, hanging like a stench in the air. "But there's nothin' to love anymore. He's a body in a box now...and I got nothin' but a string of memories...and they'll fade and die like him."

"No," Harley said, "there's as much of Aaron to love now as there ever was, Ernie."

Ernie shook his head with a mechanical finality, and Harley and Christa knew that he would speak no more. In unison, they retreated a step. Harley looked up to the tree tops, found a final trace of velvet light in the uppermost branches as it brushed the smattering of leaves clinging resolutely in the face of the coming winter. Only the hint of a breeze teased the leaves. The night would be proper for November—still and frosty, with a diamond-studded black sky. It would be a night of sadness enshrouded in beauty.

Harley spoke softly to Christa. "Let's go back to the house. I'll come back here and stay with him after you get settled in."

They returned to the house in silence, carefully picking their way through the woods. In the kitchen, Christa sat down heavily at the table, rested her head in both hands, her elbows braced on the table. Harley stood beside her, his hand patting her shoulder. "You need to get what rest you can, Christa. Gather your strength for the coming days. I'll take care of him tonight. There's really not much we can do tonight anyhow."

She nodded in agreement, then stood. "I'll get you some blankets and fix a thermos of coffee."

"You want Mom to come over and stay the night with you?"

"I appreciate the offer...I know she'd be glad to do it, but I'll be all right. I just need to lay down. I'm bone tired." She looked away, found a single windowpane and framed Aaron's face in it. "God help me...I feel more tired than sad right this minute. How can that be? How?"

"Don't ask questions of yourself now. Take your rest, I'll watch over Ernie."

Within fifteen minutes, Harley was back at the creek. He unfolded two of the wool blankets and draped them around Ernie's shoulders, gently forcing the statue-like figure forward and tucking the folds between his body and the creek bank. Ernie made no response, his gaze fixed on the opposite bank. Harley chose a big hickory twenty feet distant and sat down on a folded blanket. He wore an old winter coat that Christa had fished out of a bedroom closet. He jammed his hands to the bottom of the deep pockets and settled his back against the rough bark.

The twilight had deepened, the two men now a part of the vast shadow that covered half of the earth, and with the shadow, the memories came to Harley in a disjointed, out-of-sequence surge: Last year's Aaron chasing down a windblown pop fly ball, then three years ago on the Bullet ride at the fair, then back to his final pig-picking before departing, then a nine-year-old Aaron at Jimmy's Restaurant after church services, the cheeseburger wider than the smiling face. Back and forth they swept Harley, until the tears came and trickled warmly over his cheeks. The tears were not for Aaron; the boy was in no need of pity, was in no need of anything the world could offer. The tears were for the living, those left behind. Christa would heal and not be diminished in any fashion, of this he was certain. But Ernie would require many tears and many prayers before he would heal.

Harley blinked his eyes clear and focused on the capped head perched out of place at the creek bank. For this night, and for many to come, the grieving father would desire neither tears nor prayers. But Harley knew that these gifts were properly given even to those who would scorn them.

The darkness accumulated, claimed the trees and the ground alongside the creek, but Harley looked up, found the radiant points of starlight.

The Ledbetter family was gathered around the supper table when the telephone rang. Margie placed her fork on the nearly empty plate and pushed away from the table. Fudd complained through a mouthful of sweet potatoes. "There ought to be a law against usin' the phone at supper time."

"The law ought to be that you answer once in a while," Margie said. "Hello."

She did not speak again for a half minute. Finally, she sat down clumsily in her chair, the telephone cord stretched tautly. "Oh, Clara… I can't believe this."

"Believe what? What's goin' on here?" Fudd asked.

Margie held up her left hand, signaling for silence. "We'll talk later, Clara. Let me know if there is anything we can do." She hung up the phone as Fudd and the children stared intently, their utensils idle.

"Put your fork down, Fudd, and swallow your mouthful."

He swallowed, looked quizzically at her. "Did something happen to Harley?"

"No, it wasn't Harley…it's Aaron. He's…gone. Killed on Sunday."

The only sound was the jumbled chatter coming from the television set in the living room. Fudd's eyes were unfocused, cast downward at a point just beyond the edge of his plate. Elizabeth's chin began to quiver, and then she burst into tears and ran from the kitchen. Tad stared at his plate, slowly shaking his head.

"The boy didn't make it," Fudd said, his voice quietly incredulous. "I can't believe…the boy didn't make it." He pushed away from the table. "I got to get me some air."

He took two steps in the direction of the back door, then paused with a hand resting on top of his head. "How's Ernie doin'?"

"Not good. Harley's over there with them now. Clara says for you to call Dorsey, tell him that he'd better figure on both of them being out for days."

Fudd shook his head, said, "I don't want to talk to anybody. You call him…tell him I'll make up for Harley and that I don't want nobody else on my side of the truck."

Fudd opened the door, walked outside into the chill. The metal yard chair sagged with his weight. Behind him the door softly opened and closed, but he did not hear it, only felt the hand come to rest on his shoulder. He turned his head, saw Tad, then reached back and touched his son's hand. "The boy didn't make it, Tad…I can't believe he didn't make it back here."

Harley did not know how long he had dozed off when the motion at the creek bank roused him. In the miserly light of dawn he watched as Ernie stood on the cottonwood root, the blankets hanging from his shoulders like an ill-fitting shroud, then slipping to the ground as the tottering figure stepped up to the bank. Harley, stoop-shouldered and stiff, gained his feet and rotated his torso in an attempt to unknot his back muscles. Ernie walked stiffly away from the creek, silently passing Harley without the slightest glance.

Harley retrieved the blankets, quickly balling them into untidy wads beneath both arms. He stopped to pick up the thermos bottle without losing his hold on the blanket under his right arm, and then fell in step behind Ernie. Five minutes into the march, Harley looked ahead at the house as they reached the edge of the woods; the light from the kitchen window beckoned the weary man. He wondered if Ernie sensed any comfort in the familiar sight, or if he was even aware of it. At least the first long night had passed. There would be more long nights for the father of the slain son, but the first was thankfully behind him.

Christa was wrapped in a terry cloth robe as she stood beside the kitchen table when the two men walked into the room. She took a step toward Ernie, extending both arms in a pleading gesture, but the sight of the haggard face, set in stone, caused her to lower her arms. Her hand brushed the sleeve of the faded denim jacket as he shuffled past her. He walked to the open door of Aaron's bedroom and closed it, and then continued down the short hallway to the master bedroom. Without removing either jacket or shoes, he draped his body diagonally across the bed and fixed his gaze on the ceiling. Christa, following closely as she chose words with which to break the silence, quietly slipped into the bedroom, but the cold eyes of her man again stunned her, and she rushed from the room.

Harley took her hand and led her back to her chair at the kitchen table. "It'll be easier when he's had some good rest, Christa. He'll come around, but it's going to take some time."

"I know that, but this brooding silence is worrisome to me. Did he say anything at all last night?"

Harley shook his head. "Only what we heard when we got there."

He studied the troubled features of the woman, saw her attempt to force a little smile that would not form. She said, "Can't life change in a few minutes, Harley? Can't it change so?" Harley squeezed her hand and nodded before she continued. "I want you to go home and get some rest yourself now. I appreciate so much what you've done for us…and I know I'll be calling on you a lot more. But he's got to come out of this dark shell before anybody can help him."

"Christa, I'll stay as long as…"

"I know you would…and bless you for it, but in the end, me and him have to face this thing together. You just remember us at the tracks in the morning."

She walked him to his truck and watched until he backed out of the driveway. Then she whispered the prayer in the morning stillness. "Lord, give me strength to deal with this…I can't lose them both."

When she walked back into the kitchen her attention was immediately drawn to the tools lying on the counter. Ernie had been in the process of repairing the kitchen window the previous afternoon, and she surmised that he must have gone to the shed for something. Then came the official dark green sedan, and the terrible confrontation on the porch, and the hammer and screwdriver passed into insignificance. Until now. He would begin to face the thing now, like it or not.

She picked up the tools and walked to Aaron's door. She tapped out the hinge pins and lifted the door free, leaned it against the wall. She then wrestled the door flat on the floor and slid it under Aaron's bed. The three hinge pins clinked softly in the top drawer of the dresser. Christa stepped back from the open doorway and surveyed the order of the room. Through parted curtains, the first strong rays of sunlight shimmered on the glass panes, and the mother and wife was glad the morning had dawned burnished in gold. She moved to the edge of the bed and sat down so that the nascent warmth of the rays touched her face. And there she rested and gathered her strength.

The newest hanger on Fudd and Harley's side of the dock had been at his job for a week, and Dorsey's guess of another week's tenure had proved overly optimistic. That the man did not report for work this Tuesday morning was a blessing. Fudd arrived at the dock only moments before the first bird was to be hung, nodded grimly at Dorsey, and then marched resolutely to his position at the loaded trailer. Fudd stole a glance at Ernie's workstation. Two men stood, nervously awaiting the arrival of the first stunned bird. Fudd gritted his teeth, shook his head. The tall, quiet man should be there, should be the one to flawlessly slice the necks of the birds. He should be the one to laugh at Fudd's jokes in the lunch room, should be the one planning the pig-picking to welcome home a son. But he was not there. He was deep in grief, lost in the unjustness of a son's death. Fudd felt helpless, angered that he could do nothing to help his friend. He did not possess Harley's gift of saying the right things, knew that he could only clutter the minds of those he longed to aid. But he could damn well hang these turkeys. And he could release himself in this place of filth and sweat and blood. And he could grieve in his own way, with the might of his hands and arms. It was all he had to offer. Today he would hang for Aaron and his parents, and for Harley, lost in the midst of their grief. He would hang for his own son, safely tucked in a classroom a mile away, a son who would marry and sit grandbabies in his lap. A son who would stand over his father's grave in the proper order of things and shed tears for the old man. By God Almighty, sons buried fathers, not the other way around. Life got so strange sometimes, so out of order.

So it was that James Elmer Ledbetter, father of a living son, labored in muffled fury, his tears soon lost in the grime that coated his face.

Gino Polites heard the singing woman's voice inside his head during the fifth night following Aaron's death. He awoke from a fitful attempt at sleep under his rain-drenched poncho, the memory of the melody haunting yet beautiful beyond anything he had ever heard. He shivered, the pre-dawn mist heavy and foreboding, clinging to him like an unwanted blanket. He had not been assigned to night watch duty on the perimeter, knew that Winfield and McHenry had been watching, had seen them talking quietly with Little Doc, the medic. Only Pima had attempted to speak to him, but he kept him at arm's length, refused to listen to his entreaties. Now his mind was a whirl of sights and sounds that made no sense, worse now with the coming of the woman's voice like some invisible angel in the mist. He held his head in both hands, caught between a desire to weep and a desire to scream. He could not remember how many days remained in his tour of duty; there were not many, his and Aaron's tours nearly coincided. He sensed that Winfield and McHenry would cover for him until they reached the base camp, then urge their superiors to cut him loose before he got someone hurt. Crazy soldiers and the jungle did not mix well.

For a fleeting moment, he considered seeking out Pima, but realized that it would be a futile search, a stupid stumble in the darkness. So he curled back into a ball under his poncho, listened to the lingering voice echo in his head.

CHAPTER TEN

Christa awoke on Wednesday morning, stiff and enervated after a long night on the couch. She had fallen asleep in a living room chair and, after having checked on Ernie, who had not moved from his position in the bedroom, decided to leave him in solitude for another night. Pastor Riggins had come to the house the previous night and proved to be a steadying influence. He said little, allowing Christa to lead the conversation when she desired to talk. He did not attempt to offer profound words of wisdom, or lengthy pieces of advice. The only counsel he offered was to urge Christa not to allow a continuation of Ernie's brooding silence. Mostly, Christa concluded, he came to grieve with her, nothing more, nothing less. He spent over an hour in the living room, yet Christa was truly sorry to see him leave.

Ernie had neither eaten nor drank for over two days, and it was with this in mind that she moved with a purpose about the kitchen. She made a pot of coffee, and soon the rich aroma permeated the house. A skillet full of bacon sizzled and popped, the meaty fragrance blending enticingly with the coffee. She placed the strips of bacon on paper towels and wiped her hands on a dish towel. Drawing a deep breath, she cast a tentative glance toward the bedroom. He had been alone for too long; she could wait no longer. He was lying on his side, facing the wall, a blank stare frozen into his face. Christa moved to the side of the bed and carefully sat down. She gently placed her hand on the side of his head and stroked the close-cropped hair above his ear. The profile of the long face was highlighted by the soft morning light. It was an easy face for a woman to love, even now, cold and lifeless.

Christa was suddenly remorseful at not having studied the features for years. She would restore life into it, one way or the other. Hopefully with tenderness, as this was her nature. Certainly, at least until the return of Aaron's body, tenderness was the only option. Two weeks or more, the Marine messenger said—too much time, far too much time. There was simply no way to make meaningful progress until they laid the body down and bade their final farewell. Yes, tender for now; she would care for the man as he was—wounded and broken—as surely as if by gun or sword.

"Ernie…my poor Ernie. Just listen to me for a minute, and I'll leave you alone. Just let me help you one little step at a time. Just live this morning with me and don't look any farther."

She took his hand in both of hers, said, "I know you have to be hungry and thirsty. Let yourself smell the bacon and the coffee. I'll help you get these clothes off, then we'll run a hot shower. I'll lay you out some clean clothes on the bed and help you put them on. Then we'll fry some eggs to go with the bacon…get something in your stomach." She paused. "All right?"

The blankness of the stare faded a bit, and she could see him attempt to focus on her face. She nodded her head in encouragement and squeezed his hand. Her heart jumped as he tipped his head forward in a tiny nod. She deftly helped him remove his clothes and led him to the bathroom.

Christa sat in measured triumph on the toilet lid as the steam began to curl over the plastic shower curtain. She bowed her head and spoke in a whisper. "Thank you, Lord, for this start. Lead me by the hand so I can lead him by the hand."

The broken man and his wife passed the remainder of the week never more than a few feet apart. She cared for him like a man suddenly grown old, stricken obliquely by the angel of death. Progress, painfully slow in its pace, was measured by the hour. First, a look directly into Christa's eyes, though only for a moment. Then, as he stole a furtive glance into the room with no door, a glistening of the eyes, quickly repelled. Finally, on Sunday morning, the gentle woman's heart was gladdened by the return squeeze from the callused hand, the grip nearly pitiful, but unmistakably a sign of feeling—a tiny crack in the stone veneer. Conversation grew to the exchange of sentences, the subjects unimportant in content, but the effort and inflection of voice great things for Christa to behold.

On Sunday morning Christa was tempted to call Harley and ask him to stay at the house so that she could attend services, but she thought better of it. Troubled waters lay ahead; she knew that she must make the most of every hour available before the return of Aaron's body, was thankful for each of the hours. Yet, with her own grief subjugated out of necessity, she was pierced by the keen desire to lay her son's body to rest in the proper order of things.

She would have one more week to use, and to wait.

Harley and Fudd labored resolutely on the hanging dock, both thankful for the sweaty travail that occupied the body, and to a large extent, the mind. The plant's appetite for the big white birds was insatiable, the droning of the shackle line a constant in the men's ears. Conversation was sparse on the line, and little more at breaks or lunch. Although Harley yearned to be of greater direct aid to Christa and Ernie, he knew that his opportunities would come, and he took solace on the tracks each morning and on his knees at night, confident that his humble supplications were heard. Fudd took no such solace. The weightier matters of life had always been an onerous burden for him—questions without answers, mighty mysteries that he considered far above himself. He wished only for the end of the ordeal, with some semblance of normalcy restored to life.

When he had first learned of the lengthy interval between the death of a soldier and the return of his body, he lamented to Harley. "It ain't bad enough that he's cut down, but his folks can't even bury him without waitin' for days on end. I know it's a long way over there, but, dang it all, two or three weeks ain't right. A man can't get over somethin' that ain't even happened yet. I swear…it won't seem real till I lay my eyes on the casket."

"I know what you mean, Fudd. That's what worries me about Ernie. Any headway Christa makes with him is likely to be tested when Aaron comes home."

Fudd shook his massive, grimy head at the injustice of it all, reached for another bird.

On Friday morning Fudd and Dorsey stood at the edge of the parking lot, peering south at the tracks. As Harley approached, the two men shuffled uneasily. The call had come last night, the fateful message spreading quickly. The body would be flown into St. Louis late Friday afternoon, and Jack Bowden, the funeral home owner, would be there to meet it. The long, black hearse would finally glide west down Highway 50 and stop on Oak Street at the brick funeral parlor where the body would lie in state until it was moved to the church building for the Sunday morning memorial service.

"It's finally gonna be over with, isn't it?" Dorsey said.

"Yes, this is it," Harley replied.

"How's Ernie doin'?" Fudd asked.

Harley turned toward the loaded trailer awaiting the hangers, thought for a moment before answering. "Hard to say. We'll know more real soon…one way or the other."

He trudged up the dock steps and around the concrete wall, soon to be lost to the unearthly murmur of the machinery.

Harley was setting his supper plate in the kitchen sink when the telephone rang. Clara answered, spoke quietly and briefly, then motioned for Harley to take the receiver. "It's Christa."

He nodded as he spoke to Christa. "Sure…yes…sure, I'll be there in fifteen minutes."

He hung up the phone, turned to his mother. "Guess she told you what's happening?"

"Yes, son, she did. I think it's a good sign that he's willing to go tonight and that he wants you there too. Shows he's reaching out to others to hold him up."

"I sure hope you're right. He's got to get this step behind him. Christa wants me to drive to the house and leave with them from there. I'm not sure when I'll get back."

They embraced quickly. Harley said, "I'm gonna put on my Sunday suit for this."

Christa heard the rumble of Harley's pickup in the driveway. She opened the front door and waited for him to hop up the steps, then extended her hands. Her smile was brave, attempted to mask the weariness. "We're about ready. He's in the kitchen. Why don't you go on in and sit with him, I won't be but a minute or two more." Harley looked into the kitchen and hesitated. "It's better now, Harley. He's talking some, and some of the bitterness is gone. We've come quite a ways from the night at Paddy Creek."

Before Harley reached the kitchen table, Ernie scooted his chair back and stood, extending his hand. "Thanks for comin', Harley. I appreciate it."

Harley closed the gap between them, took the big man's hand in his. "Bless your heart, Ernie, it's real good to see you up and around."

Ernie motioned for Harley to sit down, then joined him at the table. Ernie said, "Me and Christa talked about this, but I'm not sure I'm up to it. She says that there just isn't any way around it…and I know she's right."

"Yes, she is right. You've got to take this step now. The worst is behind you, and we've got to keep moving forward. I'm proud to walk with you…and I'll be there every step of the way."

Christa entered the room and stood motionless for a moment, looking first at Ernie, then Harley. "It's time to go to town."

"I'll drive us," Harley said, instantly regretting that he had not driven his mother's car. "I don't know what I was thinking when I left the house. I should've brought Mom's car."

"Oh, Harley, it doesn't matter a bit," Christa said.

Harley slid behind the wheel beside Christa as Ernie shut the passenger door. The engine churned to life and soon the colorless gravel surface of the county road stretched beyond the hood. A minute passed in silence before Ernie spoke, his voice little more than a whisper. "He would've wanted us to come to him in a pickup."

Christa nodded silently, laid her hand on Ernie's knee.

Harley said, "Yeah…he would've."

Silence again claimed the cab as Harley turned the truck south onto the shiny asphalt pavement of Highway 87. Five miles slid steadily under the wheels, and then Harley cranked the wheel for the final turn into the funeral home parking lot. He switched off the ignition, looked at his passengers. Ernie was hunched forward at the shoulders with both hands clasped tightly in his lap. His head was raised, eyes locked on the building. "I can't believe he's in there."

Christa spoke firmly, but gently. "Ernie, we've talked about this before. Aaron is not in there…just a casket holding his body. You've got to hang onto the difference. We've come too far now. Our son is in a real place…but this isn't it. All we're going to see is the casket that holds an earthly body he doesn't need any longer." She paused, prayed silently for the right words. "We said goodbye way back when we put him on the bus to Fort Wood, Ernie…we said goodbye to that body and that face…and when we see him again, it'll be even more wonderful. We just have to wait longer than we want to."

Inside the building, Jack Bowden reached into his hip pocket and pulled out a clean white handkerchief. He tilted his head, sought the precise angle that would most clearly define the fingertip smudges on the Plexiglas viewing top of the casket. With smooth strokes, he drew the handkerchief back and forth until they disappeared. Secure in the knowledge that he had done everything possible to set the stage for a comforting viewing by the bereaved, Jack walked briskly toward the lobby and the sound of the front door opening. Though he would hide it well in the years to come, Jack Bowden would never completely forgive himself for the error of omission that was about to be revealed.

He entered the lobby, walked first to Christa and embraced her. He turned to Ernie, shook his hand, said, "You folks take your time, this home is yours for as long as you want." He stepped aside, extending his arm toward the service parlor. "You go right ahead when you're ready, folks."

With Christa and Harley each linked to an arm, Ernie took six steps into the room and peered down the twenty feet of carpeted aisle before raising his head to look straight ahead. The rasping sound that arose from his throat stunned both Christa and Harley, and it came simultaneously with the collapse of Ernie's legs. When his knees hit the floor the rasp changed pitch, became a wail of agony. "Noooo! Noooo! I can see him! I can see his faaaace!"

Christa's shock was horribly twofold. She too was unprepared to see the profile of her son's face, but far worse was the instant realization that Ernie had plunged back into the abyss. Her mind reeled in momentary confusion as she and Harley struggled to get the sobbing man seated in a pew alongside the aisle. Jack rushed forward to aid Harley with the stricken man, allowing Christa precious moments to gather herself.

Jack shook his head in frustration, said, "Folks...I'm so sorry...I didn't realize that it would...I should have said something...I..."

Christa reached out and grasped Jack's forearm, squeezed it gently in reassurance, but her attention was already directed to Ernie. "Ernie, listen to me. Nothing has changed...nothing has changed about anything we talked about." She wrapped her arm tightly around his shoulders as his upper body rocked to and fro.

"I already said goodbye...already said it," he sobbed. And then, like a man possessed, he tore away from Christa and bolted for the door. She rushed after him, with Harley close behind. They found him leaning against the passenger door of Harley's pickup.

"Ernie..."

"Your God's askin' too much, woman. Too much!"

"Ernie, listen..."

The words were jagged spurts: "It's not enough that He's killed him? And now I've got to see him in a box...all laid out in death...after all this time?"

"Ernie, stop blaming God. God didn't make him join the Marines... it was his choice...a man's choice. God didn't stir up this war, men did! He went a man, and he died by a man's hand!" She paused, the fingers of her right hand opening like the petals of a flower, then closing back to her palm. "I'm so sorry that this has set you back...but, nothing has changed from where we were yesterday unless you let it."

He looked directly at her now, eyes hard and cold. "All that fine church prayin' by you and Harley and the preacher and...and he's dead in a damn box anyway. That's all I know for sure...and I know for sure because I just saw my boy's face in there!"

Christa, now in tears, turned to Harley with a pleading look. He stepped forward and attempted to gain eye contact with Ernie, who had shuffled two steps away from the truck.

"Ernie, I've stayed out of this till now, but there's something you need to know. Aaron wrote me a letter a while back, and the main reason he did was to ask me to help his mom with you if something happened to him. He was worried about how you'd take it. I don't know if he felt some warning or what...but it gave him peace to ask me. Now, I never figured I'd be standing here outside the funeral home with you two, but here I am. And it hurts me so...and would hurt Aaron so...to see you condemn God and the finest Christian woman I've ever known."

Harley ran a hand over his bare head, waited, searched Ernie with a fading hope, found nothing. "There's nothing you can do to make her or me stop caring about you and loving you...and we're gonna see this thing through."

Ernie looked up, focused on a point far above and beyond the top of the truck, as if to allow Christa and Harley a clear view of the transformation of his features. Slowly, in agonizing increments, the long face returned to the stone etching that had first appeared on the creek bank. He then walked stiffly to the truck and climbed in.

"Harley, would you...just drive him home and sit with him until I get back? Jack will take me home."

Harley nodded. She filled her lungs, exhaled deliberately, and with the back of her hand wiped away the tear stains on her cheeks. "I'm going back in there for a while."

She turned and walked carefully toward the front door, the yellow glare from the street light bathing her as she passed under it. On she went—one black, low-heeled shoe after the other—up the steps and through the open door and, finally, down the red aisle until she stood before the stately coffin and looked past the translucent covering. The familiar, handsome features were framed between neatly-trimmed black hair and the high collar of the dark blue full dress uniform. The lustrous buttons were lined in perfect order beneath his chin. She tenderly placed her right hand on the cover, as if to caress the body sealed from her world.

"Son…son…the natural order of things got turned around, didn't it?"

She prayed with her eyes open, fixed on the face. "Lord God, don't let go of my hand now. We'd come a long ways, and now that's lost. Give me and Harley the right words to say to him. If we can't get through to him…who can? You know him better than I do…but who could it be but us? I always thought it would be Aaron here, but his work is done." She paused, drew in a long breath. "My heart is heavy, Lord. You'll have to carry me through. Please carry me through this trial and reveal Yourself to my man who has a heart of misery."

She stood for several minutes before turning and walking up the aisle. She did not notice the tall Marine in full dress uniform standing twenty feet away, silent and still at parade rest in the shadows of a side room.

Harley was sitting at the kitchen table when Christa returned. He opened the kitchen door for her and led her to the table, where they both sat down.

"He went back to the bedroom, I'm sure." Christa said.

"Yeah…he did."

"He say anything at all?"

"Not a word. I tried a couple more times, but it wasn't any use."

She stood, placed a hand on the edge of the table for support, the toll extracted by the last hour evident from head to foot. "Well… thanks for staying with him. There isn't any reason for you to bother any longer."

"Christa…I just wish there was…something I could do. I'm not used to feeling helpless."

"Then just hold me. That would help a lot right now."

Harley gathered her in his arms and held her while she sobbed, did not attempt to stop her, rocked her gently from side to side. He said, "Gramps claimed that every tear shed by the brokenhearted was collected by God and given back somewhere down the line as a tear of joy. Yours will be changed over someday…I know they will."

By eleven o'clock Saturday morning, the kitchen table and all of the counter space was covered with an assortment of food dishes brought by friends. Although each of those who came was asked to come inside, only two had actually entered the house for brief conversations. Under normal circumstances, friends of the family would have filled the house, partaken of the food, and milled respectfully about the kitchen and living room, much in the manner of a wake, although not known as such in rural Missouri. But circumstances were not normal, and by now everyone close to the Bates family knew of Ernie's bitter heart. So they came with a few tried-and-true words of sympathy and left them at the door with their food offerings.

Christa was moved by the gifts of food, but could not help but feel some distress at the waste that would no doubt occur. It was a minor dilemma in the midst of major dilemmas. She sat without appetite in a kitchen chair surrounded by the aromatic bounty and pondered the next twenty-four hours. The funeral home would be open from seven until nine that evening in order to receive those who wished to pay their respects and have an opportunity to speak to the family. The thought pricked at her: she alone would constitute "the family." That not one of either her or Ernie's parents were living was yet another fact to fit into the mournful arabesque of the day to come. Beyond that, the near certain knowledge that Ernie would not even attend the main memorial service scheduled for the church sanctuary was a weight that she refused to calculate, and she willed it into a phantom burden, cast into the future.

More food-bearers came during the afternoon, with bowls and casserole dishes and pie plates now covering a card table pressed into action. She called Harley to ask if he would watch over Ernie while she attended the visitation service, and she reminded him not to eat a bite at his home.

He arrived just before six o'clock. Christa ushered him into the kitchen and waved a hand at the food. "You try to make a dent in all this, and for Heaven's sake, take all you can carry home for you and

Clara. It's a plain shame...all this fine food here to feed a woman with a lump in her throat and a man sick with grief."

"My appetite isn't much better than yours. I'll take some home."

She shook her head, turned around as Harley helped her into her coat. Words were no longer necessary, and with an exchange of small, grim smiles, she left.

Pastor Riggins, alongside Jack Bowden, waited at the front door of the funeral home, and both greeted her with a sturdy hug. Riggins said, "Jack told me about Ernie's reaction last night. I figured you might like someone to sit with you in the line."

"Pastor, I would appreciate that. I would be honored to have you sit with me."

They proceeded into the main room, and Christa looked down the center aisle at the casket. It appeared to her as a mural, undulating slightly up and down with her measured steps, growing ever larger as it framed the back wall. The casket was engulfed in a glorious array of floral arrangements, dominated by exquisite splashes of reds and whites, reaching nearly to the ceiling on all sides. In cadence, they halted a step in front of the casket. Christa touched the fingers of her right hand to the lucent cover.

Though she did not speak with a tone that defied death, it was a tone that clearly identified her as its foe. "I expect that he will look a lot like that across the Jordan...in his prime and all."

"He will be something to behold, Christa, sure enough," Riggins said, "but won't we all."

It was when she turned to her left to be seated that Christa saw him. The young Marine in the regal black uniform jacket stood ramrod straight in the corner of the small alcove. He had obviously been lost in the trying events of the previous evening. Christa had respectfully declined the full military funeral, but had voiced no objection to a formal escort. And now, to her chagrin, she realized that she had promptly forgotten him. She caught his eye and walked directly to him, extended her hand as she read the nameplate on his chest.

"I'm not sure of your rank, soldier Birdsong, you'll have to help me."

"Staff Sergeant Travis Birdsong, ma'am."

"Please forgive me for not noticing you last night...I'm sure you were here. My husband is not dealing with this well at all, and..."

"Mrs. Bates, there's no need for an apology. I'm at your service... and I wish there would have been something I could have done to help last night."

"Thank you, Travis. You're only the second Marine that I've met, and you both have had tough duty. There is something that you can do for me tonight. I want you to stand proud over there by my son's body while all the townsfolk pay their respects. A handsome soldier like you surely doesn't belong back in the shadows. Will you do that for me?"

"It would be my great honor, ma'am."

"Where are you staying? Is everything taken care of?"

"Mr. Bowden has kindly seen to all of my needs, ma'am, and then some. I had a room booked at the little motel on Highway 50, but he insisted that I stay with his family."

"Yes, that doesn't surprise me. That's good. Well, I'm going to go sit down and get ready to shake a lot of hands and hug a bunch of shoulders, and you'd better get ready to do the same. Folks around here think pretty highly of soldiers."

She returned to her seat and waited in silence as the loose column of mourners began to shuffle respectfully toward her.

CHAPTER ELEVEN

The Sunday dawn arrived in hushed splendor. The faintest of breezes tenderly nudged the smattering of dry oak leaves clinging resolutely to the battered sentinel tree at the edge of the driveway. The sunlight, still subordinate to the biting chill left by darkness, would soon swell, yellow and warm, and conquer the yard.

Christa was not cold, but it felt good to tug the collar of the terry cloth robe snuggly about her neck as she stood on the front porch. November had been kind in her latest offering, and this pleased the woman who would bury a son at mid-morning. She awoke an hour before dawn with the words of the hymn on her lips. She remembered no dream of which the hymn had been a part, yet it filled her soul wholly, having now become far more than a song. Her son had crossed the stormy Jordan, and she would one day follow. The man lying in the house staring blankly at the ceiling could see only the stormy waters, not the far bank.

She spoke to the sky. "Jordan's stormy banks…yes, Lord, they are that, aren't they?"

The song would be for Ernie and Aaron, the living and the dead, yet neither would hear it. She hummed the tune as she wondered why it had come to her in the night. How could it be for Ernie if he would not hear it? Still, she knew beyond all doubt that she was to sing it. The words and the tune had become a part of her, a flowing current in her brain, and they would spill forth with all of the energy that she could muster.

Yes, when the glorious early winter sun was high in the southern sky, when they were all gathered around the casket one final time, lost in the sea of stones, then she would sing…oh, God Almighty, she would sing as she had never sung before.

She returned to the bedroom, did not look at Ernie's blanket-covered form, and switched on the closet light. It was a day to dress defiantly—a white dress with a dark blue belt and shoes to match. There would be no somber black wrapped around her this day, not while she stood on resurrection ground. Not while she sang her hymn.

Harley knocked softly on the front door, his mother at his side. Christa greeted each of them with a hug and a cheek kiss. She held Clara at arm's length, said, "Clara, I thank you so much for staying here with him…I know you want to be with us, but…"

"Christa, I'm happy to finally be able to help in some way, and I want Harley to be there for you. Simple as that."

Christa looked down at the floor for a moment, then sidestepped to the counter and picked up a small brown paper sack containing all of the shotgun shells and rifle cartridges in the house. Worried fingers fidgeted with the sack, crimping its already neatly folded top, and then she held it out to Harley. "May God have mercy on me for even thinking such a thing that…seems so crazy…so desperate."

Harley took the sack, said, "It's the right thing to do. There's no need to ask for mercy." He turned to Clara. "There's not much chance he'll even leave the bedroom, but if he does, just show yourself, let him know he's not alone."

She nodded in reply. "We'll be fine, go on to town now. I'll be praying from here."

The three voices from the kitchen carried indistinctly to Ernie, but he registered each, knew that one belonged to Clara Raines and that she had accepted the watch duty. So it would be her that misfortune had claimed for the fateful day. The thought had first passed over Ernie the night before like a frigid wind, but with the passing of each hour the wind diminished, was warmer now—a mild presence in the room—no longer foreboding. The voices were silent, the back door had opened and closed. He uncurled his fingers against the bed spread, looked down at the smooth black handle of the big Case pocket knife.

He slipped his thumbnail in the notch of the main blade and swung it open, touched the tip of his forefinger to the sharp tip, thought of the quick jab through the soft flesh of his neck, and on into the great artery beside his Adam's apple. The task would be performed outside; there was no need to cause unnecessary trouble. Sooner or later, he would hear Clara's footsteps lead to the bathroom, then he would be free to slip out into the back yard. He reached up to his neck, pushed two fingers against the steady throb. There was a grim symmetry that could not be ignored: the spiller of blood would become the victim of his own hand, would bleed out in the same fashion as had the thousands of doomed creatures, would bleed out in the same fashion as had his father.

That he now reasoned with what felt to be stunning clarity was a little mystery lost in the greater mysteries. Or was it just another ruse perpetrated by the powers of the universe, one final dark prank that would serve them as amusement? Was it the Satan of the Bible, cackling with treachery? Or perhaps it was his wife's God beckoning him, forgiving him in advance, understanding his pitiful weakness? These things, the man could not know. What he did know, what was as clear to him as a beacon of white light, was that when he saw the beautiful face of his son in the casket, his desire to be one with him was irresistible, and that it did not matter whether both father and son became a part of some blissful eternity or were lost in the black void of nothingness. Just to be one, in light or darkness, in Heaven or Hell or nothingness. Just to be one.

The small vehicle caught Harley's attention as it chugged to a halt at the curb on the opposite side of the street. He had just stepped out of the church building for a breath of fresh air and perhaps a short walk to ease the tension; the service would not begin for another fifteen minutes, and there was nothing he could do inside the solemn place to be of any real aid to Christa. She sat with Pastor Riggins in the small alcove to the rear of the sanctuary, engaged in quiet conversation. For Harley, the aura of the place was discomforting—a sanctuary for worship flipped upside down in mourning—and it was from this atmosphere that he sought refuge in the cold, cleansing breeze.

The car, a Volkswagen Beetle, would have been conspicuous on Oak Street in California, Missouri, even without the large peace symbol crudely spray-painted on the driver-side door. What paint remained on the body was the color of a ripe banana. The left rear fender was missing, leaving the rusted wheel well exposed. Harley studied the vehicle with an uneasy curiosity as the occupants stirred within the cramped space. Both doors sprang open at once, and three bodies uncoiled and began to stretch their limbs. The driver appeared to be about twenty, and was clad in a military fatigue jacket that had been stripped of the shoulder insignia. A black cloth band was wrapped around his head, with long brown hair gathered into a pony tail lapping at his collar. Harley watched as the man surveyed the church building, obviously paying no attention to the fact that he himself was being watched from the church steps. The other two members of the trio were partially hidden from sight as they knelt on the sidewalk behind the car. Harley heard hammering, amateurish and without rhythm, and then the muffled curse as the inexpert carpenter nipped a finger. The intrusive cadence began anew with less vigor, and ceased after several more blows. It was when the two youths emerged from behind the car with their handiwork that Harley registered the stab of apprehension. They had assembled a wooden poster board that bore its message in heavy block lettering. Although Harley could not yet discern the wording, he knew what the theme would be, and his heart sank.

Harley doubted that they had any intention of entering the building, but he knew that they would take highly visible positions near the front steps. When the mourners filed out at the conclusion of the service, the protesters would raise their voices and their poster. Christa would walk from the building directly into the chants and shouts. Harley's mind churned with possibilities regarding the effect on Christa. There would be no visible reaction, but no doubt more agony would be etched into a mind already burdened. She carried too much sorrow already, this gentle woman. Whatever the outcome, no good could come from any demonstration. The protesters would find no sympathetic ears, and harm could come to them. Let them sound their protests on the campus in Columbia, or at the capitol building in Jefferson City, but not at the very feet of a mourning mother. No, it could not take place on Oak Street, in front of First Baptist Church in California, Missouri. Not today.

As the three huddled at the front of their car in final preparation, Harley turned his head toward a familiar vehicle pulling quietly to a stop in the parking lot to the north of the building. The Ledbetter family emerged, one from each of the four doors, and gathered near the front bumper for a final inspection from Margie. Ties were straightened and clothing smoothed out, and soon after they began their walk toward the building, Fudd spied Harley. When they reached the front steps, Fudd shot Harley a glance, then said to Margie, "You all go on inside. I need some fresh air with Harley for a minute or two."

Margie began to usher the children up the steps, but not before glancing furtively across the street at the strangers. Fudd waited until they were out of earshot before speaking. "Is that what I think it is over there?"

"I'm afraid so, Fudd, and I know as well as you that it's not gonna work out. But let me talk to them for a minute without you getting riled up. We don't want any commotion of any sort for Christa's sake. I think I can make them understand. I just want you to stand here and stare at them, all right? Don't take your eyes off of them. But just stay here…please."

"We'll try it your way, but my blood's heatin' up some already."

"Fudd, think about Christa…no commotion…not here."

The protesters began their march across the street. With a final up-and-down motion of his hand aimed at Fudd, Harley walked to meet them at the curb. A denim-clad boy, younger than the leader, carried the sign. The third member of the group was a woman of about twenty, who would have been attractive had she allowed herself to be. Her hair was tangled, her features hardened in defiance. She wore military-style clothing similar to the leader, and a black arm band of the same material as the man's head band.

The wording on the sign screamed in bold lettering:
STOP THE INSANITY—HE WAS SLAUGHTERED FOR NOTHING!

The leader eyed Harley, smiled grimly as he read the sign. "The *truth* hurts doesn't it, man?"

Harley ignored the question and looked directly into his eyes. "Son, I don't plan to argue the war with you. I'm not smart enough to figure out all of the 'whys' of the thing. But I am smart enough to know that all you can do here is hurt people who are already hurt too much."

He cocked his head at the woman. "Listen to this crap, will you?"

She smirked, said, "Did you think he came over here to throw out the welcome mat, Anthony?"

"Look, man," the leader said, "we got every right to protest this crazy war anywhere we choose, and this is a real good place, seems to me. This little wide spot in the road just coughed up a healthy kid for no good reason, and there'll probably be a football stadium full of corpses just like him before it stops."

"Like I said, there's no use in us arguing the war. Nothing you do here today will keep one more soldier from dying. Go to Washington, or go camp on some politician's doorstep. You can't do anything here but hurt folks." Harley gestured, palms up, in a final attempt. "Please… just let us bury our dead in peace."

"No can do, man. We won't let him be buried in peace. That's the problem. Let him be buried while we wave this sign around and talk to people, and maybe some of them will catch fire and spread the word."

Harley raised his head and looked for a moment into the sky above the man's head before replying. "Well, you've got your principles, I can see that for sure."

The three exchanged triumphant glances as Harley paused. "There's just one more thing. Most important principles in life have a high cost, and this protest of yours is one of them. Your cost is standing behind me there by the steps."

Fudd had remained motionless during the conversation, just out of earshot, but now he glared hotly as six eyes became riveted on him, and he could feel his face begin to flush. Harley said, "This big fellow isn't much of a talker about serious things that weigh his mind down. Right now he's all torn up inside, partly because there isn't much he can do for the parents of the dead soldier. They've been friends for a very long time, you see. If he thought my speech making fell short of the mark...well, I doubt that I could do much with him...if you catch my drift."

The leader said, "Oh yeah, man, so now you're going to sic your pet bulldog on us, is that it?"

"Son, you know you've got a real talent for annoyance. I'm not threatening you at all." Harley paused, drew an even breath as he asked God to turn His head for a pure, white lie. "I'm just trying to tell you about something beyond my control. I'm trying to tell you that the man over there feels as strongly about his principles as you do yours."

The three studied Fudd again, who now realized that Harley was having some difficulty. His fists closed slowly as the shade of his crimson face darkened a degree. The close-set eyes reminded the leader of a painting of a grizzly bear he had once seen. The visage of the big man was a strange composite of sadness and rage, at once puzzling, yet terribly foreboding. The knots of flesh and bone poking from the suit coat sleeves looked more like crude instruments than hands—clearly, they were not normal human appendages.

Harley spied the sign he was looking for: the leader's Adam's apple bobbed in, then out as he swallowed. "It's not a pretty sight, I know. I don't even want to look at him when he gets like this. In the space of about a minute, he'll mangle you two boys and do enough damage to that little car that you might have to walk back to where you came from." He waited, let them shuffle their feet for a moment. "Those are the facts of the matter. What'll it be? I won't stand here much longer, and when I walk away, you're on your own."

The woman wrapped her fingers around the leader's arm and started to speak, but he shook it off before she could utter a word. He said, "What a bunch of hayseeds...they're not worth a scuffle. Let 'em plant their soldier boy."

With the pronouncement, the trio began the retreat to the car. As they neared the vehicle, Harley's voice wafted, softly and without malice, toward them. "The truth is a hard thing to find sometimes."

Harley walked back to the steps and spoke to Fudd in subdued tones, patting him on the back as they climbed the steps. During the course of the last several minutes, a dozen people had arrived, with three of the men having witnessed the end of the scene from the porch.

As he passed behind Fudd, one of the men tapped Harley on the arm. "I can't believe they thought that would work out…here."

"Oh, Dan, they saw their error pretty quick…pretty quick."

Strains of organ notes floated toward the men as the big front door opened and swallowed them into the building. Christa was seated on the first row of pews with Sergeant Birdsong. Harley and Fudd joined Margie and the two children in the pew directly behind them. The presence of the casket pervaded the sanctuary. Several of the larger floral arrangements had been transferred to the church building with the casket, swathing it with grand splashes of red and white that gave it the appearance of being upheld by the hundreds of delicate petals rather than the underlying metal framework.

Jack Bowden began the service by singing all four stanzas of *Just When I Need Him Most*. Christa had requested the hymn when the order of service was prepared. "Sing it for the living, not the dead," she instructed. The strong tenor voice was vibrant, and after he finished and took his seat, Christa, with an unobtrusive movement of wrist and hand, gave him the thumbs-up signal that she herself had so often received through the years.

Fred Riggins walked to the lectern and spoke for less than ten minutes. His scriptural reading was from his beloved Luke, and he tied the words and meaning of the resurrection to both Aaron and his late wife—pupil and Sunday School teacher—now forever reunited. After offering a prayer of benediction, he looked down at Christa for a moment, a little nod punctuating their silent communication.

"Christa has requested that each of you join us at a brief graveside gathering. She would like to say a few words and…sing a hymn for us all. She needs us all there. You will understand why, I promise."

Fred and Sergeant Birdsong escorted Christa outside and on to the waiting limousine. The pallbearers, six of Aaron's high school classmates along with Harley and Fudd, performed the task of placing the casket into the long black hearse for the final journey. The mourners filed to their cars and pickups and fell in line behind the limousine and the hearse as they proceeded down Oak Street toward Highway 50. As the westbound drivers respectfully pulled onto the shoulder and stopped, the long line of vehicles, headlights aglow, crept inexorably toward its destination.

The limousine rolled to a halt on the narrow gravel road at the point nearest the gravesite. Jack turned to Christa and Sergeant Birdsong in the back seat. "We'll wait a few minutes here until everybody has had a chance to park and gather around."

Christa nodded in silent agreement before peering out the window at the gravestones. Beyond them, north of the railroad tracks, the plant loomed, washed white in the brilliant sunlight. The black asphalt parking lot was empty, save for two crows pecking busily at a scrap of trash. Christa's eyes drifted back to the stones. The plant and the cemetery sat atop the highest elevation in Moniteau County, and the wind was a constant—a keeper of the stones—ever cleansing the hallowed place. Somehow, the feathers blown from the plant did not threaten desecration, had never become the eyesore that many originally feared. They had come to belong as much as the fescue grass and the hickories and the oaks, and the woman in the limousine did not mind their presence. She watched as they twirled in ones and twos from across the tracks.

"Harley's Jordan tracks," she mused aloud. Her reverie was disrupted by the opening and closing of the door as Jack departed. "Oh...Travis, I'm sorry, got lost in my thoughts."

"Yes, ma'am, I understand."

He was curious about the names he had just heard, did not dare address her, but he had no control over the silent energy exuded by his curiosity. Christa touched her fingers to the sleeve of his coat. "I'll declare, Travis, I've lost all manners. Let me tell you about these tracks. Look out your window. See the man standing behind the last chair on the left?" The soldier nodded. "He's one of the finest and clearest thinking men I've ever known, and right now, he's the best friend I have in this world. Every morning before he goes to work in that turkey slaughter house over there, he stands on the tracks and prays. I asked him a long time ago why he picked such a curious place. He said it was a perfect place to be reminded of the order of things—work and life and people on the north side...and then crossing over to the stones on the south side. Kind of like crossing the Jordan River, in a Bible sense, he said. Not as pretty as a river, he said, but it would do for him. Said they were his Jordan tracks…and…I told him that I didn't reckon it was such a curious place to pray after all."

"I don't have much Bible learning, ma'am, but you do make it sound real."

"Oh, it is real, son. It's as real as the steel in those old railroad tracks."

A little silence grew; Christa felt the shift of his weight on the seat, sensed again the force of his thoughts. "Speak your mind, Travis, I'm the one who started this."

"It's just that…I've seen death up close…and, I surely don't mean any disrespect, ma'am, but it sure seemed to be a final thing."

Her lips formed a smile, small yet sturdy. "You listen close to my song here in a few minutes, study on the words in the days to come. Just do that for me, would you?"

"Yes, ma'am, I'll try."

Jack approached the hearse and opened the door on Christa's side of the vehicle, and then waited for Travis to join him in escorting Christa to the assembly of people gathered in a loose half circle.

"Thank you both," she said, motioning for them to join the others. "I won't be needing a seat today."

She stood in front of the casket and allowed her gaze to sweep over the quiet group for a moment as she composed herself. Harley stood beside Fudd, encircling his back with an arm, as did Margie, snuggled tightly against the side of her sorrowful husband. Christa did not look away from the expansive face, clouded with grief and confusion. It was simply one more burdened soul to be lifted, one more reason to strengthen her resolve.

"I know it's not normal to speak…let alone sing…at your own loved one's funeral, but I'm moved to do it, and if God gives me strength for the next few minutes, I will do it. The pastor warned me that it might be a hard thing to do, but I'm going to do it as best I'm able."

She looked at Fred Riggins for moment, and then said, "The pastor told you that I had something to ask of you today. It's no secret that my Ernie isn't coming to grips with Aaron's death. Truth is, he's never come to grips with seeing the Lord as the truth. He's a kind and loving man, but there is something inside him that keeps his heart hard about all this. I've not been able to do much with him the last couple of weeks, but I've never stopped praying…and here is what it's come down to."

She paused, looked down at the casket before refocusing on her friends. "In the dark this morning, I woke with a hymn in my head so strong that I couldn't stop thinking about it. It came to me that I should…must, really…sing it here today—just why, I'm not sure. I know it has to do with Ernie and Aaron both, and I know Ernie is not here to listen to it. That's where you all come in. I'm asking you all to pray for Ernie while I sing. Just hold him up to God. That's what I'm asking of you. Aaron doesn't need prayers or anything else we can give him…but his daddy does."

The mourners listened in rapt silence as the woman spoke in even, steady tones, her voice pleading, yet filled with power. "I'm going to sing my song now. It's got four verses and I'm going to sing them all. I'll just sing the chorus once at the end, and you sing it with me. You'll know the words."

She touched her fingertips to the casket and looked across Highway 50 and the rolling fields beyond, and then she began to sing.

"On Jordan's storm-y banks I stand,
And cast a wish-ful eye
To Ca-naan's fair and hap-py land,
Where my pos-ses-sions lie.

All o'er those wide ex-tend-ed plains
Shines one e-ter-nal day
There God the Son for-ev-er reigns
And scat-ters night a-way."

He heard Clara's soft footfalls pass by, and then the closing of the bathroom door. The time was at hand. An urgent drone—machine-like and powerful—filled his brain, but far greater than the din was its sinister energy, and it quickly spread downward, filled his core, his arms and legs, and finally the fingers of his right hand as they secured the handle of the knife. Catlike, he slipped from the bed and carefully turned the doorknob, opened the door an inch at a time, then carefully closed it behind him. He repeated the process at the back door in the kitchen, turned to squint for a few seconds into the late morning sunlight, and after a dozen long strides, rounded the corner of the tool shed. He pressed his back against the rough wood, allowed the energy to claim him.

Christa sang on, and to Fred Riggins, it was the voice of an angel. The flesh at the nape of his neck tingled as he struggled mightily to pray, but the only word he could utter was "Ernie." It would have to be enough, this lost man's name, for the power and the glory of the angel's voice would allow him to say no more.

And so it was with all who prayed—only the man's name could be spoken as they were swept away.

"No chil-ing winds nor pois-nous breath
Can reach that health-ful shore
Sick-ness and sor-row, pain and death
Are felt and feared no more.

The great drone in his head subsided, then vanished, only to be replaced with a silence so profound that it was equal to the drone, but only for a moment. For then came the hiss of the voice. *Do it now, poor and weary man. Bleed as your father bled, bleed as your gun-shot son bled! Chase after them!*

When shall I reach that hap-py place
It is your only chance at happiness. Do it!
And be for-ev-er blest?
Happiness…for-ev-er…your only chance!
When shall I see my Fat-her's face
Your father awaits you in the spirit world, as does your son!
And in His bos-om rest?
Do it! Cross over! Rest awaits on the other side!

He closed his eyes and arched his neck to the left as he tilted his chin upward, felt the faraway sting of a metal point, felt the gathering tension of bands of muscle in his arm and hand. A shout of agony arose in the air, but to his dying day, Ernie Bates would never be certain that the shout spilled from his own throat. His right hand and arm were locked grotesquely behind him, high and over his shoulder, and he jerked his body to the right to relieve the pain. It was then that he saw the five-inch blade of the knife buried to the hilt in the hard wood siding of the shed. He wrenched the knife handle sideways, breaking off the blade, and then, with the last measure of a waning strength, he hurled the handle into the field. Trembling legs failed him, his back sliding roughly down the wall, until he sat awkwardly on the ground.

He listened carefully, fearfully, but the only sounds he heard were of the world he knew.

Then came the final chorus, but it was only Christa who sang. The mourners performed the only task given to them, formed the only sound that they could utter in raspy whispers and little groans and pleas. "Ernie...Ernie...Ernie..."

I am bound for the pro-mised laaaand
I am bound for the pro-mised land,
Oh who will come and go with me?
I am bound for the pro-mised land.

Through eyes misty with tears unknown since childhood, Travis Birdsong watched as a single white feather danced through the grass, hovered for a strangely long moment over the open grave, and then was whisked away on the wind.

Christa watched from the back porch steps as Harley drove the little Chevrolet sedan down the gravel driveway. With a final wave, she turned and entered the kitchen. Clara's report that Ernie had remained quietly in the bedroom came as no surprise. She sat down at the table, locked her fingers, drew in a long cleansing breath as she closed her eyes. The toll extracted by the last three hours had left in its place a heaviness, an indefinable weight leaning on her bones. The memory of the service just past was a slow weaving of sound and color and motion—the gleaming black of the casket, flowery swatches of red and white and yellow, the words of the hymn faintly echoing over the stones, the precise cadence of the honor guard, the gravity of the tightly folded triangle of United States flag on her knees—all now, suddenly, oddly, bits of the past. She opened her eyes, blinked away the images and sounds, thought only of the silence of the house, the silence of the bedroom, would tolerate it no longer.

She pushed away from the table and walked to the bedroom door, swung it open to the sight of the empty bed, the long curl of his body impression visible in the bedspread. The electric jolt of panic stunned her momentarily, wiped the slate of her brain clean, and seconds passed before she willed herself to think clearly. *He must be at the creek…yes, dear God, let him be at the creek.*

She ran to the coat rack beside the kitchen door and snatched down Ernie's old jacket, poked her arms into the sleeves as she toed off her dress shoes and worked her feet into a pair of scruffy tennis shoes. She trotted across the back yard, but when she passed the tool shed, the unnatural silhouette in her peripheral vision caused her to jerk her head sideways.

"Ernie!"

Christa knelt beside him, made a quick visual inspection, and except for the lack of a coat and shoeless feet, nothing appeared amiss. He did not turn to face her; his head tilted slightly forward, eyes cast downward without focus. She covered his cold cheeks with her hands, and then gathered both of his hands, squeezed his fingers.

"Ernie, are you all right? What…what happened here?"

He gave no sign of acknowledgement, and Christa again wrapped her hands around his cheeks, said, "Look at me…talk to me, Ernie." She turned his head, looked directly into his eyes, saw the glimmer of focus follow a blink. She pushed his shoulders forward, worked her arm behind him. "Come on now, you're cold to the bone. Let's get you up and back to the house."

She coaxed his feet under his body, and with the aid of the shed wall, helped him stand, then took off her coat and draped it around him. "Good…good, you're doing fine. I'll hold onto you."

They shuffled for only a couple of steps before he stopped, turned his head back toward the building. It was when Christa felt the shiver pass from his body into hers that she knew some evil had visited the air around Ernie in the quiet place behind the shed, had scraped against him as surely as sleet in a winter storm. The shiver was in her spine, but it passed quickly, became only a harmless remnant about which she desired to learn nothing more.

The melody of the hymn returned to her, filled her, and she hummed the notes as she guided her broken man toward the house.

No chil-ling winds nor pois-nous breath
Can reach that health-ful shore...

CHAPTER TWELVE

Three minutes had slipped past midnight at the base camp. Sounds of fitful sleep permeated the close air of the tent. Six cots lined the perimeter, each laden with a Marine who had not known such modest comforts for fifteen nights. Gino occupied the cot nearest the tent flap, and as he writhed on the canvas bed, his moans grew to a crescendo.

"Gino, stop it!" Pima gave his cot a quick shove. Gino shot bolt upright and stared through the darkness toward the sound of Pima's voice.

"You hear that, Pima? You musta' heard it!"

"I didn't hear nothing, man. How can I hear your nightmares?"

"Pima, I'm tellin' you I heard a voice…singin'…I wasn't dreamin', I swear."

"Shhh," Pima whispered, "you wake Eberhart again, he's gonna beat the crap out of you." He poked a finger into Gino's arm. "Let's go outside."

The dank air closed around them as they picked their way from the tent on bare feet. They walked ten paces before stopping shoulder-to-shoulder. Gino clamped his hand around Pima's forearm. "You don't believe me, do you. Think I'm totally nuts, right?"

"I'm not sure what's nuts and what's not anymore, Gino…but come on, man, it was just a dream." He shook his arm free. "You just got days to go before you're outta this hole…days!…get a grip on it."

"It was a woman's voice."

"Oh, jeeeze…

"It was a religious thing...you know...a..."

"Hymn?"

"Yeah, yeah, that's what it was...a hymn, like Aaron was always tellin' us about him mom singin'."

"Gino, can't you see it was just a dream...Aaron, his mom, him all the time bragging about her voice? Don't you see, man, you just can't let this thing go. He was my friend too...jeeeze, I loved the guy...he was...pure, better than the rest of us, and I don't like dealin' with it either, but what else can we do? Just go nuts? You think he'd want that, huh? We just go nuts and ruin the rest of our lives?"

"But I heard...words, Pima, and I don't know the words to any religious hymn!"

"About what? What were the words you think you heard?"

"I don't THINK, I KNOW. Storms...banks...God...it's all jumbled now...some guy named Jordan..."

Jordan.

Pima felt a flutter in his chest, like a tiny bird in a sack. He reached out, touched Gino's shoulder, said softly, "I'm sorry."

"For what?"

"For doubting you."

"And now you don't" Gino huffed a mirthless laugh. "I'm as crazy as I was ten seconds ago."

"You're not crazy." The silence of the night gathered around them, broken only by the distant hum of the command post generator. "It's not a guy's name...Jordan. It's a river, in a hymn."

Gino sat down abruptly, drew his knees to his chest. "I don't know if I can deal with this, man...I just don't know."

"You can, but there is only one way. You have to go to Missouri and find his parents. You will have no peace forever unless you do."

"I don't want to...I just want it to let go of me."

"You must not fight the Spirit. He is like the wind, and you cannot run away from the wind."

"I'm tired and I'm scared."

"You will be given strength, and your fear will be taken from you."

A sound escaped Gino's chest, a mixture of weariness and resignation. "I hope you're right, cause if you're not, they'll lock me up in a loony bin someday soon."

Two hundred and fifty yards separated the railroad tracks and the two men from the fresh grave. Only a mound of clay soil covered with flowers identified the site.

Fudd jammed his hands into his coat pockets. "Harley, I still get goose bumps just thinkin' about her singin' over there yesterday."

"It wasn't a normal thing, there's no doubt."

Fudd began to speak again but fumbled to a halt. Harley sensed the big man's effort to properly express himself, but remained silent. "Harley, you think...I mean...you reckon I could've prayed over there yesterday with the rest of you all? I heard everybody sayin' his name. 'Ernie...Ernie...Ernie' and before long, I'm sayin it too, and it's like it ain't even my voice, and Christa's singin' fillin' my head...oh, I don't know. I must've just got caught up in it all somehow..." His voice trailed off apologetically, as if he had defiled something sacred.

"Fudd, times like that...you just can't explain. You sure don't have to feel uneasy about being a part of it. You've been close to that family for a long time, and some of those feelings are bound to come out."

Partially satisfied with the explanation, Fudd struggled to ask the initial question again. "But you reckon I was really..."

"Yes, Fudd, you were praying...just like the rest of us."

Several seconds of silence passed before Fudd said: "Dang, that's kinda scary, ain't it?"

"Only if you let it be. God isn't lurking around so He can scare people who pray to Him."

"No, I reckon He ain't at that."

They both looked again to the southeast and the tiny oasis of flowers. "Time to go hang some birds, Fudd."

The big head nodded slowly, and the men began to move in unison toward the plant.

As the first birds were hung, Harley watched Dorsey move to the killer's position just beyond the shocking table. Ernie's replacement was a stocky, square man named Vince Peters who was originally hired as a hock cutter. But to his surprise and dismay, only a week had passed before his transfer to Ernie's lonely post. He was assured that it would be for a few days only, and that Dorsey would keep an eye on him, lending assistance as needed. The few days had turned into many days, and he had not yet grown comfortable in this strange and demanding task. He had quickly mastered the hock cutting, his powerful hands and forearms slashing the keen-edged knife through the leg joints. There was really no way to botch the job—just hack away until the scaly limb was free in your off hand, drop it, and hack off the other leg. But the throat cutting was entirely another matter. Government inspectors griping and moaning at Dorsey, who in turn would indelicately urge more precision with the cuts, muffled curses cast in his direction…no, this was not a good thing for Vince Peters, this throat cutting. To the chagrin of both, he and Dorsey had become permanent fixtures at the position, and both wondered dozens of times each day how long it would be before the tall man of sorrows returned to his room of blood.

And each morning in the house on the gravel road off of Highway 87, the scene unfolded as a painful duplicate of the preceding day. Ernie would eat sparsely, mechanically, and speak in single words or short phrases. To any question asked by Christa requiring more, he would simply turn and walk away. He passed his days in the woods, though far from the cottonwood root at Paddy Creek and the deer stand in the big burr oak.

This Monday morning would likely be the same as the others, Christa told herself as she looked at him across the kitchen table, his face the usual brown study. She touched the tines of her fork against her plate, tapped a little beat in time with the steady churning in her brain as she maneuvered the final pieces of the plan into place.

"Harley tells me that Dorsey is having a terrible time trying to make a throat cutter out of the new hock man. Seems like he's not much good at precision work. According to Harley, he won't last much longer."

"They'll find somebody."

"Well yes, Ernie, they will have to find somebody else, that much is certain. But in the meantime, Dorsey's in the frying pan trying to manage the hangers and cover for this fellow too. Like as not, the next one won't be any better than the first, and Dorsey will be back in trouble all over again."

She paused to glance at his face as he wiped the napkin over his mouth. He began to fidget with the napkin, ever so slightly, and the response did not go unnoticed.

"They need you, Ernie…even if you don't need them. You do a job that's not pretty, and it's more than other men can handle day in and day out. Everybody in that plant…mothers and daddys with kids, all of them…they depend on you fellows out there doing the dirty work on the dock. Things get messed up in a plant like that and sooner or later, it's the workers who suffer…the little people."

Ernie looked directly at her for a moment before lowering his eyes back to his plate. He tapped the fingers of his right hand lightly on the table as he spoke.

"Whatever."

"What does that mean?"

"I'll go back if you want."

"Ernie, it's not so much what *I* want as what I want *for you*."

"Said I'd go."

Christa looked away, slowly pushed her fingers across her brow. The victory was small and hollow, and she felt only a tiny surge of confidence that a forward step had been taken, and she clung to it until it faded away.

Ernie scooted his chair from the table, took down his coat from the peg, and left the house. Christa watched him through the window until he disappeared into the woods.

Harley steered around the guard house and into the parking lot, aiming the rounded hood of the vehicle toward the row of spaces nearest the dock. The pace of his heart quickened at the sight: the old blue pickup was parked in its usual space, and Ernie sat behind the wheel. Harley parked beside Ernie's pickup, hopped out and walked to the open window.

"Ernie…it's real good to see you back. You've been heavy on all of our minds for a long time."

The long face was gaunt; he had lost considerable weight during the ordeal, and the age in his eyes was striking. Without turning to Harley, he spoke haltingly, with little feeling. "I been staring…at this place since first light. I…I'm not sure I'm going back in there."

"We sure wish you would, Ernie. You need to do something with yourself, and we need you real bad. Come on…let your hands get to work. Let your friends be your friends. Just take it an hour at a time, and before long the day will pass, and after a few days, you'll start to feel better about yourself. You'll see."

The tractor-trailer rig bearing the first load of turkeys rumbled past them and into the receiving bay, dirty white feathers following in its wake.

"I'm not gonna be much for talking."

"They'll all understand. We just want to see you back with us, Ernie."

Ernie swung open his door and got out of the truck. Harley patted his shoulder as they began to walk toward the plant. They were in the break room when Dorsey and Fudd walked in. Both men had spotted Ernie's pickup and were ill at ease about the prospect of encountering him for the first time since the tragedy. They glanced simultaneously at Harley for some indication, and he understood.

"Come sit down with us, boys," Harley said as he motioned for the two men to share the table. "Ernie's gonna give it a try today. He knows that we're glad he's back, but for now, he just wants to work on the birds, and not think about anything else. Just get lost in the birds."

Ernie stared at the table, and for a moment, Harley thought he discerned the desire to speak, but it quickly passed, if it ever existed at all. Ernie stood and walked from the room, the silence trailing behind him like a cool breeze.

"Great day, he looks awful," Dorsey said. "Musta lost twenty pounds."

"Dang sure does," Fudd said.

"I'm surprised he's even here," Harley said. "It'll take a long time for him to be himself. He's got things bottled up inside that we can't even dream of."

"I wish we could say somethin' to him," Fudd said.

"No use for now," Harley said, "just give him some room."

The other crew members arrived and the work day began amid the squawks of the birds and the drone of the machinery. Ernie grasped the first head to reach him, and made the cut with automatic precision, as if nothing more than a day had passed since he had last performed the task. The angry buzz and pop of the electricity arose from his left and filled his familiar space as the ruffled white forms—ghostly and still—filed before him. The blood from the first bird mingled with that of the second, and the second with that of the third, and soon splatters formed a jagged ribbon of crimson gore on the concrete, and as the first hundred passed, the ribbon widened, and after the first thousand, it covered the floor of the blood room.

Ernie took his morning break in place at his work station, and his lunch break—sans food—in the yard outside the dock. He passed the remainder of the week in this manner—detached from all human contact, mechanical and precise at his labor. Christa began each day with hopes of some small sign of change, but nightfall always brought the same gloom to the bedroom as had the day before. They shared the same bed, but it was an awkward union, devoid of touch. Any attempt to steer the conversation toward substance pushed him deeper into his cocoon of silence. Inexorably, the toll mounted until she fought the urge to scream at him, to go into a rage for life itself, to test him for a spark of passion—even anger—anything. Anything but this. Anything at all. But she did not scream at him, although she knew that it would have been justified. It was all beyond her now; God had seemingly chosen to stay His hand. Yet there was nothing more that she could do. Just pray and believe that darkness would turn to light, even though she could not imagine how.

Another week drug by without change, and the tone of her prayers changed from urgency to desperation. Harley and Fred Riggins were the rocks of her life, snuffing out the first signs of resignation in her demeanor. She spoke with one or both daily, and though neither man would allow her to speak of dark scenarios, she knew that they wrestled inwardly with their fears that the man who had been reduced to a flickering candle would decide to put out the flame altogether.

Christa Bates could no longer ignore the stark possibility: the foul spirit in the air she sensed that day behind the shed—the narrowly dodged unspeakable evil—could have been the grinning head of the Angel of Death.

CHAPTER THIRTEEN

He came on Sunday morning with the first snowfall. Christa heard the car engine from the kitchen and walked to the living room window. The dirty yellow hulk of Norris Hagen's taxicab squatted in the driveway. The rear door opened and a short man climbed out onto the edge of the driveway. The tires crunched the gravel as Norris slowly backed away. The man's dark green fatigue jacket was unzipped and flapped gently in the wind over the crumpled sea bag resting against his right leg. His heavy eyebrows were barely visible under the bill of his cap, which was pulled down to shield his face from the wet snowflakes that swirled about like frosty butterflies before perishing as they touched the snow-covered ground. The only discernable movements were from dark eyes that darted furtively from one corner of the house to the other.

Christa's eyes clouded over as she matched the face of the young man to the one in the photograph in her top dresser drawer. She fumbled with the knob as she hurried to open the front door, and then stepped out onto the front porch.

Gino averted his eyes for a moment and drew a long, uneven breath in anticipation of the long-awaited meeting. As the woman drew near, he looked at her, through her, saw only himself, as if in a mirror, saw the image that she saw—a flesh and blood uniformed reminder of a young soldier, alive and well. She was only short steps away now, and Gino forced himself to blink away his own image, see only hers. The snowflakes fell into her hair and melted, leaving glistening speckles of moisture that danced on the black ringlets. Her expression was a composite of joy and pain, the smile brave and genuine, eyes windows to lingering sorrows.

"Mrs…Mrs. Bates…I…uh…"

Christa silenced him with a shake of her head, then gave him a quick, sturdy embrace. "It's all right, Gino, I know who you are, and I'm glad you've come. There's nowhere you could be more welcome than here. Como on inside, please."

Gino picked up his sea bag and she took his arm as they walked to the house. The warmth of the living room and the aroma of coffee greeted him as he stepped into the house. The front door clamped shut behind him, quickly followed by the sound of another door shutting from inside the house.

"I'll bet you must be hungry. Let me get you something."

"No…I…uh…ain't very hungry, but that coffee smells real good."

"I'll be right back. You make yourself comfortable."

She returned with a steaming mug and handed it to Gino, who wrapped both of his cold hands around the ceramic warmth.

"Thanks."

He sipped the coffee carefully, blowing gently across the top of the mug. His nostrils flared as he inhaled the bouquet. "For a young fellow, you look like a real coffee lover, Gino."

"Yeah…I guess I am. Been drinking it since I was a little kid." He glanced at Christa, dared a little smile. "My Aunt Rosa…boss of the family, says it fights off sickness in the lungs."

Christa chuckled softly. "Was she right?"

He nodded, huffed the semblance of a laugh under his breath. "So far, I guess."

The force of the silence came on cat's paws, grew suddenly, claimed the room as an unwanted guest. "Anyway…I know you must be wondering why I came here…and I won't be here long…but…aw…jeeze, I knew what I wanted to say to both of you…and now I'm sputterin' around like a fool…"

Christa got up from her chair, sat down beside him on the couch. "Look at me, son. I'm not a very good liar. Never have been. I'm telling you the gospel truth when I say you're as welcome as anyone could be in this house, for as long as you want to stay. You take your time about what you want to say and when you want to say it."

Christa paused to gage his reaction, perceived it as positive. She gathered her thoughts, decided that there was nothing to be gained by delaying what must be said. "Gino, Aaron's daddy is not dealing with his death…in a proper manner. Truth is, he's dealing with it very badly. He's always been a quiet man, but he's too quiet now. The heart's gone from him…and me and some close friends have tried just about everything we can think of to lead him out of his darkness."

She paused, saw the fork in the road of life looming directly ahead. The safe road would avoid placing any responsibility on a very young man whom she barely knew. She offered up a wordless prayer, turned away from the safe road. "Your being here is not going to make things worse…believe me. He'll be glad you're here even if he can't bring himself to say it for a while." Christa feared that it was a white lie, though, in truth, it was hope—pure and white—that hung in the air.

"Mrs. Bates…I don't know…"

"Gino, you've been traveling for a long time, and you must be worn out. You just rest for a few hours, and have supper with us, and we'll take it one step at a time, okay?"

Gino nodded, no longer attempting to hide the weariness in his shoulders.

"Now bring your bag and come with me."

He followed Christa to the doorway of Aaron's room. Gino stood still, looking first at the doorway and then at Christa. "It's his room, isn't it?"

"Yes…yes it was. Now it's anybody's who is a guest in our home… and you're exactly that. He'd be proud for you to rest yourself here, don't you think? Besides, the only other bedroom is ours and you can't have that one." She smiled. "I'm going to have to put you to work for a minute first. We've had some trouble with this door, but I think it's all right to hang it again. Help me slide it from under the bed."

They set the door on its hinges, and Gino held it in place as Christa retrieved the pins from the dresser drawer. She slid the pins into the hinges as far as they would go. "That'll do for now. I'll get the hammer and tap them down later. If you want to wash up a little, the bathroom is right across the hall, and there are clean towels on the rack."

"I know I look pretty rough," he said, running his fingers over the stubble of beard."

"Gino, I've seen ten miles of beard in my time, and never minded a whisker. You just lay yourself down for now. You need some sleep more than anything else."

He nodded, walked to the edge of the bed and sat down cautiously. Christa moved to the door and began to close it before pausing. "Don't suppose Aaron ever mentioned my chocolate pies?"

Gino smiled for the first time since entering the house, and it pleased Christa greatly. "No more than four or five times a day," he said, the smile faint now but still touching his lips.

"When you wake up, you'll know why." She closed the door softly.

Gino's gaze slowly swept the room as he attempted to deal with the lingering unease. The room bore little resemblance to the room of his youth, which had been shared with two older brothers. This room had but one owner. It was small and orderly, yet comfortably functional, each object in its proper place and well cared for. The bed felt firm and inviting, and was anchored with four tall corner posts. A baseball glove was perched atop one of the posts at the head of the bed. A St. Louis Cardinal pennant was displayed prominently across one wall—a long, brilliant slash of red—and stood in stark contrast to the painted white plaster behind it. The dresser was plain, sturdy, and of ample size, with a half mirror mounted on top. A small statue of a ball player, perhaps eight inches in height, stood alone on the dresser. Gino walked to the dresser and picked it up. The plastic figurine was well made and remarkable in detail. The red Cardinal insignia emblazoned the front of the white uniform, with the stirrup socks disappearing into black cleats. The cap was perfectly positioned on the player' head, with a face of distinctive features, anchored by a strong nose. A yellow baseball bat was poised at the ready in the left-handed hitter's hands, but his batting stance appeared hunched over and uncomfortable to Gino, who decided that this was the only flaw he could find in the otherwise handsome model.

"Number six," he mused aloud, studying the numeral on the player's back. "Must'a been one of his favorites."

He carefully replaced the figurine with the strange crouch and returned to the bed. He unlaced his shoes and pinched them off with alternating jabs of his toes, and then stretched full length on the mattress, crossed his arms behind his head on the pillow. The wall facing him was the only one that he had not studied. It was bare except for the small, oval-framed painting of Christ. As Gino studied the serene face, he imagined himself as Aaron, looking at the face a final time before falling asleep each night. The weariness had nearly consumed him now, his body a flat stone on the bed.

"You and your Jesus man, Missouri boy," he whispered to the spirit of the room. "I still can't see him as a foot-washer."

The image grew indistinct, and he felt the corners of his mouth begin to form a smile as sleep, ever tender in its conquest, defeated him.

Harley heard the phone ring as he opened the back door, his mother following a couple of steps behind him. He walked to the kitchen counter and picked up the receiver. "Hello."

"Harley, it's Christa. We've got company over here. You remember the picture with Aaron and two of his buddies?"

"Sure."

"Well, Gino, the short fellow on his right in the picture, is sleeping in Aaron's bed right now. He came late this morning."

"Has Ernie seen him?"

"Yes, I think he has, but he slipped into the bedroom before Gino saw him. Harley, I don't exactly know why, but I'm real glad he came. He was bone tired, and we didn't talk much before he laid down, but he's got important things to say…I just know it. Anyway, I did manage to tell him that Ernie was having a bad time, and that bothered him I know…"

"Christa, I'm happy he came too. Ernie…well, he'll just have to face him, and the sooner the better."

"I know, Harley. Would you come over and meet him? I'd feel a lot better if you were here when Ernie meets him."

"Just tell me when to be there."

"I'm sure he'll sleep a good while, so why don't you wait two or three hours or so. Besides, I'm going to try to talk to Ernie some before he wakes up."

"All right, I'll see you later."

"Thanks, Harley...and plan to eat supper with us."

She hung up and stepped quietly into the short hallway. The two closed doors separated her from a man with whom she had shared most of her life, and a boy whom she had known for less than an hour. Yet, the three were bound together somehow—swept up in life's mysterious vortex. And each life would know change, perhaps great change, within the coming hours.

She whispered a prayer in front of the bedroom door. "Lord, let some good come of this. Please, it's time some good came to this house."

She turned the doorknob and stepped into the room. Ernie was sitting on the edge of the bed with his hands twisted into a jagged chunk of flesh and bone. He did not look up as Christa approached.

"Ernie..."

He cut her off with a strained voice that spat out the words. "Why'd he come here for? I don't want to know anything else about what happened over there. Hasn't even been a respectable time!"

Christa registered the distinctive flip of a switch inside her head, saw red burned against the back of her eyeballs, and though a faraway voice told her to flip the switch back off, she ignored it, let it fade into the red.

"Just listen to you! Always you, you...you! Don't you think anybody else feels hurt? Don't anybody else's feelings mean a thing to you anymore, Ernie? I don't know why this boy came to this house, but I do know I'm glad he did, and by glory, he'll be made welcome here even if you've lost all the manners you ever had! This boy's got things on his mind and he wants to talk to us, for heaven's sake. He didn't come here to torture you. He's been slap in the middle of all that killing for the past year too, and who knows what his feelings are. But I'm telling you, mister, he's found a resting place here, and you can stay holed up in this room for however long you want, and it won't change a thing."

She paused for breath, surprised by the torrent of words loosed from her mouth. Ernie appeared shocked, and she saw his features change, was not certain that they softened. The red rage lost its form, leaked from her so quickly that it left her dizzy for a moment. She knelt in front of him, placed her hands on his.

"Ernie...oh, Ernie..." A great sigh escaped her and she accepted the sound it made as a momentary respite from the storm. "He didn't belong to you. He wasn't your little boy anymore. He was a man who chose his own path, chose to be a soldier of his free will, in a time of war, and he died young. God only knows, it seems like a horrible waste...but we can't judge all that, can't deal with all that. We have to live on...we can't stop living, Ernie. He wouldn't have wanted that and you know it."

Slowly, his head ratcheted toward her, his lips a thin tight line. "Ernie, answer me one question. Has all that love you had for Aaron just died? Did we bury it with him?"

His eyes flashed to her face and all the bewilderment and doubt in his heart were in them. "Woman, you think about him, and you see your heaven in the clouds. I think about him...and I see that box with a window in it, and I see his face one more time in death. You believe you know where he is, and I'm glad for you...I really am. But all I can see is our dead boy in a box, and how can I give love to that?"

She bowed her head to rest on the knot of hands in his lap and did not speak, wished to hear a high wind in the tree branches, or the clean call of the whippoorwill, or the lovely murmur of laughter from a yard full of friends, but she heard only silence.

"We'll deal with your doubts in God's time...that's all I can tell you for sure. But the boy in Aaron's room is alive and in the flesh, and I'm asking you to treat him with the same respect you'd give anybody else. Do that for me, please...and for him...and for Aaron. It took some courage for him to come here, I know that for sure." She paused, said, "And it took some love too, Ernie...it took some love."

She stroked his head soothingly, the anger within her only seconds ago now little more than a strange memory, as if it had occurred long ago. "Harley is coming over in a little while to meet Gino and eat supper with us. I've got some cooking to do now. Why don't you get cleaned up before Gino wakes up."

Ernie heard her simple request, spoken in a conversational tone intended to mask the underlying plea, but Christa Allen Bates was absolutely incapable of deception, and he felt a tiny surge of love—old and deep and true—commingled with pity, was not certain which was stronger, was not even certain that the two emotions could coexist. He was certain that an indefinable element of his being departed with the spirit in the air behind the shed, and he wondered if he would ever know of its composition, or if it would ever return to him.

Christa stood motionless as the seconds oozed by, resisting the growing urge to say something else, but she left the room in silence.

It was three o'clock when Harley rapped his knuckles on the back door. Christa peered through the glass top of the door and motioned with a flour-covered hand for him to enter.

"Come in and sit down, Harley. Let me get this beef in the oven. Put your cap and coat in the hall closet…I'll treat you like a real guest for once."

She slid the big metal pan into the oven and closed the door, washed and dried her hands, then took a chair at the kitchen table opposite Harley. She reached across the table, patting his forearm in silent thanks.

"Reckon Gino's still asleep?" Harley asked.

"Out like a light. I just looked in on him and he was flat on his back and the bedspread was smooth as glass."

"Ernie come out yet?"

"No…no, he hasn't. But I went in and…well, I ended up scolding him, I suppose I'd have to say. He started in on this boy for coming here so soon and, well, it just got all over me. I lit into him pretty hard, but I don't regret it one bit. Maybe he needed it. Anyway…it's done. He either comes out or he doesn't."

"I figure he'll come out to see him. He's had a little time to get over the jolt of it. Probably working out for the better, the boy sleeping for so long."

"I hope you're right. Deep down, he's got to want to hear what Gino's got to say no matter how much it might hurt." She quickly turned her head to one side, lifted her chin, then again looked straight ahead, as if wiping clean her slate of thoughts. "How is your potato peeling these days?"

"Just hand me a knife and give me elbow room. I don't figure I can mess up 'tater peeling too bad."

"Good. I'll boil and mash them last thing while I cook the string beans. Beef roast, string beans, potatoes and gravy, and chocolate pie… reckon that'll do? I could put on…"

"Christa," Harley held up his hand, "table fit for a king."

"I suppose it'll have to do. I'm going to freshen up a little while you work on the spuds. I'm a little nervous just now."

She rattled in a drawer, handed Harley the paring knife. She paused in the doorway, removed her apron, looked back at him. "Harley, this all just can't turn out bad…it just can't."

"It won't, Christa. This boy didn't come here by accident."

She nodded in reply, then stepped into the hallway.

When Christa returned, Harley had completed his chore, and he proudly displayed a bowl full of peeled potatoes, cut up in small chunks and ready for boiling. Christa puttered around the kitchen as Harley began to set the table. With the opening of a bedroom door, both looked in unison toward the hallway, but only Christa knew that it was the door to Aaron's room. She wiped her hands on her apron and stepped into the hall.

"Hey there, feel better?"

"Not sure yet," he said, running a hand over his hair. "I really sacked out."

"Shows you needed it. Now the bathroom is all yours. A hot shower will make a new man out of you. When you're finished, join us in the kitchen. There's somebody that is looking forward to meeting you, who Aaron mentioned a time or two, I'm sure…Harley Raines. He's going to have supper with us."

"Yeah, he did talk about him a lot…I remember the name. Well, I guess I'll try to knock the crud off my body."

"No hurry."

Gino turned and made his way down the hall.

Harley overheard the exchange, said to Christa as she returned to the table, "Seems like a nice kid."

"Yes he does. Aaron wrote that he came from a rough background—some trouble with the law and the like—but you could never tell it from what I've seen so far."

"I imagine it's not too hard to get in trouble in the big city. Anyhow, there's no way that he came back from over there the same as he went."

"No doubt of that."

Twenty minutes later, Gino stepped tentatively into the kitchen. He wore the only clean clothing in his possession—faded blue jeans and a wrinkled short-sleeved shirt. He looked first to Christa in apology. "This is all I got clean right now."

Christa dismissed his concern with a little toss of her hand, then said, "Gino, this is Harley Raines, the dearest friend of this family."

Harley stood, extended his hand, and took a step toward Gino. "It's my real pleasure to meet you, Gino. You look just like the picture I've seen. Welcome to Missouri."

Gino returned the handshake, said, "Thanks, Mr. Raines…"

"Make that 'Harley,' for heaven's sake, that mister has an old sound to it."

"You two sit down here and keep me company while I finish up," Christa said. "Fresh pot of coffee brewed up there." She motioned toward the counter. "Harley, pour us all a cup please."

Harley filled three mugs and sat them down on the table. "Chicago is home to you I understand."

"Yeah…that's where I grew up. Not sure where I'm going now though."

The silence threatened to build up, and Harley quickly changed the subject. "Well, you're in Cardinal country now. You ever follow baseball any…the Cubs or the White Sox?"

"Never did before I went to Nam. Then Aaron…he was always trying to explain the game to me, and this last World Series came and he about drove everybody nuts trying to find out how it was goin'…" He paused, smiled at the memory. "He did love baseball."

"I reckon I'm the cause of that for the most part," Harley said.

"He didn't get it from his parents," Christa said.

"He was really pis...uh...pretty mad for a couple of days after the last game," Gino said. "Kept talking about why a player ran across home plate instead of sliding, or something like that."

"Oh, yeah," said Harley, "I know what that was all about. Lou Brock was the player's name, and he should've slid. I'll explain that to you before you leave. We might even have to play a little catch if the sun comes out warm one of these afternoons."

"Careful, Gino, you'll get hooked if you don't watch him close."

Suddenly, Ernie's towering frame filled the doorway, and three heads swiveled in unison. Christa quickly moved to Ernie's side as the two men stood. "Ernie, this is Gino Polites, Aaron's friend from the service."

Gino pushed away from the table, nearly toppling his chair. He looked up into the tall man's face, and extended his hand as he approached him. "Mr. Bates...I'm glad to meet you...uh...Aaron, he was always talking about you."

Like a statue with a single moving part, Ernie's long right arm rose, fingers slightly curled, but they only hovered for a frozen moment before the arm retraced its path to his side. Christa could not bear to look at the boy's face, could only hope that her husband would feel the longing within her that burned as surely as heat from the edge of a fire. She looked up into Ernie's face. His lips were slightly parted, as if words he could not utter were hidden deep within an unlit shaft reaching to his soul, and she knew that the fire in her own soul could not touch his.

Gino lowered his hand, then his head, and walked out of the kitchen into the hallway. Ernie walked to the back door, quietly opened it and left the house. Harley stood, said, "Which one do you want me to go to?"

"The boy...the boy. Tell him something...anything, Harley, to make him stay."

She snatched a coat from the rack, flinging it over her shoulders as she swept through the open doorway.

Harley found Gino in Aaron's bedroom, hands jabbing the crumpled uniform into his sea bag. Harley moved to the corner of the bed, clamped a hand around the post.

Gino said, "If you'd drive me to the bus depot, I'd appreciate it. Or I can hump it, doesn't matter…I'm used to humpin' miles at a time."

Harley sat down on the edge of the bed, locked his fingers together in his lap, waited for Gino to finish stuffing his bag and zip it shut. "Sometimes…in this strange life, fellas who barely know each other have conversations that mean a lot." He paused, smoothed a crease on the bedspread. "This is one of those times…I hope."

"There's nothing to be said. You saw what happened in there."

"Yes…yes I did, and it wasn't what you think."

Gino's dark eyes darted at Harley and then back down to his bag. "How do you know what I think?"

"It's not hard to put myself in your place, and I know what I'd be thinking. It would seem like an outright rejection. That about it?"

Gino nodded.

"Well, you're wrong. It was just one more step toward dealing with all this. He loved his son so much I can't put it into words…and seeing you, the soldier who was Aaron's friend over there…I didn't really expect him to handle it very well the first time. If you leave now, without him ever having a second chance with you…" Harley shook his head, pursed his lips. "I'm asking you from the bottom of my heart, and Christa is too, if you'll stand with us and try to help him. I know that we have no right to do that, but we really don't have a choice at this point."

Gino ran his fingers over the top of his bag, then sat down on the edge of the bed. "I gotta tell you…I'm not the most…together…human being myself right now. I came here to find peace with some strange things that happened over there." He looked up at the framed painting of Christ, smiled grimly. "I'm not like Aaron. I'm not a believer in his Jesus. Oh, he tried…they, really. Him and an Indian buddy we called Pima…Jesus boys, I called 'em. But not in a bad way." He looked up at the ceiling, then lowered his head in unison with the sag in his shoulders. "I just wanted some…peace."

"I'll tell you the truth, Gino, there are many things in this life that I'm not sure of, but right now I'm sure of one thing. If you leave now, Aaron's daddy will never know peace, and you might not either."

Harley stood, placed his hand on Gino's shoulder. "You're going to have to be soldier a little longer…in a different way. Come on, let's go back to the table."

Christa had followed Ernie to the rear of the shed, stopping an arm's length behind him; neither of them had moved an inch. Ernie faced away from the building, his head tilted slightly upward toward the trees at the boundary of the yard. She blinked against the cold wind, did not know or care if the moisture in her eyes was the result of the wind or a dying ember of emotion. It was all beyond her now, turned loose like a frenzied bird that she was no longer capable of holding without crushing. It was frightening beyond anything she had ever experienced, this barrenness of the soul, but equal to the fear was the weariness—a living, breathing, consuming monster that had claimed a part of her despite all of the entreaties to God.

Just walk away…don't torture yourself anymore.

The words swished through her head, nearly one with the sound of the breeze rushing past her ears, and Christa Bates did not know if they came from God or Satan. She began to tremble, at first only in her fingers, but it quickly spread to her arms, her torso, down through her legs. She gritted her teeth, battled the nerves and muscles that acted with wills of their own, until she was certain that she could turn and walk away. After a single halting step, Ernie's voice stopped her.

"I saw the other side, woman…almost crossed over right here."

Christa turned around, reclaimed the step. "Talk to me, Ernie. In the holy name of Jesus, talk to me."

He walked stiffly to the wall of the shed, began to run his fingertips across the rough wood, his eyes intently following their path. Christa moved to his side, waited, mesmerized by the strange searching. As if drawn by a magnet, his fingertips homed in on a few square inches of the wood, then stopped; only the tip of his right forefinger moved back and forth.

"Feel that."

Christa reached up and touched her finger to the spot, moved it side to side over the metal edge that protruded a fraction of an inch from the wood.

"My knife blade," Ernie said.

Christa nodded, lowered her head. A tiny, cold hole opened in her gut, and she knew that it would grow larger, was powerless to stop it.

"One good hard cut…than some bleedin'…would all been done."

Christa swallowed the wave of nausea, clutched Ernie's arm to steady herself. "Don't stop…get it all out."

"I was ready. Wanted to go to the boy…just on the chance I might find him."

"You wouldn't have found him, Ernie."

"Maybe not, but I was ready to try."

"What stopped you?"

He shook his head, said, "It was my arm and hand that slammed the knife backwards in that wall…and my arm and hand that threw it into the woods…but it wasn't…me."

She took his cold hands in hers, raised them to her cheeks. "It was the hand of God…had to be."

"Or the hand of some force that…that wants to hurt me for a while longer."

"No! No! It was not that, Ernie." She pressed her head against his chest. "We've passed by something here…or it's passed by us, doesn't matter. It's gone forever…if you'll just let it be."

He raised his hand behind her, touched only his fingertips to the soft denim of the jacket, as if to surreptitiously fathom the level of love remaining in the reservoir of his soul. He increased the pressure of his fingers, allowed her to feel them against her body only for a moment. He could not justify more, would not lead her down a path whose end he could not yet see, might never see.

The touch of his fingers was electric to Christa, if only for an instant, and she did not attempt to cling to it, recognized it for what it was. She said, "I know it won't be easy, but you have to deal with Gino. Remember what I told you. He came here out of love…and he came with courage. He's a boy…alive, yes…a reminder, yes. But so be it. He's broken in his own way, Ernie, just like you…and me…and everybody on this earth. We're all broken in our own ways."

She hooked her arm around his waist, gently nudged him toward the house.

CHAPTER FOURTEEN

Gino and Harley were sitting at the table when Christa led Ernie into the kitchen. Harley gave Gino a reassuring nod as they pushed away from the table and stood. Without hesitation, Ernie walked directly to Gino and extended his hand, his long fingers engulfing the boy's. The handshake was dignified, nearly formal, but everyone knew that a great chasm had been crossed.

"You're welcome here, son…for as long as you want to stay."

"Thank you, Mr. Bates."

Ernie gestured toward the table, spoke softly, "You all…please, eat your supper. I need a little time to myself, and I want to clean up." His chest rose and fell with the long breath. "There'll be time to talk. No hurry now."

They stood still as Ernie left the kitchen, then cast inquiring sidelong glances at each other until Christa said, "My goodness, we look like the three stooges doing a skit."

Relieved, Gino huffed a little laugh, clung to the simple joy of it as it rippled through him. Harley smiled, nodded his head at Christa, said, "Except we're a lot better looking."

"That's not much of a brag, Harley," Christa said.

They all laughed now, unafraid of the sound. Harley tilted his head back, sniffed the air. "Gino, I smell two wonderful things in here, and I bet your nose is as good as mine. One is roast beef and the other is…" He paused, waited for Gino to fill in the blank.

"Chocolate."

"As in chocolate pie, that is."

Christa said, "Well, if you two will set the table, I'll bring out the source of those nice smells."

"I've never heard a better offer," Harley said.

They had sat and talked quietly in the living room for nearly an hour before Ernie joined them. He padded in on sock-covered feet; he wore a clean set of denim overalls and a flannel shirt. In his right hand he carried a single slice of white bread folded over a piece of roast beef. He nodded a wordless greeting, then sat down in a chair in the corner of the room.

Christa glanced down at the photo album, felt a twinge of apprehension with the knowledge that this was the first time Ernie had been near it since Aaron's death. But she pushed the feeling aside, looked at Ernie, then said, "I thought Gino would like to see some old pictures…of all of us."

Ernie nodded again, said, "Sure."

Although both Christa and Harley continued to narrate, several minutes passed before Gino again felt comfortable asking questions about the subjects in the album. Then Harley, with a wide grin, reached down and tapped a forefinger on a photo of Fudd leaning against a stack of hay bales.

Gino said, "I'll bet that's the big guy with the funny name…Fudd, right?"

"None other," Harley said, "One James Elmer 'Fudd' Ledbetter."

"What's with the hay?"

Harley said, "If you'll look close, you can see he's really gassed. If it was in color, you'd see a dark shade of red on his face, and that's because he just finished arm wrestling with Aaron." Harley looked at Christa, said, "To this day, I'm not convinced he didn't let Fudd win that last match."

"Me neither," said Christa.

"Aaron talked about the guy quite a bit, but I don't remember anything about the arm wrestling."

"It started out when Aaron was a tyke," Harley said, "just playful. But that last one wasn't just playful."

Gino turned the page, looking from side to side at the black and white Polaroid shots. "Lots of picnics, huh?"

Christa said, "We call them pig-pickins' around here. Ernie smokes a whole hog in his big cooker…our friends from the plant bring their favorite dishes…a real feast."

"And guess who eats the most, by a long shot?"

Gino smiled. "Fudd, I'm sure."

"An absolute legend in his own time," Harley said. "Some pretty good eaters from that plant bunch, but he's in a class all by himself."

Christa said, "Gino, you'll have to visit them soon."

"Why not tomorrow?" Harley asked.

Christa raised her fingers, looked at Gino. "I'll drive you in…after you've slept in as long as you want. What do you think?"

Gino resisted the urge to look at Ernie, then said, "Sure…I'd like to if it wouldn't be a lot of trouble."

"No trouble at all," Christa said.

"The trouble would be if Fudd heard you were here and I didn't talk you into coming to see us. So you'd be doing me a real favor, trust me."

"Okay."

Harley clapped his knees with his hands then stood up. "Done deal then. Well, I've got to get back to the house now. Thanks for the wonderful supper, Christa, and Gino, we'll see you tomorrow."

He reached down with one hand and clasped Christa's fingers, and with his other hand patted Gino on the shoulder. As he walked past Ernie he said, "See you in the morning, Ernie."

He paused at the door, looked back over his shoulder at Gino. "See if Christa can find you an old shirt to borrow for tomorrow."

Christa raised her eyebrows. "I'll bet I know what that's all about."

Harley put a finger to his lips as he slipped through the doorway.

Gino cast a quizzical glance at Christa, who said, "Loading dock secret…but you'll have fun."

"I guess I'll have to trust you on that."

"Yes you will." She stood. "I'm going to have a go at those dishes and pans in there."

Gino said, "Been a while since I pulled KP, but I'm good help."

Christa waved a hand toward the kitchen. "I think I'll take you up on that, then we can finish the album, and after that you can watch TV if you like…stay up as late as you want. Me and Ernie turn in pretty early."

Christa opened the bedroom door, her eyes drawn to the yellowish light seeping through the small lamp shade on the night stand. Ernie sat in the rocking chair in his customary position, facing the window. He did not turn around when she entered the room. The bedroom had become a place of acute silence, broken only by the faint wooden creak of the old rocker and the rustle of clothing and bed covers. Spoken words were unnecessary tools in the grim practice of life within the four walls.

Christa closed the door, stood with her back pressed against it as she studied his profile, wondered if the last five hours had altered the complexion of his soul. With the wondering came a surge of disgust, and although she could not precisely assign its origin to a single event— could not even assign it to Ernie himself—she knew that the silence of the room must end.

"You can ignore me if you want, but I'm going to talk in my own bedroom…now, and whenever else I feel like it…even if it's to myself." She stepped forward, sat down on the edge of the bed, allowed the liberation to well up within her, strengthen her. "You stood with me, Ernie, and vowed 'till death do us part,' but that meant one of *us*…*us!* It didn't mean *anyone* else…not even our precious son." A great sigh escaped her, and with it the low moan of her spirit. "Ohhhhh…Ernie… I suppose we could go on like this for years…just trudge on and one day forget the touch of our lips…our fingertips on our skin…just fade into old age with no joy, no caring…like two candles blown out by the wind." She shook her head, set her jaw. "But I refuse, Ernie…I refuse to accept that."

She raised her head and filled her lungs with air. "We've lived and loved and worked and laughed and cried and raised a fine son and helped friends and accepted help and…on and on, Ernie. We've done all this together…together, for twenty-five years! And now, together, we've lost the precious son, but I'm not ready to die yet…and with the power from Jesus Christ, I will not let you die in the shell of your body, Ernie Bates!"

The rocking chair no longer creaked. He spoke softly, toward the window. "Your good book says they slaughtered your Jesus on a cross... but by his power, you're gonna save me."

"He arose, he is not dead."

"There is a spirit world out there, I do know that for sure. But I only know the dark side. Maybe it swallowed up Jesus back then... maybe he was just a man."

Christa moved to the opposite side of the bed, near the rocker. "He was a man, but he was *God* too, Ernie...God come down here to save us."

"But they slaughtered him."

"Because He *let them*. And He did not stay dead. He arose, Ernie. People saw the empty tomb, but what's a thousand times more than that, people saw Him *after* the cross. Why do you only believe the witnesses who passed down the story of His Crucifixion? Why not the people who told of His resurrection after they saw Him, talked with Him?"

He lowered his chin to his chest, said, "Woman, I don't know what to believe just now. I'm tired...tired of thinking...remembering bad things...hoping for things I'm not sure of...just bone tired." The rocker began to creak, found a slow rhythm. "Go on to bed, I just want to rock tonight...don't want to think anymore."

Fudd drug an unwilling eighteen-pound tom out of the coop and positioned it for hanging. When his targeted shackle approached from the right, he effortlessly dropped the bird's feet in place. "Harley, you reckon this boy'll show up here, sure enough?"

"Said he would, Fudd. It'd be good for him and Ernie both."

"Reckon he'll eat dinner in the break room?" Fudd asked in reference to Ernie, who had yet to eat with the crew since his return.

"Don't know. Might...just might."

As Fudd hung his final turkey and ducked under the shackle line he glanced at the vehicle stopped at the parking lot gate. "Hey, ain't that Christa's car?"

Harley craned his neck and looked through the dock opening. "Yep. And that's Gino getting out."

Both men waited on the dock as Gino warily approached the door. When he spotted Harley, his pace quickened and he threw up his right hand in greeting. Harley waved and motioned for him to join the men on the dock floor. Gino clambered up the stairs.

"Welcome to the turkey plant, Gino. I want you to meet my friend, Fudd Ledbetter."

On cue, Fudd stepped forward and quickly wiped his filthy right hand on his slightly less soiled shirt before extending it in greeting. Gino's hand was consumed in the massive chunk of callused flesh, and Fudd pumped it vigorously. "Howdy, Gino. Harley here has been tellin' me about you."

"Pleased to meet you, Mr..."

"Crapsakes, Harley, you tell him to call me that? It's just Fudd, son...just Fudd. Last fellow to call me 'Mr.' was a doctor, right before he did somethin' terrible to me."

They all laughed as Harley shook his head at Gino. "I tried to warn you."

"Come on," Fudd urged, "let's get them ham boxes down. My belly's been growlin' like a panther for an hour."

Fudd finally released Gino's hand. After shielding the hand from view behind his leg, Gino quickly flexed his fingers in an effort to return the blood flow to normal levels. Harley looked into the blood room where Ernie was removing his apron. Fudd led Gino into the break room, clapping him on the shoulder like a long lost friend. Harley walked up to Ernie as he stepped up to the main floor level.

"Gonna have a bite with us, Ernie?"

Ernie hesitated for an instant, then said, "I reckon so. I'm going to get a pack of crackers and a Pepsi from the cafeteria."

"Good, we'll see you in a minute."

"Fire soup!" The booming voice rolled from the break room. "Harley, Gino claims he ain't hungry, but he might change his mind when he gets a whiff of this."

Fudd unscrewed the plastic lid of his thermos and inclined his head slightly before inhaling the heavy aroma.

"Dangnation if that's not chili I smell in there!" Dorsey roared as he banged open the door.

"Meanest stuff this side of south Hades, boss man. You're just jealous 'cause you don't have some of your own."

Harley said, "Dorsey, this is Gino Polities, Aaron's friend from the service."

Gino stood and exchanged handshakes with Dorsey. "Welcome to the dock, Gino. Glad you came to visit us."

"Thanks."

Fudd watched as Harley unwrapped his sandwich and took the first bite. "Judgin' from the skinniness of that sandwich, Harley, it must be peanut butter again. I can't figure out how you can work up enough energy to hang these big buzzards eatin' that stuff."

"Fudd, a man doesn't have to eat meat every time he has a sandwich you know. There are other things that go between bread slices."

"There ain't supposed to be. That's why there's a heap more meat processin' plants than peanut butter makin' plants."

"How do you know that, Fudd?"

"Just good common sense, I reckon. Heck fire, I bet the biggest peanut butter plant in St. Louis ain't no bigger than my barn. Man's gotta feel what he's bitin' between the bread slices, for pity's sake."

"Don't pay any attention to all that, Gino," Dorsey said, "it's like this every day."

The door opened and all eyes turned to Ernie as he walked into the room. "Howdy, boys," he said, reaching for a metal chair. He sat down quickly and began to fumble with the cellophane wrapper of a pack of crackers.

"Got half a sandwich here, Ernie," Harley offered, pointing to the uneaten portion of the sandwich.

"It's not a real sandwich, Ernie, cause it's not got any meat in it," Fudd said. "If you want somethin' to taste, dip into this here chili."

Ernie raised his hand defensively. "I'm not up to that yet, but thanks anyway."

Ernie turned to Gino. "Christa fix you a bite at home?"

"Yes, sir. Roast beef sandwiches and a couple more pieces of that chocolate pie."

Fudd moaned. "Lord have mercy, boy. Don't mention that pie when I'm lookin' at Hydrox cookies for dessert."

Gino chuckled. "Sorry, Fudd. It is something special. I'll think about you when I have some more at supper."

"Harley, you didn't tell me he had a mean streak," Fudd said as he slurped a spoonful of chili.

The banter continued, the minutes melting away. Dorsey pushed away from the table and opened the door. "I'll check and see if they want us to start back yet."

Fudd was energized by Ernie's return to the break room despite the fact that the tall man had spoken only a few words. He perceived it as a major step toward normalcy. It was a far cry from the Ernie of old, but it was a beginning. Fudd reasoned that the boy was a positive influence, though it did seem strange to him that he had come to Aaron's home.

"Come on, Gino," Fudd said, "let the two best turkey hangars in the country show you how it's done." Fudd headed for the door, tossing words over his shoulder. "Heck, maybe in the whole dang universe, what you think, Harley? They hang these buzzards overseas, you think?"

"How would I know that? Who can say."

"Well it doesn't matter…who could be better than us anyhow? Ha! Ha! Haw!"

Gino stood a safe distance and studied the actions of Fudd and Harley as they began to fill the moving shackles. The motions were smooth and unhurried, and it seemed as if the large birds were acting in concert with the men who sealed their doom. Upside down the right hands slid into the coops, coming out each time with both of the bird's legs firmly secured. The creatures were instantly tucked against the hangars, with an open wing pinned to the right hip. Finally, in a flash of motion, the feet were jammed precisely into the small "Y" frames of the shackle, and then the process was repeated, machine-like, and with little variation. Not so difficult as one might imagine, Gino thought to himself. He wondered why Fudd had bothered to brag so loudly.

"Want to try one, son? You look fairly stout." Fudd issued the challenge as he stole a glance at Harley. Gino looked around the dock and shrugged his shoulders. "Don't worry, Dorsey don't care." Fudd knew is was nearly, if not completely, a lie, but he trusted his ability to prevent a calamity. "You might like it so much you'll want a job. Duck under the line over there." Fudd pointed to the end of the dock where the moving line descended steeply from the opposite side of the trailer. Gino carefully made his way to Fudd's side.

"You been watchin' pretty close, huh? You probably got it already. Just nice little toms…maybe seventeen or eighteen pounds…nothin' to it really."

Fudd looked over his shoulder at Harley who was shaking his head in resignation at the trap. He could see the corners of the big man's mouth begin to twitch as Gino eyed the coop.

"There's not but one rule for beginners to remember," Fudd intoned solemnly. "Protect your private parts."

Gino nodded at the ominous warning before he inserted his right hand into the coop. He succeeded in grabbing both legs, but as he congratulated himself on the initial victory, one of the legs slipped from his grasp and churned piston-like at the dried dung on the floor of the coop. As the first of the foul pellets ricocheted off his cheek, Gino released the other leg and swiped at his face with both hands. With great difficulty, Fudd suppressed an explosion of laughter and addressed the faulty novice.

"That was good, Gino, you almost had him on the first grab. They're a little stronger'n they look. Just hold tighter next time."

Gino wiped his face on his shirtsleeve and selected another target. Again, he connected with both legs, and he squeezed mightily. The bird flopped cooperatively to the coop floor, and Gino began to drag it forward. The coop he was working was chest high, and he was bolstered with the thought that it was about in line with the shackles. "Get a leg in each hand and hang this thing," he mumbled under his breath. He managed to grasp a leg in each hand, but forgot to hold the bird close to his body. The turkey instantly sensed an opportunity for escape and began to beat its long wings with all his might. Intent on hanging the bird before further problems arose, Gino staggered toward the shackles, blinded by the filthy wind churning against his face. He squinted through the minor storm of feathers and debris, peeking at a single shackle moving at what appeared to be an incredible speed. Just as he began his lunge at the moving target, he felt a muscled arm wrap tightly around his shoulders and stop his movement. He felt the turkey being lifted from his hands as he strained to see Fudd's laughter-contorted face.

"Haw! Haw! He! He! Danged near got it done, boy. I'll swear if that wasn't one of the best first tries I ever saw. Harley, he might've hung him, what cha' think?"

"Just might've, Fudd, just might've at that."

Gino had already retreated to the safety of his original position on the dock, and was shaking his head in amazement at his brief but engrossing encounter. He caught his breath and smiled sheepishly. "Sure didn't look that hard from here."

"We've heard that a time or two, ain't we, Harley?"

Dorsey banged open the evisceration room door and, with one look at Gino's bedraggled appearance, knew exactly what had just transpired. "Son, I should've known better than to leave you out here with him."

"I kinda wanted to try I guess," Gino said.

"Now, boss man, you know I wouldn't let nothin' happen to him," Fudd said.

"Come on with me, Gino," Dorsey said. "I'll give you a proper tour of this place. Let's check out Ernie."

They approached Ernie's position, but first passed the hiss and pop of the electrical stunning table. "Does that thing kill 'em?" Gino asked.

"Nope, just quiets them down for Ernie. Good as he is, even he wouldn't be able to cut half of 'em if they were flapping all over the place. The cut's got to be just right for them to bleed out."

They stood between Ernie and the stunner, watching the man wield the crimson-stained blade like a surgeon's scalpel. There was little motion involved in the task—just hands and arms—yet there was a peculiar grace about the gruesome chore that demanded Gino's attention.

"It's all feel…in the hands," Dorsey said. "No two birds exactly alike…and he cuts them all perfect. Doesn't matter if he's fresh or bone-tired. All the same…number fifteen thousand gets cuts as perfect as number fifteen." Dorsey looked sidelong at Gino. "I'd bet my tongue in a vice against a five dollar bill that there's not a surgeon in St. Louis that has hands better than his."

Ernie glanced for a moment at his small audience than quickly resumed his work. Gino noticed the look, but could not read anything into it. The big hand with the chain mesh guard reached for yet another turkey; Gino wondered how many more thousand times it would reach out before the shackles were empty for the day.

"Come on, let's check out the gut line," Dorsey said.

Only a single metal door separated the receiving dock from the feather picking machinery and the hock cutters, with an identical door leading to the evisceration line. As Gino stepped through the doorway, Dorsey handed him a paper cap and motioned for him to put it on. The contrast from the grime and feathers of the dock was stark. Long florescent light tubes hung from the ceiling, illuminating every crevice in the windowless cavern. The uniforms of the workers were white with short sleeves, and covered with white plastic aprons. The odor from tons of blood and offal, mixed with endless gallons of water, was not nearly as foul as Gino had anticipated, more of a clinging, oppressive dampness that seemed to permeate his body.

They walked slowly down the line as Dorsey pointed out the various operations performed on the white naked carcasses. The "drawers," Dorsey called the four women who went about the gruesome business of pulling the wad of intestines from the body cavity. Two of the women were obviously veterans at the chore, and paid no attention to Gino or Dorsey. Small but powerful hands reached into the cavities and steadily pulled the mass forward. Gino judged the other two women to be no older than himself, and he could see the embarrassment in their faces as they struggled, and he sensed that their unease was due more to the fact that a young man was watching rather than to their fumbling. The government inspectors poked and prodded not only at the entrails, but the entire carcass. Each had a knife-wielding trimmer stationed at his side. At the slightest motion of the inspector, some offending part was deftly severed and dropped into the waste trough below the line. Just beyond the trimmers, the giblet cutters used long scissors to cut the organs that would be stuffed into the neck cavity before final bagging.

The next station was manned by two long-limbed fellows handling long hoses. Dorsey called out over the din to Gino, "The lung suckers." Gino watched intently as the taller of the two men thrust the metal end of the hose into the body cavity and twisted his wrist with a controlled violence as the lung tissue was drawn out. The muscles and tendons in his right forearm rippled like elongated creatures living just beneath the skin. The man looked over his shoulder at Dorsey, and then to Gino.

"Bring a rookie for us, Dorsey?" he shouted.

"Naw, R. C., this young fellow here is too dang good for the end of a lung hose."

The big man threw back his head and roared in laughter as Dorsey and Gino walked past. The only remaining manned station on the line was the final inspection stand. Dorsey explained that this lonely soldier was charged with the responsibility of checking the carcass for any imperfections before it was released into the chilling tanks.

"Easy job when we got good birds and no rookies on the line, but it's bad news when we're running sorry birds. They put two of 'em up there when R. C. takes vacation so they can rake out all the lungs that get missed with the hoses."

The final process was brutally simple and efficient. As the carcass passed this station, the head was caught in an ever-narrowing slot in a metal table, with the result being a neat amputation that maximized the neck length. The turkey was then dropped from the line into the cylindrical chilling tank that churned its contents of turkeys and ice water with huge slowly revolving paddles.

"They stay in there for about forty-five minutes or so," Dorsey explained. "Government won't let them soak up but so much water though…always testing the weight differences with tagged birds." He smiled. "The water sells for the same price as the meat."

The tour moved to the packaging side, where the final product was vacuum bagged and sent on its way to the blast freezers. "We'll just peek into the blast freezers when they take in another load. Colder than the North Pole in there, I'll tell you. Then we'll go back to the dock where the real men work…according to Fudd."

After a quick look into the freezer, Dorsey clapped Gino on the shoulder and they began to retrace their steps. As they passed the neck cutters, Gino again glanced at the older of the two men operating the air-gun clippers. The first time past the station, it appeared to Gino that the man spent as much of his time watching the younger man as he did at performing his own task. The pattern continued to hold true, and Gino wanted to ask Dorsey about it, but reasoned that there could be only one reason: older men watched younger men who were in harm's way. Gino remembered the way Sergeant Winfield's hawk eyes followed soldiers new to the treachery of the jungle. The look was the same here, exactly the same.

The tour ended in the main lunch room with Dorsey buying Hershey bars and Pepsis. Dorsey smoked half a pipe full of tobacco as they made small talk. He exhaled luxuriously, his mouth forming a loose oval as the thick cloud of smoke drifted to the ceiling. He emptied the bowl into a small metal ash tray and carefully placed the pipe in his right rear trouser pocket.

"Be another twenty minutes at least before afternoon break," Dorsey said. "You can wait back in the dock break room for the boys or go outside and walk around for a while. I got a couple of things to tend to."

"I think I'll go outside for a while. A little air sounds pretty good."

"It does take a while to get used to the smells around this place." Dorsey huffed a little laugh. "I guess it took me a good two or three months before I didn't think about my nose."

Gino pushed open the exit door to the rear of the big room and walked a few paces onto the sidewalk that formed a perimeter around the building. The afternoon air was crisp and pleasant, the stout breeze in his face a sweet respite from the heavy odors of the plant. He walked slowly along the rear wall of the vast chalk-colored building, its enormity a presence hovering over him. He stopped at the corner, his eyes drawn to the railroad tracks that paralleled the south side of the property. An old barbed wire fence, overgrown with tangles of long grass and withered vines, separated the railroad right-of-way from the property beyond. Gino turned west, resuming his leisurely pace. He walked nearly half the distance of the wall before he again glanced south at a point where the overgrowth on the fence thinned out. He stopped abruptly and squinted at the two gravestones now in view twenty yards beyond the fence, then quickly picked his way across the gravel bed of the tracks and jumped over a shallow drainage ditch near the fence line. The two stones had multiplied to hundreds—row after orderly row—reaching two hundred yards to the east and one hundred to the west.

He spoke aloud: "You're out there somewhere, ain't you, Missouri boy?"

He had planned to visit the grave before leaving town, but now that it lay before him somewhere—beckoning, yet foreboding in its grim victory—he was less certain. The thought was disconcerting: He had not sought it out; rather, it had found him. But the place could not be ignored, the pull of the stones nearly gravitational. The rusty strand of barbed wire creaked as he pushed it down and slid his body through the narrow space. Ten paces from the edge of the stones he stopped and began his visual search. It seemed like a large cemetery for such a small town, and he figured he would have to move several times before locating the one grave that mattered to him. His search was brief. On the first sweep to the west, a tiny splotch of color caught his eye. Focusing intently on the spot, the pace of his heartbeat quickened with the realization that he was looking at a small American flag dancing in the wind. He approached it steadily, yet warily, and soon he could see the earth, naked and brown, and the weathered flowers near the base of the stone. As he drew near, the delicate popping of the little flag rose with the wind, and at first Gino looked only at the flag and the ground, but the shiny gray of the tombstone beckoned. He raised his head to the stone.

AARON WAYNE BATES
BORN JULY 15, 1949
RELEASED FROM EARTHLY BONDS NOVEMBER 9, 1968
*STANDING IN THE ROARING OF THE JORDAN,
COLD TO THE HEART WITH ITS DREADFUL CHILL,
AND VERY CONSCIOUS OF THE TERROR OF ITS RUSHING,
I CALL BACK TO YOU WHO ONE DAY IN YOUR TURN WILL
HAVE TO CROSS IT, "BE OF GOOD CHEER, MY BROTHERS
AND SISTERS, FOR I FEEL THE BOTTOM, AND IT IS SOUND."*

Gino's eyes blurred, but he snapped his eyelids, would not allow tears to form. Slowly, he sat down at the foot of the grave and drew his knees under his chin. He stared at the words cut into the stone. "Man, it should've been me, Aaron. Never been worth nothin' much to nobody in my whole life…and I'm above the ground when all the shootin' finally stops for us…and you're under it."

He looked down at the tiny scar on the tip of his right forefinger. "That close to stoppin' the bullet myself…man oh man, Aaron…your God don't make much sense to me at all. Just messes with us, and then one day, it's over…just over."

Gino rocked to and fro in the dead grass of early winter, pondered questions for which he had no answers. The strange admixture of memories from the past year swirled about the place—hearty laughter and screams of agony, the bloom of youth and the pall of death, the acrid smell of cordite and the green, wet odor of the jungle—and he could not sort them out. The shafts of afternoon sunlight filtered through the barren trees and warmed the side of his face. He moved his head slightly to the south so that he could feel the warmth cover his entire face, and he yielded to the memories as he did to the sunlight.

The powerful air horn of a diesel engine drifted toward him with the west wind, and as the drone grew louder it chased the memories in front of it, swept them from the tracks and the graveyard. The sleek engine pulling the afternoon freight thundered past, bound for St. Louis before nightfall. Gino stood, felt the magnetic pull of the great steel beast as he walked to within twenty yards of the rumbling cars. The earth reverberated with the countless fleeting tons, and he could feel a fraction of the energy transferred upwardly through his feet and legs, into the core of his body. The massive steel rails, seemingly unmovable only minutes ago, groaned eerily as they undulated under their burden. Boxcars and flatcars, they filed by, laden with the demands of a nation, and then the caboose appeared, dirty red and forsaken by the proud engine, and finally the tracks fell silent and unyielding once again.

Gino squeezed through the fence and walked to the tracks, knelt down at the edge of a cross tie. He reached out with the fingers of both hands, lowered them until he felt the heat radiating from the track. Only moments before, a force of incalculable power had passed by, and yet the only residue was a warmth that would dissipate within minutes, leaving the track cold and dead and still. *Cold and dead.* "Is that you, Missouri boy…cold and dead? Gone down the tracks to a place I can't find?"

He retraced his path to the grave, walked behind the stone and ran his fingers over the rough hewn top. Aaron's death words whispered inside his head. *"Why do you seek the living among the dead?"* He caught his breath, wondered if the woman's singing would return to him, did not know if he desired or dreaded it. But only the whoosh of the wind filled his ears.

Gino stood at the steps of the dock opening and watched as the last of the turkeys were hung on the line. The three men on the far side of the trailer walked away first, disappearing beyond the truck at the opposite end of the dock. Fudd and Harley filled the gaps in the line on their side, then headed for the break room. Five minutes later, Fudd bounded down the steps as Gino backed out of his way.

"Well, what'd you think of the gut line, Gino?" Without waiting for a reply, he continued, "Cleaner in there, but it'd drive me up the wall like a crazy woodpecker if I couldn't move around some. Same old job on every dead bird. Crapsakes, I'd a heckuva lot rather mess with 'em dirty and alive—fightin' a little with you. No two birds the same. Makes the day pass quick."

"I suppose I'd take it your way too," Gino answered. "It's a little too close for me on that line in there."

Harley trotted down the steps and walked toward Gino and Fudd. "Fudd trying to make a hanger out of you I imagine, isn't he?"

Gino smiled and nodded.

"Harley, I swear, we could make something outta this young buck. I'll bet I could work with him a half day and he'd be hangin' the dickens outta these buzzards."

"I figure he'd do all right," Harley said. "Well, I got to get on down the road." He looked at Gino. "You…uh, you want me to run you on back? Ernie'll be a little while hosing down the blood room."

Gino knew that the offer involved more than a ride. "No…I…want to wait for him."

"Good," said Harley, "see you guys later."

Fudd swiped a hand through the air, said, "I'm outta here, too."

Gino waved, said, "Later." He sat down on a concrete step. Ten minutes later, he turned to the sound of boots on the dock, then stood as Ernie approached, his worn denim jacket flopping in one hand.

"Let's head north," he said. Gino fell in step with him until they climbed into the pickup. Soon the tires whined steadily on the asphalt of Highway 87, became one with the comforting drone of the engine. The tone of the engine grew louder as the truck began to climb the long hill leading to the gravel road intersection. Ernie downshifted in preparation for the turn. Suddenly, a tractor-trailer rig loomed at the crest of the hill, and as it passed, Gino saw that it was a turkey truck, the metal coops crammed with knots of dirty white feathers. Ernie completed the turn and the tires crunched over the gravel road.

"Goin' to the plant, I guess," Gino said.

"Yep, going to the plant." He paused, added, "last ride."

Last ride. The words hung in the close space of the cab as Gino weighed them on the scales of his brain. *Sooner or later everything that breathes takes a last ride. Aaron Wayne Bates did.* He looked out the window, tried to lose himself somewhere in the rolling fields beyond the road bank, but he did not travel far. He suppressed a great desire to lean his head against the strong shoulder of the man who had infused life into Aaron, to ask him of last rides, and where they led. Instead, Gino felt his lips form a tiny rueful smile, certain beyond all doubt that the man was as devoid of answers as he was.

CHAPTER FIFTEEN

Christa pushed open the back door as the pickup crunched to a halt in the driveway. As Gino and Ernie approached the house, she called out, "How about a cup of hot cider?"

"I think I'll pass," Ernie said. "Got a couple things to tend to in the shed." He ambled toward the tool shed.

Gino said, "I'm not exactly sure what it is, but if you cooked it, I'll try it."

The kitchen was filled with the aroma of apples and cinnamon. Christa filled two mugs with the steaming honey-colored liquid and sat one in front of Gino on the kitchen table. He lifted the mug under his nostrils and inhaled. "Sure smells good."

"My mother claimed that it's good for whatever ails the body or soul, and I've come to agree with her over the years."

Gino took a careful sip and nodded his approval to Christa.

"You get the royal treatment at the plant?"

"Oh yeah...fellow named Dorsey took me around all over the place. Some pretty tough jobs in there."

"That's a fact. Don't suppose Fudd tried to get you to hang a turkey?"

Gino shook his head at the recent memory of his brief encounter with the big bird. "How did you figure that?"

"I know Fudd Ledbetter, and I know that would've been a temptation he couldn't resist."

"I watched them for a while and figured I could at least hang it up there somehow, but I'll be dam...but I didn't get it up to the holder. It's tougher than it looks."

"There's not an easy job in there, but that plant has been a godsend to this little town. Lots of folks with steady paychecks that never had any before it opened."

An easy silence claimed the kitchen, broken only by the soft whoosh of air blowing across the tops of their mugs. Images flickered through Gino's brain—workers and turkeys and great steel machines and the shackle line droning steadily onward—but these images faded, yielded to the pull outside the plant walls, and the gravestones floated across the back of his closed eyelids. He opened his eyes, sat the mug on the table.

"Are you tired?" Christa asked.

He shook his head, looked down at the mug.

"Thinking, then?" she said, but it was not truly a question.

"I...I saw his grave today. Across the tracks from the turkey plant."

Christa tilted her head up, filled her lungs, said, "I'm glad you did, Gino."

"I was walking around outside the plant, and just looked across the tracks, and there it was...the cemetery. I...uh...didn't think a town this size would have more than, but anyway...I swear, I *knew* it was out there. Like it found *me*. I know I should've waited and gone proper with you...but..."

"Gino, there's no need to apologize, maybe alone is the way it was meant to be for you." She reached across the table and patted his hand.

"Mrs. Bates, those words on the stone...where did you find them?"

"I didn't find them. Aaron found them three or four years ago... read them somewhere, he said, and wrote them down on a slip of paper. He stuck it in his dresser drawer after he showed it to me. I'd forgotten all about it until they wanted to know what to carve on the stone. And I knew right then what to do. I copied the words on another piece of paper and took it to them." She smiled. "Not because of the writing...

Aaron printed like a typewriter when he wanted to…but because I thought they might lose his copy, and I couldn't abide that thought."

Gino looked up, fixed his gaze on the window over the sink. "He tried to talk to me about God, and heavy things. Him and a Pima Indian guy who was just like him…a believer and all…but I wouldn't let them. Always joked my way out of it, or tried to make them sound silly. Aaron never pushed me. He'd just say that it would be clear to me someday." He shook his head. "And now…it doesn't make any sense at all. It should've been me that got shot, and Aaron who lived. I've never been a whole lot of good to anybody in my life."

"Don't sell yourself short, Gino. Aaron had a pretty good eye for good people. It wasn't an accident that you two became friends."

"Mrs. Bates…I got some things on my mind that I've got to unload, and I don't think I can do it but once. I…I was with him when he got hit. I heard his last words…and things have happened to me since…"

Gino, it's all right…it's all right. We want to hear every word you brought us, and we'll be beholding to you always for having the courage to come here. But hold on for just a little longer, please. Ernie needs to hear what you have to say. If you can wait another half hour, it would mean a lot to me. Let me call Harley too. He's as dear as a blood brother to both of us, and he's tried to help Ernie through this bad time. Would it be all right if he came over?"

Gino nodded in agreement without raising his head. "If you want him to be here, that's fine by me. I'm okay…for a while longer anyhow."

He listened as Christa spun the telephone dial and spoke softly for only a few seconds. She hung up and turned back to Gino. "Let me pour another mug of cider, and you rest easy for a while. He'll be here soon, and I need to talk to Ernie for a bit."

Gino wrapped his hands around the ceramic warmth and closed his eyes. It was beyond him now—all of it—and the burden weighed him down. But only for a while longer, only for a few minutes more. Then he would attempt to make peace, and if not peace, at least a truce with the sounds and images that would not leave him.

Christa peeked through the open tool shed door and walked softly to the side of the familiar figure hovering over the workbench. "Ernie, this boy's got things on his mind that he can't hold back any longer. He wants to talk to us now. He...was with Aaron when it happened. He doesn't think he can make his peace until he tells us what happened. I called Harley and he's coming over directly. He's been a part of this thing from the beginning."

Ernie stared straight ahead, and in the hard light cast by the naked bulb, Christa watched his jaw muscles contract. He shook his head steadily. "No...no...he can tell you and Harley. I don't want to know any more about it. Doesn't matter how it happened...just that it did."

"Ernie, that's not all of it. Aaron spoke to him before he died, and I think all of us need to hear it firsthand. We owe that to this boy...and to Aaron."

He reached up and pulled the string on the light switch; the faint ambient light replaced the harsh glare. "How can it seem so long ago... us raising him and all? I used to sit him up on this bench and let him hammer at a nail. Couldn't have been more than five. He was always wanting to hammer at a nail. He'd take the hammer in both hands and flail away till he beat it crooked, and then make me start another one and he'd do it again." He paused, a great sigh escaping his body. "Where did it all go, woman, all those good years?"

"They were the best of times, Ernie, there's no doubt of that. I can't bring them back for you. God knows how much I would like to...but it's not in my power."

"I feel awful old...old and tired."

She placed a hand on his shoulder. "Just come in the house with me, please."

He reached up and lifted the hammer from its hook, the coarse flesh of his fingers and palms rasping faintly as they slid over the old wooden handle. "My daddy let me drive a nail once in a while, and then, if he was drinkin', cuss me for driving it crooked."

The reference to his father wafted in the air like a strange scent; the man was long dead and buried, though not like a blood relative. Ernie, along with the entire county, had seemingly disposed of Clarence Bates like a flesh and bone weapon used in his own suicide. Christa could not remember a previous reference to the man. She waited for him to say more, but he only allowed the hammer to slide through his fingers and clank against the workbench.

"Please."

He lifted his hands in a gesture of apathy, said, "All right."

Gino sat at the kitchen table as they opened the back door and walked into the room. He glanced up nervously at Ernie as the tall man passed the table and continued toward the living room.

"I think we'll sit in the living room," Christa said to Gino, touching him on the shoulder. "Harley will be here in a few minutes, let's wait here for him."

Before Christa could pull out a chair, Harley's pickup rumbled to a halt in the driveway. Christa met him at the door. "Thanks for coming, Harley." She took both of his hands into hers. "We're going to sit in the living room."

Christa wrapped an arm around Gino's shoulder and led him into the living room; they sat down on the couch. Ernie was hunkered down in a vinyl-covered chair in a corner. Harley took a chair in the corner nearest Ernie.

Christa said, "Gino, you just start anywhere you like and say what's on your mind. We know it's not easy…but you've come a long ways to be with us, and now you know you're among friends."

Gino laced his fingers tightly, leaned forward with his forearms on his knees. "I came here because of two things…three, really, counting our buddy, Pima." He paused, swallowed. "Aaron said words when he died that don't make sense at all to me. I could've wrote it in a letter, and asked you about it…and probably would have if the other things…the dreams… hadn't happened."

He raised his head, sucked in a quick breath, bolstered by the sound of his own voice. "We were movin' into a ville—a village—when it happened. I was on point…leading the platoon, and Aaron was behind me."

Ernie said softly, factually, "It was a quarter to seven in the morning, wasn't it?"

Gino looked at Ernie. "Yes, sir…it was…just about that time."

Christa and Harley exchanged glances as a moment of stunned silence grew into several seconds. Christa said, "Please…go ahead, Gino."

"The top sergeant, he was a little spooked by this village, and he had us going in different than usual. But nobody was real worried. We'd been through there before, hadn't been shot at. When we got to the edge of it, I headed for a little clearing in the bush. I got to twenty yards of the other side when I saw movement in a clump at the base of a big tree. I yelled and pointed, but before I could aim my rifle, he opened up. It was a three round burst…full automatic. Two went in the dirt, but the other one grazed the tip of my finger and the bottom edge of my helmet, and…that was the one…that hit Aaron. I never even returned fire. I just hit the ground and looked behind me and saw him on the ground. He was hit…in the chest, and he was layin' on his back."

Christa dabbed at the corner of her eyes with a knuckle. Harley was hunched forward with his chin resting on folded hands. Ernie remained motionless, his gaze pointed toward the window on the opposite wall.

"He never showed any sign he was hurt. He just looked…surprised for a few seconds, then when he couldn't get his breath I knew it was bad…and it got crazy then…me screamin' and yellin', and the Sarge in the middle of us…and Little Doc, and then Aaron said something to Pima…not sure…then Aaron reached up and pulled me by the sleeve right up to his face." He paused, clenched his jaws against the great swell of emotion. "I swear to all of you…I swear…he didn't even look worried then, like he didn't have a care in the world, and he looked at me and said, 'Me and Pop always liked the dawn…it was dawn when the angel said…why do you seek the living among the dead?' And then he died."

Christa blinked tear-filled eyes, did not mind the trace of the tears on her cheeks as she looked at Harley. He smiled, as if in benediction.

Gino's voice was little more than a raspy whisper now. "What did he mean by that, Mrs. Bates…what did he mean?"

Christa opened her mouth, but could not overcome the burning in her throat. She simply opened the fingers of one hand toward Harley.

"Aaron believed in Christ who was crucified on the cross and was raised up on the third day. On that first Easter morning a woman went to the tomb so she could take proper care of his body, but his body wasn't there, and she thought somebody had stolen it...and she was full of grief. But there were two angles near the tomb who saw her and one said, 'Why do you seek the living among the dead?' You see, Gino, Aaron took comfort in the empty tomb. He knew that Christ conquered death, and because he believed in Him...that he would conquer death too."

"I'd never let him talk for long about...God things," Gino said. "He'd just say that one day I'd understand the truth...somehow."

Harley looked at Ernie, who stared impassively ahead at the window, then said, "You said there were two reasons why you came back."

Gino's cheeks puffed as he shot a stream of air, shook his head. "You'll probably think I'm crazy...they did back there, all except Pima. Back at the base camp, after Aaron got hit, I had dreams so real that I couldn't shake 'em—I'm not even sure that I wanted to shake 'em. It was always a woman's voice—the most beautiful sound I ever heard in my life—and she was singing a song about a river...and Aaron told me about...you...singing in church. I couldn't make out the words real good, but one sounded like 'Jordan.' And Pima, he knew right off, wouldn't tell me anything more...just said I had to come back here if I was gonna find peace. And then, when I saw the words on the gravestone..." His voice trailed off. "It scares me some, I don't mind telling you."

"God forgive me for doubting," Christa said, "God forgive me." She turned to Gino. "Yes, I do sing some. I sang the song about the river at Aaron's funeral. I can't do it now, but I'll sing it for you sometime soon, I promise, and then you can decide if you've heard it before."

She pushed up from the couch and walked to Ernie, knelt in front of him, rested her hands and head on his knees. He stared straight ahead at the window, made no move to acknowledge Christa's presence.

"Let's get some air, Gino," Harley said. Gino nodded, then they stood and walked away.

Christa raised her head, said, "It wasn't an accident, Ernie...him coming here. You can see that, can't you? It's not some silly fairy tale.

There is a spirit world, and the good side of it is stronger…you have to accept that. You've seen the dark side, I know. In the precious name of Jesus, see the light."

"The only…light…I see is *here*, on this earth. Our years, then the years with the boy…all *here*. It all sounds so beautiful…the light you claim to know." He released his body backward, slumped into the chair. "And before all that…yeah, the dark side. I know all about that."

"I know you had a rough boyhood, Ernie. Lots of people have. You're not the only one."

Christa sensed a strange energy course through his body and enter hers through her hands and arms, then into her core. Still, she was stunned by the softly spoken declaration.

"How many of them killed their daddy?"

"It…wasn't you. Everybody around here knew your mother…had to defend herself."

"Everybody knows a lie."

She looked at his face, peeled away the years, saw the face of a frightened boy. "It doesn't matter now, Ernie…whatever took place back then."

"I took up a bread knife that got knocked to the floor, swung it at his shoulder…missed high…it went clear through his throat. I killed him. Momma made me promise to go along with her story."

Christa took his hands in hers, said, "You should have told me long ago. I could have helped you get past it."

"I was past it, when I was young. It was like a bad dream that faded through the years…until…"

"Until Aaron."

"Then I started thinkin' about it…not often, but it began to hurt when I did. If

I would've just jumped on him, left the knife be…I was strong for a boy."

"But that's just it, Ernie, you were a boy, a boy seeing his mother hurt. *Anything* you would have done was justified." She shook her head. "A boy…trying to save his mother."

"No, it was more than that. For a few seconds, I hated him…and that's when I picked up the knife. I hated him long enough to swing a knife at him…and that was long enough."

"This remembering is of no use, Ernie. It doesn't have a thing to do with where we are right now."

"Maybe you're wrong. Maybe the dark side, or the light side… doesn't really matter…required a price to be paid, on account of my hate."

"No. It is not so."

The clock in the hall chimed its tiny melody, then blended with the silence in the room. Christa got up, walked a couple of steps toward the door, spoke without turning around. "I want to go to the cemetery, Ernie…with you, and Gino and Harley. I want us all to go now. I'm not sure why…I just want to."

She waited, listened as he shifted his weight in the chair. "You will go sometime, Ernie, no matter what you feel now…you will go sometime. Let it be now…for me."

She was suddenly aware of the hall clock, its faint ticks marking the seconds oozing by. The vinyl cover of the chair crackled as he stood. "If you want."

Harley and Gino turned toward the door as Christa emerged, followed by Ernie. She said, "I want us all to go visit Aaron's grave. Harley, will you drive the Chevy for us?"

"Sure."

Christa handed him the keys and the four began to walk to the carport. Gino hesitated as they neared the car, uncertain of the proper seating arrangement. Christa motioned for him to join Harley in the front seat as Ernie opened a rear door for her. A half hour of sunlight remained and though the day was still pleasant, the late afternoon breeze foretold of the night's coming chill, and the warmth of the car was welcome.

Eight quiet minutes later, Harley maneuvered the car around the courthouse square and onto Oak Street, then on to Highway 50, and soon the cemetery came into view. The slanting rays of sunlight filtering through the trees and shrubs bored low from the southwest like beacons from a hundred lighthouses and touched the soft hues of the gravestones, pointing the way to the seekers.

As Harley turned into the second entrance road, he saw a pickup truck in the distance and a solitary figure standing thirty yards into the stones. As he closed the distance, a smile touched his lips.

"Fudd's here."

Christa leaned forward and peered over the front seat. "Bless his heart, it is him."

Harley parked behind the pickup and hopped out of the car, raised a hand in greeting, and after a slight hesitation, Fudd returned the gesture. Harley waited for the others to join him and they quickly walked to the grave. In his hand Fudd held a small American flag, and he twisted it nervously in his thick fingers as he shifted his bulk from one foot to the other.

Christa said, "Fudd, it's so good to see you. Thanks for coming. I'd been wondering who put down the pretty little flag…figured it was someone from the V.F.W. It's mighty nice of you."

"I hope you don't mind…I know I shoulda asked first, but…I didn't think you'd mind. I got me a bunch so I could keep a fresh one out here. I ain't much for flowers and…well…it seemed like he had more'n enough of those." He paused, his big right hand cutting a swath through the air. "I just came by to put down a new one. The first one was already a little nipped on the edges. Sure hope you don't mind…reckon I'll be goin' now."

"Stay with us a while, Fudd," Christa said.

Fudd twisted his fingers over the tightly rolled flag as he searched for the proper response to the invitation. His voice was nearly lost in the wind. "Well…I…I'd be proud to stand with you all, Christa…mighty proud. I did think the world of this here young'un. I did for a fact."

Harley stepped forward, drawing even with Fudd at the foot of the grave. "You suppose you've seen the last of him, Fudd?"

Fudd's fingers worked their way up and down the flag as the question hung in the air. "Aw, Harley, you know I'm not much at questions like that. I hope I ain't seen the last of him…I surely do hope for that…but…"

"You *hope* you haven't, and Ernie *hopes* he hasn't, and Gino, he *hopes* the same thing, but none of you think you can know for sure."

Harley raised his eyes from the tombstone and looked a the barren trees above and around him. He continued to speak in a steady tone, like that of a confidant sharing his innermost secrets. "Look at these trees, dead for the winter, yet come May they'll push leaves out that will shade this whole place. Nobody doubts that, do they? But you might claim that you've seen it before, every spring of your lives—so what's to doubt? But you've not seen a dead man rise." He paused, toed the ground with his shoe. "That's what it's really all about, isn't it? A man always wants to see things for himself. Only natural. Well…Aaron…he sleeps like the trees of winter…only for a while, and before you leave this place, I'm gonna do my level best to give you things to see. Things that just can't be ignored." He tugged on the bill of his cap, reset it squarely. "Aaron himself asked me to try."

"Not long ago he wrote me a letter, the first and only one he sent directly to me. Always talked to me through his letters to you two." He nodded to Christa and Ernie. "But this letter…things were weighing heavy on his mind. The fighting was worse than he would let on to you two, and he was worried…not for himself…but for his daddy, and for you, son." He looked directly at Gino for a moment, and then toward Fudd. "And you, Fudd…he'd always wanted you to know the truth too. So…he asked me to do what I could to help Christa if something happened to him." He shook his head. "Not been much good so far."

He glanced at Christa, who remained a few steps behind the men, knew that she was praying for him with open eyes. "So you fellows want real stuff, huh? Not fairy tales. All right, let's talk about real stuff. Let's talk about dying and speaking your last words on this earth. Gino, you ever see other men die in combat?"

Gino swallowed, drew a jagged breath, did not wish to be dragged into the choppy waters. He began with a nod, said, "Two. I saw two others besides Aaron.."

Harley waited only for a couple of seconds, then said, "And…?"

"One…he was screamin' for his mother till it was over. And the other one…he was cussin' the VC…spittin' blood with the cuss words."

Harley said, "But Aaron...he's telling you about the first Easter morning with the last breath he's got. He remembers a Bible verse, and leaves that with you. Was he talking crazy, Gino? Was he babbling without knowing what he said?"

"No. He was talkin' as clear as I am, only lower."

"That seems like real stuff to me," Harley said. "Firsthand telling from a man who was there with him. No fairy tale. And how did it come to pass that Gino came here and told us all this? Remember Christa's song at the funeral, Fudd? Ever hear anything like that in your life? Remember hearing Ernie's name floating all over this place? And Gino, halfway around the world has these strange dreams about a woman's voice singing about a river...and look down there at the words on the stone...words that Aaron found years ago in a book somewhere and wrote down on a scrap of paper. And here we stand today...and you three doubting for the lack of *real* stuff?"

He paused, looked at the ground beside his shoes, shook his head. No one else stirred. "Let me tell you one more thing about real stuff, and then I'll shut up and say no more. Not a soul knows about this except me and Mom. It's about the first time that I was shown there are powers that go beyond this world. It happened the night my granddaddy passed away. I was ten, and I loved that old man so much it hurt. He'd been getting weaker for a long time, and the doc said that his time was about up. I used to lay with him in bed, curled up on the covers down at his feet, with my head against his leg. The day he died, he asked Mom to put an empty chair in the room with him, and she asked why. He told her he did that when he was a boy, when things bothered him...set out a chair for Jesus, he said...and that he felt the need to do it again.

So Mom put an old chair in there with him, just inside the door, and it seemed to please him. I curled up with him that night after Mom put a blanket over me and I remember him reaching down and scratching my head with his fingers before I went to sleep. When I woke up...somehow, I just knew he was gone, and I sat up in bed and looked at his face before I saw the chair. It wasn't over by the door...it was right there next to the bed, and his hand was laying in it, half open, like someone had been holding it.. Mom must've come in the night and moved it close, sat with him for a time, I figured. He hadn't been strong enough to get out of bed for two weeks. It wasn't till after the funeral that Mom asked me why I'd moved the chair closer to him. When I told her that I hadn't moved it, she looked me straight in the eye to make sure I was telling the truth, and then she smiled when she saw the look on my face...I still feel the chills on my neck. *Somebody* had moved it, I told her...*somebody* did it. And she just looked at me, still smiling, and said, 'Jesus must have sent somebody to take Grandpa home, son. Don't be afraid of that.'

"So, I lost my fear...knew that I'd gotten a peek at the other side, you might say. I know it sounds far fetched...and I know that some folks would say I'm just spouting nonsense in the wind." He looked at Ernie and Fudd. "But you two have known me for many long years... long enough to know that I'm no windbag."

He removed his cap, slid his fingers through his hair, and replaced it with a tug on the bill. "I'm about all talked out now, and I'm sure that doesn't hurt anybody's feelings. But I say one last time...I don't know a thing about fairy tales. I do know something about real stuff, and part of what I know is that Aaron told you all in death what he couldn't tell you in life."

Harley made a half turn away and paused, extending his right hand to the tombstone. "Truth is...he believed...and now he sleeps for a little while with the trees of winter." He completed the turn, his shoes a whisper in the colorless grass as he walked toward the car.

"Amen. Amen to all that," said Christa as she turned from the grave and followed Harley.

Gino shook his head, jammed his hands into his pockets, said, "Well...kinda laid it on the line, huh?"

"Yeah," Fudd said, "he hardly ever has much to say, but when he gets wound up, there ain't no holdin' him back. My wife claims he's sorta like a priest, or a preacher man. Me...I been hangin' birds beside him for years, and sometimes I don't think I really know him...the real him. He's got somethin' I ain't got...that much is a solid fact. Him and his old railroad tracks over yonder. Every mornin', prayin' at the tracks...his old Jordan tracks, he calls 'em."

"What's all that mean?" Gino asked.

"He does it there because he believes he can see this life on the north side and the next life on the south…here." Fudd swept his arm toward the rows of gravestones.

"A month ago, I'd have said he was crazy," said Gino. "Now…now I don't know what to say." He hunched his shoulders against the gathering chill and walked quickly away.

Fudd expelled a long sigh. "I'm getting' cold, Ernie, and my mind's overloaded to boot. I'm goin' home."

Ernie nodded silently, glanced at Fudd's back, then walked toward the car.

The engines of the two vehicles churned to life in unison, and within a few moments, the crunching of the tires on the gravel faded away. Only the sound of the wind lingered as it whispered through the stones.

Christa stood in the living room, did not know which way to turn. Ernie was in the back yard, ten steps from the house. Gino strode back and forth on the front porch, the wooden cadence of his shoes drumming in her ears, and then it ceased, the imprint of the sound still in her brain as the door knob turned. He walked a cautious half circle around her, hands jammed deeply in his trouser pockets, before stopping.

"What's on your mind, Gino? We know each other pretty well by now."

"I think I ought to go on back to Chicago now. I've been here longer than I ever planned already, and…"

"Gino, I understand if you want to get back to your family and your own home and all, but there's no hurry on our part."

"I doubt I'd be missed much if I stayed away forever. I got into more than my share of trouble in the last few years." He shrugged his shoulders. "I'm not very close to anybody back there. I just need to move on…go back to the city where I belong."

"I'll bet that there are stronger feelings for you back there than you think. Don't sell your family short, but like I said, you're more than welcome to stay here as long as you like."

"That's really nice of you, and I know that you mean it…but…" His voice trailed off with another shrug of his shoulders.

Christa stood silently, waited for him to look at her. "So you've done what you came to do, found all your answers?"

He shook his head, looked down. "Don't suppose anybody ever finds all the answers."

"That's very true, but some can be found."

"Not the hard ones."

"Even some of the hard ones."

He raised his head, the hint of a rueful smile on his lips. "I don't think I can win this argument."

"If it is an argument…it's with yourself, and those are pretty hard to win."

Gino turned, retraced the half circle to the door. "I'll call tomorrow about the bus schedule."

"Whatever you want, son."

He wrapped his fingers around the doorknob. Christa said, "I'll ask only one favor before you leave."

He turned his head, said, "Anything."

"Anything…that covers a lot of ground. Are you sure?"

"I'm sure."

"Don't leave until after the church service this Sunday. I'm going to sing a solo in your honor."

He looked down at the door knob. "No need of that…singin' in my 'honor,' as you say."

"Well, that's my decision, Gino. That's how I want to do it."

"You…won't say my name…in there, will you?"

"I most certainly will."

His fingers slipped from the doorknob, tapped against the metal plate for a few seconds. Christa said, "You backing out on me?"

He re-gripped the doorknob, turned it as he shook his head. "I'm not backin' out."

Christa walked to the kitchen sink, looked out the window past the long shadowy form of her husband, and then skyward. Only tattered remnants of clouds floated past the frosty brilliance of the half moon as it cast a pale glow over the landscape. For Christa, the moon was the crown jewel of the heavens, not the mighty sun. The sun could not be viewed directly, for its power was too awesome for human eyes to behold. But the moon offered a brilliance that could light a path or illuminate a landscape, yet an earthbound admirer could look directly at it without being blinded. The moon took just enough light from the great sun and softened it and beamed it earthward, so that frail humans could accept it and be one with it. The moon was like Christ, the woman believed—an intercessor for mankind to an almighty God who could not be directly beheld.

"Yes," she whispered, "the gentle light of the world."

Ernie stood now behind the tool shed, a few steps from the shrouded tree line. He did not know how long he had been in the yard, but it did not feel like a long time. The thoughts swirled inside his head without forming a pattern, and he had made no effort to coax them into a cohesive form, nor had he made any effort to resist the dark thoughts or cling to the good ones. He stood in the chill of night like a man sifting through mud and pebbles in a stream bed, the light insufficient, yet still hoping to see a tiny flash of gold. The wind parted the clouds, spilling more of the moonlight over him, and he felt a tug, looked up, tried to smile.

He turned and walked to the back door of the house, opened it a few inches and poked his head into the space. "Christa."

She walked quickly to him, said, "What is it, Ernie?"

"I'm going for a ride."

"Where?"

"I'm not exactly sure…just…not far." He nodded. "I'm all right, I just need to be by myself for a while."

"Whatever you want, Ernie."

He had lied after a fashion, but he did not feel the weight of a lie, the clear imprint on his chest. The old pickup engine droned steadily down Highway 87 toward town and the processing plant, and the only thought in Ernie Bates's head was that he had never been inside the plant when it was dark.

Leon Patten looked up from the tattered pages of *Life Magazine* and peered through the dirty glass window of the guard house at the twin beams of headlights as they splashed whitely through his little yellow-lit space. He blinked twice before jamming a forefinger against the electrical tape that secured the hinge of his glasses. With his tongue, he rolled the chew of tobacco from left to right, tucking it firmly into the fresh cheek. He squinted, focused through the dim light of the parking lot on the tall figure ambling toward him. Leon registered no unease; occasionally, an employee forgot to tend to a final chore and returned after hours, or left something in the lunch room. Besides, he was nearly certain that only Ernie Bates would loom so tall. He felt his cheeks release the squint when he recognized Ernie's face outside the window, and he reached up and slid it open.

"Evenin', Ernie. Forgot something, I reckon."

Ernie looked down at him for a moment, nodded slowly. "Yeah… that's right."

"Well then, you know…" There was no need to finish his sentence. Ernie had already turned and taken two steps toward the plant. Leon squinted again, tongued the chew of tobacco to his other cheek, then spoke as if Ernie was in the guard house with him. "It'll be a while 'fore you're yourself again, Ernie."

There was no night light in the blood room; the only illumination spilled weakly from the moonlit dock. Ernie stood motionless at the edge of the concrete containment, waiting patiently for his vision to adjust. The starkness of the room was revealed to the man in ever-decreasing shades of gloom, but in the end, the gloom refused to be erased, cast its shadow on the floor and walls. The blood of millions of creatures had stained the floor, and an uninformed visitor, looking down now as Ernie did, would have been certain that a worker had done a poor job of sloshing black paint on it. But Ernie knew that the black was once red, knew that the dark splatter marks jutting two feet up the walls told of death meted out by a knife in his hands. He stepped down into the containment, squatted on his heels and ran his fingertips over the smooth floor, conjured up the dank smell, the mechanical roar of the plant. It was the roar in his ears that morphed into a discernable voice, the great engines of the plant losing their mechanical edge, yielding to the whispers of the dark spirit that flew on silent, invisible wings.

Ernie locked his hands around his knees, began to rock to and fro, knew that he should stand and run, but he could not, and instead pitched sideways onto the unyielding floor.

"The one who spoke in the cemetery was a fool. Your beautiful son bled out in the grass as these creatures bled out on this floor."

Ernie clenched his jaws, rolled his head from side to side, said, "No…no."

"Your son, the creatures…your FATHER…all bled out…all bled out in death…forever."

"No…not forever…it can't be."

"It is so, you pathetic fool. You are a creature wallowing in the bloodstains of other creatures. There is no difference in the end."

Ernie pushed up to his hands and knees, shook his head in a futile effort to shake loose the evil, now as palpable as the dark floor. He willed his legs to bear his weight, staggered toward the shackle line and latched onto one of the metal frames, jamming his hands down into the Y-frames. He lost his balance and his weight pulled him downward, locking his wrists in the frames.

"Perfect."

When he heard the powerful thrum of the huge electric motor, the hair at the base of Leon Patten's neck stood on end. But it was not that sound alone that caused him fear. There was something else, a strange keening, as if the voice of the night wind was a living thing intent on drowning out the sound of the motor. The magazine slipped through Leon's fingers as he shoved his chair away from the counter.

The initial tug of the shackle line jerked Ernie completely off of his feet, and with each succeeding lurch the pain in his wrists intensified. He opened his mouth, knew that he cried out, but could not hear it above din that reverberated through his head. He turned his head to the left, saw the line snake its way around the tight curve leading to the steel cylinder that contained the de-feathering machinery, with its opening made for large birds rather than men. The pain was gone, replaced with numbness so complete it was as if he had never possessed hands, and with that horrific thought came the realization that very soon he—in fact—would not possess hands. The great roar consumed him; his body was being dragged in the fashion of a beast, its prey secure in cruel teeth. Twenty more feet until fresh blood would stain the floor.

Leon had not run for a very long time, and neither his legs nor his lungs were serving him properly. He coughed, spat out the wad of tobacco. He reached down with his right hand to secure the holstered revolver that flapped irritatingly against his thigh. With his left hand he poked at the frame of his glasses, which slipped down his nose each time the heel of his boot jarred against the ground. When he was a hundred feet from the building, he stopped as if he had reached the edge of a cliff. A guttural moan rose from his chest as he beheld an explosion of brilliant light that filled the receiving dock area. Leon Patten was certain beyond the slightest doubt that he was witnessing the beginning of a conflagration that would consume the entire plant, and he was equally certain that Ernie Bates had just been burned alive.

Leon dropped to a knee, looked away from the blinding light, gathered himself to turn and run back to the guard house and the telephone. He sucked in a quick breath as he stood, but he did not turn around. For an instant, the image of the light remained, then faded, and the bewildered man blinked hard against the unbelievable: darkness and silence had claimed the plant. He lurched forward, ran to the dock and clambered up the concrete steps. His shoulders brushed the shackle line, leaving in his wake a metallic ripple as he neared the blood room. Leon found him sitting on the floor near the mouth of the de-feathering machine, his hands slowly opening and closing in front of his face.

"Ernie! Ernie! Are you all right? What happened? Lord God A'mighty…what happened here?"

Ernie rubbed one wrist, then the other before looking up at Leon's face. He shook his head, said, "I…I'm not sure."

"It had to be…electrical…breaker box…big wire…" He sniffed the air. "I don't smell nothing, I swear, but…what the…" His voice trailed off for a moment. "Why in the world did you turn on the line, Ernie?"

Ernie shook his head again. "I didn't turn anything on."

"I heard it, Ernie…the big motor. Heard it with my own ears."

Ernie ran his fingers over his face, then reached up with one hand, allowed Leon to pull him to his feet. He took a careful step to the line, touched a shackle with his fingers. "I didn't say it wasn't on, Leon. I said I didn't turn it on."

Leon poked at his glasses, made a wet, sputtering sound before filling his lungs for another attempt at speech. "Wheeew…now, Ernie, confound it all…that don't make a lick of sense. And the light…Lord God A'mighty, didn't it about blind you?"

"I remember something…something, but it wasn't a light."

"Have mercy." With a thumb and forefinger, Leon pushed his glasses from the bridge of his nose, tilted back his head. "Let's get out of here. I'm gonna call and have Warren Wells come down here and check everything out."

"You can do that if you want, but he won't find anything wrong."

Leon had to work at keeping pace with Ernie's long strides, and when they reached the guard house Ernie strode past it, leaving Leon with one hand in the air. "Hey, Ernie, you need to stay till Warren gets here. He might want to ask something about this thing."

Ernie stopped, turned around. "I've already told you all I know, Leon." They locked eyes, the seconds oozing by. "He won't find anything wrong."

Leon watched as the tall man slowly turned back around and walked toward the pickup, and he continued to watch until the red dots of the tail lights disappeared into the night. He walked through the open doorway of the guard house and flopped down in his chair, his right hand groping spider-like for the pouch of tobacco lost in the pile of magazines and papers. He attempted to breathe evenly as the fingertips of his hand pinched and formed the chew, but his fingers went limp. His head crept to the right until the telephone stared back at him, the smudged listing of necessary numbers pinched under the corner. Leon squinted, located the number.

POWER PLANT EMERGENCY 796-2120

His hand settled over the receiver, sweaty palm tapping the black plastic. He got up, walked a few steps toward the dormant building, studied the awesome serenity, the halo of enveloping darkness, pierced only by the dingy, weak yellow of the yard lights. Leon Patten was not a religious man, invoking the Deity for purposes of expression from time to time, in the fashion of most other men he knew. But he harbored no illusions about the spirit world, good or evil. He knew that a flash of light and sounds that he had never before seen or heard should be stored fresh in his brain, but as he attempted to retrieve them, it became clear that they were lost to him, would never return.

"Crazy dadgum power surge, that's all it was, Leon, you old goofball."

Although he was unaware of his journey, Leon drifted along at the edge of the spirit world, ignoring the tug of his soul to delve deeper, to seek the truth of the white light. But he would not allow it, and his astonishment quickly ebbed into little more than a memory, and it was with great relief that he turned away from the world that made no sense, slipped back into his little guard house. He would never speak of the incident with anyone for the remainder of his life. Leon Patten would live for eight years before the searing stab of pain tore through his shoulder and neck, but before he would lose consciousness, he would remember the light, and wonder what it was as he died.

Christa glanced at the clock in the hallway as it intoned the twenty-third hour of the day. She had sat quietly in the living room since Ernie had departed. At first, with the rumble of the pickup engine fading down the road, she had braced herself for a toilsome vigil. But as the minutes collected and turned into the first half-hour chime on the clock, no burdens came, and she sat in contented silence. Later, Gino came back inside, and they exchanged good nights as he went to his bedroom.

As the chime hung in the air, she heard another familiar sound, saw the flash of headlights whirl through the room. Christa waited for several minutes, but the back door remained closed. She got up from the corner of the couch, took two steps toward the kitchen, then stopped. It was with no regret that she realized there were no more words to offer him, no more pleadings, no more tearful urgings. It was as if she had been relieved of duty, a weary soldier who had stood watch far too long. She retreated to the bedroom, quickly slipped into her night gown and under the covers and fell asleep.

CHAPTER SIXTEEN

Margie walked softly into the living room and glanced at the long, sturdy face of the late-night newscaster as the authoritative voice recited the latest casualty counts from Vietnam. Fudd was draped over his old recliner, footrest extended in support of sock-covered feet.

"What's so heavy on your mind tonight?" Margie asked.

"Wadda you mean?" Fudd huffed. "I'm all right."

"Don't seem all right to me when you only eat what a normal man would at supper, and have no more to say than you did."

"How am I supposed to talk with them two jabberin' like blue jays?"

"You've always found a way to slip a few words in, seems to me."

"Have mercy, woman, can't a man rest peaceful in his own livin' room? Crapsakes."

The newscaster's voice claimed the room for a minute before Margie spoke again. "Went to the cemetery today, didn't you?" She did not shift her gaze from the television set.

Fudd shot a glance at her and paused a moment before answering. "Yeah...yeah I did. Put a new flag down."

"It's nice of you to do that. I know Christa appreciates it. Ernie will too...someday."

"Maybe he appreciates it now."

Margie looked at Fudd. "He was there...at the grave?"

"Him and Christa and Aaron's buddy from the war, and Harley... all of 'em were. Drove up while I was changin' the flag."

"That's the first I heard about Ernie facing up to Aaron's death. I still can't believe he didn't even come to his own son's funeral."

"He was awful messed up, Margie. He lived for that boy, you know that."

"I know. I'm not trying to be hard on him, I just…"

"Anyway…I ain't sure why Harley was there, but he got to talkin' to Ernie and the boy, and, well, I reckon me too, about believin' in the next life and such, and it put me to thinkin' some." He tapped his toes together, locked his fingers together in a great wad of flesh and bone. "Dang. You know how he can get when he starts talkin' about serious stuff. Like the night at the fair when I was about to smack Bud Alexander up the side of the head. You can't help but listen when he gets talkin' like that. I'm not even sure how he got off on the next life back there at the grave…but he dang sure did."

He lapsed into silence for a moment, collecting his thoughts as he rubbed his temples methodically. "He can sure make it sound real, I'll tell you that."

Margie turned her head away from the television, looked at Fudd. "Lord knows, he is good with words, but did you ever stop to think that maybe he can make it *sound* real because it *is* real? No man, him or anybody else, can make something real out of something that's not. He can just lay it out better than most people. And I'll tell you another thing. Fred Riggins can lay it out for a person to see, too. Since me and the kids have been going to services some, I've come to like that man a lot. Wouldn't hurt you none to come along once and a while."

Fudd ignored the entreaty, his gaze remaining locked on the television screen as he spoke. "He shoulda' been a preacher…that Harley."

"I'm telling you he is, Fudd. He's just not had any formal schooling in it. That's the only difference."

The newscaster's narrative rumbled to a halt, only to be replaced by the blare of an automobile commercial. Fudd said, "He sure coulda' passed for one a couple hours ago."

The Saturday lunch table conversation was pleasant. Mainly, Christa and Gino engaged one another about the wide gulf between city life and country life. They agreed that Chicago was the equivalent of the far side of the moon compared to the outskirts of California, Missouri. Ernie ate sparingly, adding a glance or sometimes a nod. His silence at the table was no longer a distraction to either Christa or Gino, both having accepted it as the equal of a prominent scar on his face. Thus, it was a simple matter: one did not stare at the scars of a wounded man.

"And the song of the birds," said Christa, "I don't think I could do without their songs. The whippoorwills and the bobwhite quail and the thrushes and the finches…and the big ones, red-tailed hawks and hoot owls…even the old crows caw-cawing in the trees. Oh my, but it's music to me. No, I couldn't do without all that."

Gino cocked his head, smiled wryly. "Only birds I remember much about are the lousy pigeons. Drive you nuts in the mornings, making that oooodle-oooodle sound up on the roof." He shook his head as the memory formed. "Uncle Telly, whew…he hated those birds. He'd sneak out the back door before breakfast in his drawers with a pellet gun…one of those good ones you could pump up about the same as a .22 rifle, and blam! it'd go and he'd ease back inside and Aunt Rosa would frown at him and he'd say the same thing every time. He'd say, 'Ders food on da ground for da alley cats, Momma. Whatsa wrong wid dat?' He must've shot a hundred of 'em while I was there. It'd work for a few days, then they'd be back, and he'd pop another one."

Christa rolled her eyes, said, "What about the neighbors?"

"Nobody bothered Uncle Telly about anything…anything at all."

Christa tapped idly with the tines of her fork at the rippled edge of pie crust as the question took shape. She blew softly across the top of her coffee mug, took a long sip. "You said, 'while you were there.' Did you…live there…for a time?"

Gino lowered his head, nodded, said, "For a long time. Me and my brothers."

Christa felt her face redden as the silence gathered, and she chastised herself even as she sought a way to redirect the conversation. "Well, anyway…I don't know why I…uh…even…"

Gino looked up. "Hey, Mrs. Bates, it's okay…really. I barely remember my parents. I was glad to have my aunt and uncle. They're good people…treated me fine. It's okay."

Before Christa could reply, Ernie leaned back in his chair and hooked a thumb over his shoulder, pointed to the kitchen door. "There's a place yonder in the woods where you can hear and see things you'll like. I can take you if you want."

Gino looked first at Ernie, then at Christa as the softly spoken words replayed in his mind. In the woman's features he saw the beginning of hope, as clearly as the glint of sunlight on a window pane, and he waited, did not dare speak or move so long as the glint was bright. Finally, she blinked, lowered her head, allowed the spell to be broken.

"Sure, Mr. Bates. Sounds good to me."

The majestic cottonwood was visible soon after they entered the edge of the woods. Ernie led the way, careful not to allow a low tree branch or bush to whiplash back into Gino. Ernie stopped at the creek bank, focused his senses on the place. He had not seen it since the terrible night following the death notification. His lonely visits to the woods had been to other locations on the creek, but never to the cottonwood. He had felt betrayed by it somehow, as if it had a life and will of its own and had conspired with a treacherous god to torment him. It seemed so long ago, and in truth it had been a great chunk of his life, though not a span measured in days or weeks or months. In the spirit world that had enveloped Ernie Bates on three occasions, time was meaningless. Only life or death mattered, and twice he had been granted life, his beloved son, death.

Death eternal, or death for just a time, Ernie Bates? You must decide.

Behind him, Gino stirred, and the question was left in the sigh of the wind. Ernie said, "Ever see a cottonwood throne?"

"I'm not sure what that is."

"Peek over the creek bank there, and take a look." Ernie motioned toward a spot located a few feet from Gino's shoes.

Gino walked to the spot and peered over the edge of the bank at the graceful curvature of the thick root. He looked back at Ernie and smiled as he nodded. "Does kinda look like it was meant to be sat on."

"Go on, try it out."

Gino slipped down onto the root and nestled his back against the earthen bank, all the while nodding his head in approval. "Not bad. Not bad at all."

"It doesn't look all that great around here right now," Ernie said, "but you ought to see it in the spring of early fall. Take your breath away, I swear it can. These trees here close in around you like tall, colored walls…and the smells, especially in the spring, like some kind of perfume. I wish I was better with words so I could really tell you."

Ernie lapsed into silence with the realization that he had strung together the longest collection of words in a very long time. The only sounds in the air were the velvety caress of water on the rocks in the creek and the low moan of the breeze in the treetops. The late morning sunlight slanted through the naked limbs and cast spidery shadows on the opposite bank.

"I think I get the picture," Gino said. "I bet it's pretty with a snow on, huh?"

"Yeah…is it ever."

The harsh cry of a blue jay pierced the sky, and Gino jerked his head in the direction of the noise.

"Old mister blue jay," Ernie said, "a man can't go too far in the woods without hearing a blue jay holler. If a man sits still long enough, he can see just about every critter there is around here. I've seen them all, one time or another. Deer, coyote, fox, possum, skunk, coon…even saw a bobcat once just before sunset. Most men grow old without ever seeing a bobcat in the wild."

"Yeah, I can see how you came to like this place so much." He paused, the thought creeping into his brain on cat's paws and then springing on him. "Only wild places I've ever known, I didn't appreciate too much. Cover and concealment for the enemy…that's what the Corps calls the thick woods. Just a place for some VC to take a shot at you."

Even as the final word escaped his lips, the regret descended on him. The muzzle flash of the AK-47 was again bright in his mind's eye, and he could hear the heavy sound of Aaron's body colliding with the ground behind him. He silently cursed himself as he thought of the man near him whose thoughts had no doubt been shoved back into sadness. The man was sharing a sacred place with him, and he had managed to defile it with his stupid tongue.

"I'm sorry...I shouldn't have said anything like that, I..."

"It's all right, son. That's not the first piece of sharp talk to come from this place, believe me. I spent a whole night here cussin' everybody and everything on the face of the earth. Forget it."

Gino nodded half-heartedly and began to gather himself to leave.

"No," said Ernie, "don't leave feeling bad at yourself. It's too nice a place for that. Besides, this place was meant for one man at a time. You can't soak up anything with me running my mouth and standing here."

He turned to leave and then nearly stopped to ask if Gino could find his way back before remembering that the young man was partly, and forever, a combat soldier who could manage quite well in a patch of woods.

Ernie had been gone for fifteen minutes when the flash of movement flickered through Gino's field of vision sixty yards beyond the bank. It looked to Gino as if some unseen hand was jerking a large white handkerchief from side to side. He stared intently at the spot as the white flashed again in the thicket. Suddenly, swatches of light brown were transformed into a distinct shape composed of graceful curves and long legs as the mature doe cautiously picked her way into the open. She raised her head and tested the breeze blowing from the creek toward her. The huge tail twitched violently now, and she swung her long neck parallel with her body and peered back into the thicket. Gino could barely discern the form of another deer, much larger, but it remained in the shadow of the overgrowth. The doe, now having scented the strong odor of man, raised her tail to its full height and vanished like a wraith into the shadows. Gino's gaze darted back into the thicket, but the larger deer had also vanished. The brief drama had played out in a matter of seconds, yet Gino felt the goose flesh form at the base of his neck. Every fiber of his being had been riveted to the performance on the grassy stage, and now, as his heartbeat slowed to its normal pace, he could feel no trace of the bitterness that had welled up within him only minutes before.

He understood what Ernie had meant now, could leave the cottonwood in peace, just as he had found it. He longed for another glimpse of the deer, especially the larger one, but he knew that they would not return. He jumped to the top of the bank and began to walk through the dry bed of hickory and oak leaves. With the first crunch of his shoes, the blue jay again sounded his shrieking alarm, and all the creatures of the forest were warned of Gino's movement.

Gino made the decision to leave the next day as he lay on his back in Aaron's bed, his head propped against the pillow. In the faint light cast by the small lamp on his night stand, the oval-framed picture of Jesus was unclear, yet the solemn features bored through the shadowiness, sought him. He could not take his eyes off the face, could not shut out Harley's passion at the cemetery, and, sounding as a chorus above these things, he could not stop the replaying of Aaron's final words.

"Why do you seek the living among the dead?

"Why do you seek the living among the dead?"

"Why do you seek the living among the dead?"

With great effort he clamped his eyes shut, flopped to his side, stared at the black void inside his eyelids.

"Can you hear me, Missouri boy? Are you among the living or the dead?"

The low whoosh of the night wind curled around the corner of the house, and Gino opened his eyes, looked out the window. A profound restlessness welled up within him, turned suddenly into agitation. He sprang to his feet, stomped to the window, balled his fingers into fists and bumped them against the pane.

"There's something scratching my insides, Missouri boy, and I don't like it…don't know what it is." His fists slid down the cold glass as he placed his forehead against it. "I want to believe you…and your mom…and your friend. I'm tryin' so hard to make sense of it all."

The wind kicked up, pushed barren limbs into the edge of the roof where they pecked like long fingernails on a table. "It's all too closed in on me…I gotta move on."

Christa expertly speared the end of a strip of bacon and turned it over in the cast iron skillet. Ernie sat at the table, a mug of coffee lost in his hands. She turned her head toward the footsteps approaching the kitchen, waited with a smile to offer Gino, but when she saw him, it wilted and she quickly busied herself with the bacon. In his hand was his sea bag, his coat draped over it.

"Morning," he said.

Ernie nodded, said, "Morning."

Christa drew in a steadying breath. "Good morning, Gino."

Gino walked to the back door, sat the bag down, and looked out through the glass top at the gently swirling snowflakes. "Second snow since I've been here."

"Yeah, they pop up early once in a while," Ernie said. "Don't usually amount to much, but this one looks like it might hang around."

Ernie pointed to the sea bag. "Looks like you're packed to go."

"It's time," Gino said.

Christa clicked the knob off and slid the skillet to a cool burner. She wiped her hands on a dish towel and turned to leave the kitchen.

"Mrs. Bates."

She stopped, did not turn around.

"Mrs. Bates…I know what you're thinking, but…I'm not backing out on our deal. I bet they'd let you sing your song at church this morning, and I'd be proud to go with you."

Christa swallowed against the burning in her throat, cleared it as quietly as she could. "Well…I…uh, suppose I do have some pull with the choir director…in special cases."

"I'm sorry I don't have a proper shirt and tie."

Ernie rapped the mug on the table. "That'll make a pair of us then, 'cause I don't even own one."

Christa slipped quickly through the doorway.

They were ready to leave at ten o'clock. Ernie returned from the carport after starting the engine. "It'll be warmed up by the time we get out there," he said to Christa and Gino, who were seated at the kitchen table. "Not as cold as you might think out there."

"Give me a minute or two, okay?" Gino asked. "I'll meet you at the car."

"Sure," said Ernie, "I'll take care of your bag."

Christa got up and walked out the back door with Ernie.

Gino stood in the open doorway of Aaron's bedroom, willing his eyes to be a camera that recorded the place for safekeeping. They would assure him that the room was his anytime he chose to return, the kind and thoughtful parents, and they would mean it, but he knew that he was seeing it for the final time in his life. And with that knowledge there was a certain gravity, a force that had pulled him sideways, rather than downward, toward the room. The bed came into focus...*click*...then the wall with the window...*click*...and then the dresser, but the shutter in his mind did not trip. The portrait of Jesus was in its proper place, but the dresser top was barren of the ball player figurine. He looked quickly back to the night stand, but it supported only the lamp. He shrugged, reasoned that Aaron's mother had slipped in after breakfast, already put it away, or perhaps moved it to her bedroom. Gino regretted that the parting image would not include the ball player, but he clicked the shutter, turned and walked away.

They arrived at First Baptist ten minutes before the start of the service. Christa greeted several friends as she walked up the front steps between Gino and Ernie, clinging gracefully to the arm of each. Once inside the building, she whispered into Ernie's ear, and he proceeded to lead the trio to a pew near the right front of the sanctuary. As she walked down the aisle, several hands reached up to seek hers, and with her left hand she brushed each one in passing. The last hand she touched was Harley's.

When Ernie stopped at the corner of the pew, she stepped aside, motioned for them to be seated, and then leaned over and whispered, "I need to find Jack for a minute. Be right back."

She returned quickly, sat down at the end of the pew beside Gino as Ruth Langdon began to play the organ prelude. Then the choir, purple and white robes flowing, streamed into their seats in the loft. Christa met the eyes of both Pastor Riggins and Jack as they followed the choir out before proceeding on to the podium. She acknowledged the slight nod of the pastor's head, the curl of a little smile. It was when Christa turned her head slightly toward the congregation that she caught a glimpse of motion to the rear of the sanctuary, near the entry. When she turned fully, she was greeted with the sight of the Ledbetter family. Fudd jammed a finger into the tight space between his Adam's apple and the knot of his necktie and twisted his head in an effort to purchase a bit of relief from the tight union of flesh and cloth. Margie spotted an empty space in the pews and quickly ushered her brood forward.

Christa drew a long breath and allowed her eyes to sweep over the choir members as they sang the opening prelude. It was complete now—all she had dared hoped for on this extraordinary Sunday morning. She was at ease now, given over to the Spirit who would strengthen her and give her breath for singing, and moisten her eyes without allowing a single tear to fall.

It was time for the first congregational hymn to be sung and Christa flipped through the pages and extended the hymnal to Gino so that all three could see the words. To the surprise of both men, she did not join in their halting attempt at song, but merely hummed the tune in barely audible fashion. After Jack made opening remarks and announcements, another hymn was sung, and again, the only sound that came from her was the soft humming. Ernie pilfered a sidelong glance, but she did not acknowledge him. Christa would sing the words to only one hymn this day; when Gino Polities heard her voice, it would be for the first time in the flesh.

The order of the service preceding the sermon flowed routinely, ending with the special music selection by the choir. As the final note sounded to a chorus of approving "amens," from the congregation, Christa beamed her approval toward the choir loft. Fred Riggins walked to the lectern, big leather-bound Bible in hand, and began to preach his sermon. The subject was thanksgiving, and he apologized at the outset for preaching on a theme that had also been addressed on the previous Sunday. But he "felt the tug," he told his flock, and he assured them that he had lived long enough to know better than to "go against the tug," about what to say from the pulpit.

Gino, his fears about sitting through a dry, or worse yet, loud, spewing of words long dispelled, sat respectfully and attentively. To his pleasant surprise, the preacher spoke in a manner that held his attention rather than one that demanded it. The half hour passed swiftly, with the theme of thanksgiving centered around the cross at "the place of the skull," as Fred preferred to call the site of Christ's crucifixion. He paused now, sweeping his gaze over the congregation before he continued.

"All talk of thanksgiving ought to come back to that place, beloved. If our Lord had chosen to exercise His power and authority and had struck down all the cackling fools around Him, instead of allowing them to carry out their grisly death wish…then there would be no need for this Thanksgiving, or any other. Ever. Our doom would have been sealed for all eternity. But His thoughts were not centered around Himself…they were centered around us, and our pitiful condition. And so, He did not strike them dead, but allowed them to butcher Him like some lowly animal. And in so doing, presented my very soul to a holy God, if I would only believe in Him, and accept the gift of salvation. This I have done. Not because I'm so smart and highly educated, and certainly not because my life is so clean and pure that I now deserve it. I have done it in the only manner acceptable to God. I have thrown myself at Jesus' feet, let the blood from his shattered body splatter down on me—undeserving wretch that I am—and thanked Him for the gift of eternal life. I took it with a repentant, humble heart…and never looked back."

He raised his eyes to the ceiling for a moment as the hint of a smile crossed his face. "And I have assured myself of a reunion with my wife, who also believed…and with Aaron Bates, who also believed. And all those who precede us across the Jordan…and I fear not death. Because I'm brave and a man full of great courage? Hardly…it's hardly that. It is because I see the truth, and accept it. So can any of you who dare to open your eyes. The only thing God will not do is force Himself on you. We are not a creation of robots. He gave us free will, and therefore we have a choice.

Has any of you seen a child on Christmas morning who opened a beautifully wrapped box containing the gift of his dreams, only to solemnly hand it back to his astonished parents? It would be a strange child indeed, would it not? Sometimes, I think that is how God must feel toward us when we reject Christ. Thanksgiving? Oh, yes indeed… there's great reason for thanksgiving. Recognize the truth…and take the gift. Don't turn your back on the place of the skull."

He looked at the hymnal that lay to the side of the lectern, picked it up for only a moment before replacing it. "You won't need one of these for the invitational hymn this morning. You won't even have to sing. We can just listen together as Christa sings us across the Jordan. It is a gift of song for a dear friend, I'm told. A friend who will leave our town today. Gino Polities was Aaron's friend in Vietnam, and we are honored to have him with us this morning. I hope that you won't mind, Gino, if we all share in your parting gift."

He smiled at Gino, and then at Christa, as he motioned for her to come forward. She stepped into the aisle, walked the few steps to the base of the stage.

"I sang this song at my son's funeral…so most of you all have heard it not all that long ago. But some of you couldn't be there…and Gino here…well, he was halfway around the world."

Christa lowered her head for a moment, then slowly raised it, and began to sing a cappella.

"On Jor-dan's stormy banks I stand
and cast a wish-ful eye, to Ca-naan's
fair and hap-py land, where my pos-ses-sions lie…"

With the first notes, the chill crept over Gino like a prickly mantle. His eyes were closed and his hands grasped the back of the pew in front of him. The sounds that once haunted him in the night now lifted him in love. The purity of the woman's voice filled the sanctuary, and those who had heard the song at the grave again marveled at the enchantment of it. Gino struggled against the trembling of his lips and the burning in his throat, and only the street fighter's instinct within him prevented him from succumbing to the great sobs poised within his chest. Part of him desired to rip at the flimsy veil that held them in, to free the sobs, to free the love that was as palpable as the wood beneath his fingers. But the fighter's heart was strong, and faint voices echoed in his ears, voices that chastised him. *Tears in front of strangers?*

Sobs of a child from a man? Where is your pride, boy? Faintly, yet clearly they whispered.

Fred Riggins stood to the side of the lectern with arms uplifted in invitation to any who would come forward in public profession of faith. But none came with the second verse, or the third, or the fourth and final. When Christa finished, she quickly made her way back to her pew and embraced Gino with one arm around his shoulders.

In the silent moments that followed, neither Fred or Christa registered disappointment, much less despair. They both remembered the words of Fred's late wife, words passed on to Christa more than once. She had told him years before, at a time when his chest still yearned to puff with pride: "Who do you think you are, Fred Riggins, that you should be allowed to see the fruit of every seed that's sown?"

And so it was today. But he knew that seeds were sown; it could not be doubted. The presence of the Spirit permeated the place this very morning with a power and majesty that transcended a mortal's understanding. And the seeds would be nurtured, and they would grow and seek the light, and one day bear fruit. These things Fred and Christa believed.

Christa lingered in her pew with Gino and Ernie, allowing the sanctuary to empty as she talked quietly with them. Harley made his way to the rear and began talking with the Ledbetter family. Christa led the way up the narrow aisle, preceding Gino and Ernie, and she stopped at the small circle of friends.

"We've got about twenty minutes to get this young man on his bus," she said.

Harley stepped forward and extended his hand. "I'm glad we met, Gino. Don't forget us after you get back to the big city."

"I just told Mrs. Bates that this was the first formal preaching I ever heard, but it wasn't really." He paused, smiled at Harley. "I've heard you."

"You heard a turkey hanger babbling in the wind compared to what you heard today, Gino, but thanks for the thought."

Gino turned to Fudd and they exchanged a strong handshake. "There's no need to worry if you have trouble findin' work up there, boy," Fudd said. "I can make a bird hanger outta you in less than a week. You'd be handlin' those big toms like turtle doves."

"I'm not so sure about that, Fudd," Gino said. He nodded respectfully at Margie and the children, said, "Good bye to all of you."

"You take care," Margie said.

The short ride to the bus stop at the Sinclair station was made in silence. The bus was parked on the side of the lot, parallel to Highway 50. During the night, state road crews had treated the snowy highway with cinders and salt, and the black grime churned up by the big tires had coated the sides of the bus, giving it the appearance of a dirty, metal-clad building. Ernie braked to a halt near the front of the bus and lifted the gear selector into park.

"I'll see how long we got," Ernie said, shouldering his way past the car door.

The low grumble of the big diesel engine filled the air as Ernie tapped on the door to gain the driver's attention. The portly, ruddy-faced man opened the door and stepped down the stairs.

"Yes, sir," he said pleasantly, "traveling with us today?"

"No, but I brought one for you over there in the car."

"Baggage?"

"Yeah, there's one. I'll get it for you."

Ernie opened the back door and pulled out Gino's sea bag while the driver lifted the storage compartment door on the side of the bus. He took the bag from Ernie and wedged it in, quietly muttering to himself as he rearranged several suitcases in the cramped space.

"How long before you pull out?"

"Be about five minutes."

Ernie returned to the car and slid in behind the wheel, brushing the snow from his bare head. "We got about five minutes or so, he says."

They all sat in the front seat, with Christa in the middle.

"Ernie, I'll declare, I can't understand why you won't wear a hat in the winter...even in the snow."

The words sounded less like an admonishment than the simple avoidance of the time at hand. He did not answer, but passed a hand over the top of his head. The snowflakes careened against the windshield, now warmed by the defroster, and slid lazily down the glass.

Christa sighed forcefully and twisted her fingers around the thin plastic of her purse handle. "Gino, there is one more thing I have to ask you, and I'm not even sure why I want to…but…"

He turned his head toward her, said, "Go ahead."

"Over there…when he died…from what you said, it seemed like there was only one soldier who shot at you all…and I don't know why I should want to know, but…did you see him?"

Gino stared straight ahead through the windshield, saw the snowflakes, but only for an instant. "I was too shook up at first, but then…I went over to spit on his body…but I never did. A skinny kid, couldn't have more than ten or eleven. He didn't look strong enough to raise the AK to his shoulder. I doubt if he ever did. The V. C. probably snatched him out of his hut the night before and stuck him there as a decoy. The main force never hit us. Must not have liked the numbers or the setup. Whatever…he was it…he was enough."

He paused, looked down, and slowly massaged his temples with the thumb and middle finger of his right hand. "What can I say? He looked like a big, black-haired rag doll layin' there. He didn't look like a soldier."

Christa nodded her head in silence and stared at her purse. "I'm sorry for having to ask you."

"It's all right, Mrs. Bates…it's okay."

"I reckon it's time," said Ernie.

"We'll walk you over to the bus," Christa said.

They climbed out of the car and shuffled through the snow to the door of the bus. Ernie extended his hand to Gino who ignored it as he reached up with both arms and hugged the tall man tightly and quickly. Gino turned to Christa and hugged her in the same fashion, but he lingered, drank in the lilac aroma wafting in the falling snow, and he knew that if he lived to be a hundred, lilacs and snow would always be one, would always be Christa Bates.

The embrace ended, and Gino turned toward the door steps. Christa reached out, tugged on his coat sleeve. "Wait a second." She reached into her purse, her hand emerging with a small, neatly wrapped object, and she placed it in his hands. "Open it on the bus. It's from Aaron." She clasped her hands over his, said, "When he was just learning to hit a ball, he tried way too hard, but then he understood, and he could do it." She smiled, the farewell clear and beautiful, and it pierced Gino. "Sometimes, unbelievers are like that."

"Better roll, folks," said the driver.

Gino nodded, framed them both a final time: first Ernie, then Christa, then together.

The door whooshed shut and the engine protested against the burden as the metal hulk rocked onto the shoulder of the highway and then into the eastbound lane.

Gino claimed a seat on the aisle near the rear; he was unaware of his fellow passengers, his hands clenching the gift. He waited, allowed the faraway drone of the big engine to push the miles behind him. With his fingertips he broke the pieces of clear tape on the wrapping. The paper rustled and the red numeral **6** appeared as the plastic statuette of the baseball player took shape. He slowly turned it over in his hands, saw the neatly folded note taped to the front, pulled it free, unfolded it.

STANDING IN THE ROARING OF THE JORDAN

Gino read only the first line, remembered the matching words on Aaron's tombstone, knew that it was the original note Christa Bates had saved from her son's youth. Gino refolded the paper and slipped it into his coat pocket. He studied the statuette, formed into the strange, hunched batting stance that had first caught his eye in Aaron's room.

The squeaky voice came from across the aisle, broke his reverie. "Momma, momma, lookie there...he's got Stan the Man."

Gino looked at the small round face of a boy stretching into the aisle from his mother's lap.

"Yes he does, son. That's Stan the Man for sure," the boy's mother said. She smiled apologetically at Gino as she attempted to wrestle the excited child back onto her lap.

"It's okay," said Gino with a shake of his head. He reached across the aisle and handed the model to the boy. The child's eyes darted furtively at his mother's face as he accepted it.

"Thank you," she said, her hands moving instinctively under her son's to form a protective cup. "Be careful, Paulie," she warned as the boy fondled the likeness of his hero with busy fingers. "We're from St.

Louis and even little boys from there know what Stan Musial looks like." She chuckled. "And he's been retired for five years."

Gino smiled back at her and watched the contented face of the boy.

She said, "You must have a friend who's a ball fan, huh?"

Gino did not answer, and the woman's fingers began to fidget over her son's as the seconds gathered.

Gino said, "Yes, ma'am…he was that."

The woman began the process of talking her son into surrendering the statuette. She managed expertly, with the child offering only mild protestations. She handed it back to Gino.

"Thanks again," she said softly, "It was nice of you to let him hold it."

Gino's nod was barely discernable, and when the woman glanced back at him a minute later, his eyes were closed and his head rested against the seat. Only tiny patches of color were visible through his fingers as they enveloped his gift.

The bedroom light had been out for a half hour, but the couple laid in uneasy silence. Ernie stirred, rolled toward the window. "When you told him he was trying too hard you were talking to me too, weren't you?"

"I didn't mind you hearing it."

He pushed the covers aside, got out of bed, walked to the window. "You must be tired of all this…tired of dealing with me."

"Tired? No, Ernie, it's not like that. A little weary maybe, but not tired. Tired is when you don't much care anymore…and it will never be like that…never."

He padded to the corner of the room, then back, looked out the window. "I do know that there is another world out there."

"So you believe in the dark one…the only one you think you've been in…but not the other?"

"I don't feel like I've ever been in the one you and Harley and John Riggins hold to."

She got out of bed, walked to his side. "How can you say that? I don't know what happened at the plant the other night, but I do know that something horrible almost happened behind the tool shed. What do you think kept you from that? I can tell you, Ernie…not exactly, but I can tell you. It was a lot of believers praying for you. Did angels swoop down and grab your hand? Or was it something planted inside you? I don't know…and I don't care which it was, just that you were stopped." She paused, ran her fingers across the window sill. "I don't expect to know just exactly how spirit things work till I cross the river." She tapped her fingers on the cold wood. "So…yes…yes, Ernie, I reckon you could say I'm a little…weary."

Ernie placed the fingers of his right hand on the window sill. "I miss both of them, woman. Aaron and Gino both. You think Gino will come back and visit us?"

She shook her head slowly, thoughtfully. "No."

"Maybe write a letter?"

"Maybe, but I doubt it."

"Then you won't ever know if he changes?"

"We did what we could while he was here. I'm thankful for that. It's enough for me."

From the edge of the yard, in a high branch of the green ash, a great hunting owl hooted his night song, and Ernie Bates heard it as an old song—rueful and true—a song of a long ago death, and he yearned to hear it now as a song of life. His fingertips traced a path toward Christa's hand. When he covered it, the warmth infused him, and he regretted that he could not remember the last time he had held it.

Christa listened to Ernie's deep, rhythmic breaths, allowed the sound to carry her to the edge of sleep. She closed her eyes and sought an image to take her beyond the edge. Aaron was with her now, the handsome face calm and serene, but she could not identify his surroundings. He appeared to be clothed in light, the side of his face awash in brilliance, and he was peering into the distance, arms outstretched, waiting. The diminutive figure, clothed in a separate light, ran gracefully toward him with arms upraised, and they met in a mighty embrace as Aaron lifted the child for a moment and then placed him on his feet. The features were delicate, with only the hint of masculinity, and when the radiance fell full force on his hair, its blackness shone like the feathers of a raven.

The wintry light of dawn came begrudgingly at the tracks, and Harley could see that it would offer little more for the entire day before skulking into evening. The snow had diminished to occasional swirls of tiny, dry flakes. His hands were buried in the pockets of the heavy corduroy coat, its collar turned up against his neck. He preferred cold mornings at the tracks; his thoughts seemed sharper, clarified in the enveloping chill. The white blanket on the ground, clean and radiant even in the scant light, purified the place for him, and he drank in the panorama. The tracks stretched from his boots like parallel pencil lines drawn on a draftsman's table, precise in their ever-decreasing spacing, until they became one in the distance.

He turned his head to the southeast, away from the wind, and aimed his eyes at the speck of color nearly hidden in the stones. He had spotted the small flag on the first morning after Fudd had set it out, but had mistaken it for a floral arrangement, and did not learn of its true identity until the afternoon at the grave. From behind him came the snowy shuffle of heavy footfalls and he turned to watch as Fudd labored up the slope, billows of breath trailing like steam from an engine.

"Thought I'd come check on you before you froze to a block of ice and got your butt run over by the mornin' freight."

"It's not that bad up here, Fudd."

The big man chuckled from his belly, expelling great clouds of vapor into the air. They stood in silence, motionless except for the slight movements of their heads as they shifted their gaze. Harley homed in on the cemetery, and Fudd squinted down his friend's line of sight. He caught the flicker of motion and color, and strained to fix the point.

"I'll be…but I swear I can see it from here," Fudd said. He stole a satisfied glance at Harley before returning his attention to the flag.

"Yep, I've been seeing it every morning," Harley said. "Look forward to it."

"Yeah…yeah, I kinda like that myself…sure enough do."

"It's a fine way to have remembrance of him. I'm sure glad you thought of it. Means a lot to his folks too."

Fudd flushed with the thought that he had pleased Christa and Ernie, and again peeked at Harley to assure himself of the weight of the praise. The only sounds were occasional drones of vehicles passing on Highway 50.

"Harley, you reckon…and I mean *really* now…a fella like me could learn to pray some up here too? Now don't answer too quick, dang it… just listen for a minute. I never been much on serious stuff, you know that…I just don't like it. Seems easier to just not deal with it most of the time…but I can't dodge it all the time. Now, I ain't ignorant so much as ignorin', you understand? After all that's took place around here lately…well, pity sake, I reckon I'm sayin' I must've changed some. I can feel it now and then, down in my bones, and it seems like I ain't so ready to chase it away…aw…mercy, I'm ramblin' like a fool…"

"No, Fudd, you don't sound like a fool to me. You asked me a question, so let me answer it. It doesn't take any special words to pray. The good Lord hears such as us just as good as He hears somebody with a world of book learning…better, I imagine. Some smart folks probably figure they've read enough books and learned so much that they can do just fine by themselves."

Harley paused, removed his cap, slowly ran his hand through his hair before replacing the cap. "First time you decide you want to try it, just give in and admit to being a stumbling human like we all are, and stand quiet and listen for a while. You'll start to get smarter by the minute." He looked at Fudd, held his gaze. "Yeah, I imagine you can manage that all right. If you just decide to go ahead and do it."

"Yeah…I think I might just try it in the mornin'. Start out from scratch sorta. Just march up here like I knew what I was doin'. Whatcha' think?"

"Fudd, I think that these tracks here can stand the weight of four feet as easy as two." Harley smiled at the wide face and dancing eyes under the bill of the dirty cap.

Fudd said, "Even if two of 'ems mine, huh?"

Harley nodded. "Yeah, Fudd…even if two of them are yours."

Fudd clamped a massive arm around Harley's shoulders, and the pair began to walk toward the plant.

"I hope we got monster toms today," Fudd crowed. "I feel stronger'n whale's breath."

The peal of his laughter rang out ahead of them, and the workers in the parking lot recognized the sound.

CPSIA information can be obtained at www.ICGtesting.com
Printed in the USA
LVOW10s1231110115

422375LV00002BA/369/A

9 781420 813609